Absolution

Tattoos and Tears – Brody

By Amiee Louise

This is a work of fiction. Similarities to real people, places, or events are entirely coincidental.

ABSOLUTION

First edition. October 2, 2025.

ISBN: 978-1968759308

Written by Amiee Louise.

"Rock stars did not invent burning out, they just do it louder..."
- The gospel according to Brody Hart (Chapter 2)

Prologue

Brody
Present Day

Absolution

(ˌæbsəˈluːʃən) (ab-suh-loo-shuhn)

1. Noun

The act of absolving[1], or the state of being absolved; release[2]d from guilt[3], obligation[4], or punishment[5]

2. Declaration that a person's sins have been forgiven.

[formal] "He had been granted **absolution for** his sins."

3. State of being absolved.

Synonyms: forgiveness[6], mercy[7], exculpation[8], pardon[9], acquittal[10].

I had begun to cherish those precious moments between sleep and wakefulness. In those moments, everything is as it was before... normal. My brain isn't scrambled, my body isn't broken, and my girl is lying next to me. I turn onto my side, reaching over to find that familiar cold, empty spot where she should be. I blink up at the ceiling and the enormity of my grim reality hits me full force in the gut. That's when the relentless, shrill ringing

---

1.   https://www.collinsdictionary.com/dictionary/english/absolve

2.   https://www.collinsdictionary.com/dictionary/english/release

3.   https://www.collinsdictionary.com/dictionary/english/guilt

4.   https://www.collinsdictionary.com/dictionary/english/obligation

5.   https://www.collinsdictionary.com/dictionary/english/punishment

6.   https://www.dictionary.com/browse/forgiveness

7.   https://www.dictionary.com/browse/mercy

8.   https://www.dictionary.com/browse/exculpation

9.   https://www.dictionary.com/browse/pardon

10.   https://www.dictionary.com/browse/acquittal

of my phone starts. It grates on every nerve in my exhausted body, and I briefly close my eyes, willing for it to stop. *I just want it to stop.* The annoying, high-pitched beep, signalling for the person on the other end to leave a message, resonates and echoes around the eerily silent room. The sound sets my frayed nerves on edge and causes a pounding throb to form in my head. I rub the pads of my index fingers in gentle circles on both of my temples to try and dull the ache. I know who it's going to be before they've even spoken. *Why won't he just get the fucking hint?* There's an audible sigh, as Sam's distinctive husky voice echoes through my silent, stark, lifeless prison.

"It's me...again, you prick! Why the fuck aren't you answering your god-damn phone? I know you're there. Pick up, you wanker, or I'm coming over there to kick your arse!"

He growls. *Fuck off, Newbolt.* The message cuts off, the red light flickers in the dark room and I try to make myself as small as possible. If they can't see me, then I'm not really here. *Really, Hart? That's what you're going with? What are you? Five years old?* I snuggle down in my bed and pull the duvet tighter around me, willing my brain to stop torturing me, just for a few minutes.

Without her, I'm in my own version of hell and it's all my fucking fault. All of it is my fault. I feel so alone, so...disconnected, so...dead inside. I don't blame anyone but myself. I was the one holding the gun, and I was the one who pulled the trigger. My face is all over the newspapers, internet, and TV, for all the wrong fucking reasons. I was the one who thought it was a good idea to get high before getting on my bike. *What the fuck was I thinking?* I slam the heel of my hand into my forehead, relishing the sharp pain that follows.

In my arrogant, narcissistic quest for self-destruction and to shield her from the man I had become since the accident, I lost the one person who understood what it was like to be broken. The only person I have ever loved and the one person who could have fixed me. It's on me that I ruined our relationship. I ruined Raleigh's life. I got her pregnant, then abandoned them like they meant nothing, when in reality, they're all that mattered. All because of a split second of madness and all because I lost control after she told me she was pregnant. I was a weak pathetic fucking coward, all because I couldn't handle hearing her tell me she had my child growing inside her.

Even after countless hours of therapy sessions, I can't even begin to explain why I'm the world's biggest fucking idiot. I put her through three months of hell while I lay in hospital in a coma. After she spent countless days and sleepless nights willing me to wake up, nursing me back to health and I told her I couldn't be with her. I broke her heart and watching the pain in her eyes was probably one of the worse things I have ever witnessed. The look of pure heartbreak and that debilitating agony and the gut-wrenching ache that I felt somewhere deep inside. I'd give my right arm to take back the look in her eyes when I told her it was over. After everything we've been through together, the fights, the tears, the arguments, and the crazy, sweaty, angry make up sex, the highs, the lows, and everything in between.

No one could hate me more at this moment than I hate myself right now. The look in her eyes, as I let her claw and punch me. I deserved every single slap, every single punch, and every single ounce of pain she gave me. It broke my fucking heart and I'll never be able to undo that. I have to make her hate me; but no one could hate me more at this moment than I hate myself right now. I have to make her forget she ever had feelings for me, because it's better this way. I can't let her give up her career, her hopes, and dreams to care for me. I won't let my injuries hold her back. She deserves so much more. They both do.

I was fully aware that life had broken me and I was no longer whole. Whoever put me back together didn't take due care and attention. I was fractured, damaged beyond repair, I had pieces missing and here I was, lying in the wreckage, a shadow of what I used to be. I had come to realise since I had been discharged from the hospital that the hardest thing isn't to lose yourself. It's to find yourself again amongst all of the chaos and right now, I'm in my own version of hell and I'm struggling to see beyond tomorrow. But I vowed for the sake of her and our baby, that I was going to try. I was going to try and slay the demons I had battled for twenty-plus years. In the beginning of our story, she was my fucking redemption. Now all I'm asking for is absolution.

1

Raleigh
Past

Someone once told me that you can't keep dancing with the devil and wonder why you're still in hell. As I think back to those words I heard all those years ago, I had come to realise that the devil didn't come dressed in a red cape and wearing pointy horns. He came in the form of a handsome, world-famous guitarist, with magic fingers, a charming smile, and a cock to die for. He was everything I had ever wished for, but like the devil himself, he was too good to be true. His smile was like a loaded gun, but I lived for those damn dimpled smiles that made his silver eyes sparkle. As believable as his disguise was to the public, I saw right through the façade. I saw the real, raw version, and he fucking resented me for it.

When I told Brody I was pregnant with our baby, I expected a different reaction from the one I actually got. I didn't expect such anger and hostility. Sharing happy news like the arrival of a new life is meant to be celebrated. I'm so fucking angry and upset right now, I can't stop the tears that roll down my cheeks. I stroke my still flat stomach while whispering sorrow-filled, incoherent words to our baby.

"I'm so sorry, jellybean, I'm so sorry, I'm sorry," I sob softly, as I stare blankly through the floor length window into the inky black, starless sky, resigned to the fact that he's not coming back, not tonight at least.

Without warning, my stomach twists and roils vehemently, as I turn and race to the adjoining bathroom. I drop to my knees, not registering the fierce pain that shoots through me, as I vomit violently into the toilet bowl. I rest my head on my forearm, squeezing my tear-filled eyes shut briefly, trying desperately to push away the crippling hurt and cruel rejection that sears my heart. A tear rolls down my cheek and I sit up, resting my damp head against the cool tiles of the luxurious bathroom, trying to make sense of the events leading up to this very moment. After a few brief minutes, I get to my feet and wearily head back into the bedroom. I lay down, exhaustion and pure anguish consuming my entire body, feeling the weight of the last hour bearing down on me, and soon, I'm a slave to sleep.

I'm unaware of how much time has passed, but I'm woken by the sound of my phone ringing. I blink a few times, struggling to focus on the brightness of the screen. As my focus begins to adjust, I look at the screen and I don't recognise the number. I look at the clock illuminating and bathing the room in soft blue light, and it says it's two fourteen a.m. *Who the fuck would be calling at this ungodly hour?* I swipe the screen and answer cautiously.

"Hello?"

My voice thick with sleep.

"Hello, Raleigh?" the gruff voice greets me warily.

"Hello, this is Raleigh," I answer cautiously, the voice on the other end of the phone unfamiliar to me.

"Love, it's Lenny, Brody's sober sponsor."
Lenny's voice surprisingly soothes me.

"Hello Lenny, is everything ok?" I ask curiously, suddenly uber aware that this man on the end of the phone is a complete stranger to me, but I oddly feel like I know him.

"It's Brody, there's been an accident," Lenny's voice wavers, and as soon as I hear those words, my stomach somersaults and the bottom drops out of my world. I sit bolt upright and all of a sudden, I'm wide awake.

"W-what happened?" I swallow back the golf ball size lump in my throat before I continue to speak. "Lenny?"

I'm suddenly terrified, as I feel the familiar bile rise up in my throat. I take a few calming breaths, and I hear him sniff, as if he is bracing himself for his next words.

"He's been in a motorbike accident, it's serious. I need you to get to the hospital now, he's in intensive care. I'm not gonna lie, it's not looking good, sweetheart."

His voice sounds weary and exhausted. I'm dazed and disoriented, as I swing my legs out of bed. The coldness of the floor as my feet hit the floor is a shock to my system. I blindly reach out to turn on the light, and it takes a few seconds for my eyes to adjust to the brightness. I get dressed on autopilot, almost robotically. I haphazardly pull on the nearest piece of clothing I can lay my hands on. I pull on a pair of cropped black sports leggings, Brody's large Rancid Vengeance vest. I catch sight of my reflection in the floor-length mirror. It looks huge on me, but it smells of him and it provides comfort and reassurance to me. I jam my feet impatiently and shakily into my white Converse.

"I've sent Sam to come and get you, love, he's not too far away. He's a fighter, our Brody, he's going to be just fine," he says reassuringly, but even as he's saying the words, I'm not entirely convinced.

***

"There's been an accident."

Those words are the worst four words in the English fucking language. The anguish and the intense knot deep in the pit of your stomach, the little voice in your head telling you *"This is all your fault."* That's exactly how I felt when I found out my reason for living and the father of my baby, had been in a motorbike accident. I spend the entire journey to the hospital in total silence, apart from the sound system in the car softly playing *Disturbed Reason to Fight*. The sound of Sam humming at intervals and subconsciously tapping on the steering wheel strangely soothing me. I can't help the soul-destroying sobs of despair, and the thought at the forefront of my frontal lobe is, I don't know how I'm going to carry on, if something happens to him. *Please don't die on me, Brody.*

Sam keeps one steady hand firmly on the steering wheel and reaches over with his free hand to stroke my knuckles, while whispering hushed words of reassurance. I turn my head to face him in the dark confines of his car and I surrender to the overwhelming burden and I allow the tears to fall free, unable to be the strong, brave woman everyone expects me to be.

I don't know how we made it as the whole journey was a blur, but we arrive at the Queen Elizabeth Hospital, to an entrance full of paparazzi and journalists. *How did they find out so fucking quickly?* For the first time in my career, I don't care if they see my vulnerable side. The man I love is fighting for his life, and I don't give two shits who knows it. They heckle and cat call to me, as I step out of Sam's truck. He tosses his keys to Jace, who is waiting at the curb for us with a sombre look on his face. There is a wordless exchange between the two men, as he catches the keys easily, nodding curtly at Sam. Sam mirrors his gesture, while quickly heading round to my side, shielding me from the glare of their lens. He wraps his thick, corded, tattooed arm around me, tucking me into his side and I smile a silent gratitude to him. As he leads me inside the hospital, I let out the breath I didn't know I was holding, and he looks at me with turbulent green eyes.

"You good, sweetheart?" he rasps, and I manage to nod, as I unconsciously cradle my stomach, without a thought for who could be watching. Sam looks down and cocks his pierced eyebrow with a look of surprise on his face.

"Congratulations?" he questions softly, aware of who could be listening. I nod sombrely, as he smiles that dimpled smile everyone goes gaga over.

"Does he know?" he asks curiously, and I nod again, my eyes full of sorrow.

"I asked him if he wanted kids, a family of his own, and he went off on this angry tirade about how he didn't ever want children. I blurted out the news in the heat of the moment, and he walked out on me."

The next thought that enters my brain cripples me and threatens to knock me off my feet. I slap my hand over my mouth, and I can't stop the tears from falling.

"Oh God! What if those were the last words I ever got to say to him, Sam?" I sob, feeling panic threatening my composure, and Sam pulls me closer into his strong arms. I rest my cheek on his pec, holding on for dear life.

"Shhh, it's going to be ok; I've got you, sweetheart."

I sob uncontrollably, conscious of people's eyes on me and the blinding flashes of the cameras around us. My heart beat starts to quicken, and I start to tremble in Sam's arms. The cacophony of the reporters and photographers seems to get louder with each minute that passes, as Sam eyes me cautiously.

"Shall we go somewhere quieter?" he whispers, so only I can hear him, and I nod, as Sam leads me away from staring, judgmental eyes. We go up to the intensive care unit in the lift, in relative silence, which I am grateful for. We are both greeted by the people close to Brody and Peyton steps into Sam's arms and cries for her best friend. She clings onto him, as if her life depends on it, and I'm suddenly hit with an unwelcome pang of jealousy. I push that thought to the back of my mind and try desperately to focus on the here and now.

I don't know how I managed to put one foot in front of the other, it is all a blur. I feel exhausted all of a sudden and I rest my head against the wall, trying to make sense of the events leading up to this very moment. I'm lost in thought, as I glance up at an older gentleman looking me over carefully, with his hands tucked into his pockets. He is average height, grey slicked back hair, pale blue eyes, wearing black dress trousers and a baby pink Lacoste polo shirt, with the top two buttons open, revealing a smattering of white chest hair.

"Raleigh?"

I nod, pulling his hands from his pockets and offers me his hand. His large, weathered hands are unusually soft, yet strong as he encases his hand in my small one.

"Lenny, pleasure to finally meet you," he says gruffly. I try to manage a small smile, as he regards me carefully.

"Pleased to meet you too, Lenny," I greet him softly and there is a brief silence, but it's not uncomfortable.

"How are you holding up, love?" he asks and I shake my head, with glossy eyes unable to speak, as a wave of emotion takes over my entire body. I'm desperately trying to swallow back the grief that's threatening to choke me where I stand. He nods in understanding, as he shifts his gaze to the floor. I manage to compose myself, if only for a brief moment.

"What happened?" I ask in a small voice, terrified of the answer.

Lenny takes a breath and looks to Jax for support. Jax awkwardly steps forward, with one hand tucked casually into the pocket of his baggy camouflage combat trousers, looking everywhere except at me.

"He was in a motorbike accident. He took a corner too fast and crashed into an incoming vehicle, which failed to stop in time. It was a hit and run, and he was found unconscious in the middle of the road, covered in blood. It was lucky he was wearing a helmet. It could have been so much worse," Jax states, almost clinically and completely detached from the situation. I slap my hand over my mouth at the thought of someone purposely driving off and leaving him lying injured and alone in the road. *Who would do that to another human being?*

"He's got a fractured skull; he was flung up in the air and hit the ground from a height. He's also got a broken wrist, fractured tibia and fibula, and a broken collar bone," Lenny adds, and I can't help the sob that escapes. Peyton pulls away from Sam and moves toward me, hugging me tightly to her. She envelopes me in her arms, her scent oddly offering a source of comfort to me.

"He's going to be fine, honey. He's stubborn, strong and even if he doesn't want to admit it, he loves you," she reassures me, pulling away from our embrace and squeezing my hand in a gesture of reassurance.

"Can I see him?"

I look to Lenny and he nods, throwing me a cautious look.

"I'll warn you now, he's in bad shape, love," he warns prudently. I nod, as I follow him and Sam down the corridor and into a dimly lit corner room.

Nothing could have prepared me for the sight that greeted me. Brody lying motionless in a hospital bed, with wires coming off what seems like every part of his broken body. I let out a strangled sob, my legs buckling underneath me, and I sink to the floor.

"Oh God! Oh God! I'm sorry, I'm so sorry, I'm sorry," I mutter repeatedly, the sight too much for me to bear. I hear heavy footsteps and Sam sits down on the hard floor next to me and pulls me into his lap.

"Shhh, I'm here, sweetheart, I'm here, shhh."

Sam and I have the same relationship as Brody and Peyton have. We have become close in the months that have passed and I'll be forever grateful for having him in my life. He cradles me close to him, stroking my hair softly, gently shushing me as he lets me sob all over him.

Sam breaks the momentary silence.

"How far along are you?" he asks curiously and I don't look up at him, choosing to mumble into his chest.

"I'm not sure. I haven't been to the doctor yet to confirm. I've been so busy with the movie I haven't had a chance. I told him earlier, and he said he didn't want to be a dad, that he couldn't infect our baby with his poison. Why would he say that, Sam? What isn't he telling me?" I sniffle, with more than a hint of desperation to my voice.

"Brody's damaged, babe. We all are in some way, but he's not had the best life. He was in foster care. He bounced from one children's home to another, and was homeless for a while, until mine and Jax's parents realised. Jamie-Leigh and Jude took him in for a few months, then he went off the rails, started doing drugs. It was recreational at first, then he got involved with the wrong people. Once we got famous, we started getting recognised more frequently, and the money started rolling in. J.D. enabled him, but he let himself be influenced by the fame, the easy access to the drugs and the women. By this point, he was heavy into drugs and was my partner in crime and for years. I let him lead me down a dark path. I could just have easily said no, but I chose that path. I know now it wasn't good for me. I knew deep down, we weren't good for each other. That it was toxic. I ended up in rehab because of it, several times. Then I met Peyton and she was it for me. I gave up that lifestyle for her. She taught me that there's good in everyone, even if you can't see it initially. He's been clean ever since he met you. You're good for him, we all see it, and for the first time in years, he's got a purpose. Now he's going to be a dad, which I'm going to rib him for, for the rest of eternity, by the way!" Sam jokes and I laugh. After a five-minute conversation with Sam, I feel like I know Brody a little better than I did earlier.

"Are you ready to get up? My legs are fucking killing me!" he laughs, and I hit him playfully.

"You're lucky I like you, Newbolt!" he winks cheekily.

"Right back at ya, Storm."

He pulls me to my feet and pulls up a chair next to Brody's bed. He gestures for me to sit down and I do as I'm bid.

"Talk to him. He can hear you. I'll be right outside, so yell if you need me."

He kisses me gently on my forehead and leaves the room, closing the door behind him with a gentle click.

The room is silent except for the dull, incessant beep of the machines.

"Hey handsome, it's me...us."

I hold his calloused hand in mine and place a gentle kiss on the back of it, feeling my bottom lip trembling.

"Please, wake up. We need you. I know it's not ideal. I know you're angry and you're probably still in shock, but I forgive you," I whisper, the tone of my voice pleading with him.

"You're the first man I let get close to me since Carter. *Fucking hell,* I can't do this without you, Brody. I feel like I know more, since Sam explained a little about why you are the way you are, but I need to hear those words from you, so you need to wake up, please, wake up. I love you, so, so much."

I cry for the broken man in front of me, peppering kisses on the back of his tattooed hand, hoping for a reaction, or a slight squeeze, anything to tell me he's still in there. As I sit next to his hospital bed, an overwhelming feeling of helplessness washes over me, as he lies there looking so pale, broken, and fragile. *My broken angel.*

2

Raleigh

I relish in the silence for those precious few moments, until the machines start beeping wildly and Brody starts convulsing. I frantically scream for someone to help him.

"SOMEONE HELP! PLEASE! SOMEONE HELP HIM! PLEASE!"

Within seconds, the room is a hive of activity, with doctors and nurses rushing to his bedside. Sam and Lenny battle to get me outside into the corridor, but I refuse to leave him. *I can't leave him; he fucking needs me!*

"No! I'm not leaving him! No! Please don't make me leave him!" I plead, as Sam cool as a cucumber, slightly bends and lifts me up effortlessly over his shoulder in a fireman's lift. He strides out of the room, with me flailing and screaming at his back.

"Put me down, you fucking ape!"

I hear him chuckle throatily, as he sets me down on a chair next to Peyton. I flash him a warning look, and he has the audacity to wink. *That bastard.* Peyton giggles girlishly and rolls her eyes, taking my hand in hers. I feel comforted by the people who are closest to Brody. I have been accepted into their family after years of feeling like I didn't belong, even in my own family.

I feel a rush of calm wash over me, even though on the inside I am far from calm. I'm fucking terrified that he's not going to make it through the night. I'm terrified that the last words I got to say to him were words of hate. I feel hot tears burning the back of my eyes and I choke on a sob, which causes a familiar roil in my stomach. I feel like I'm going to throw up. I quickly get to my feet and run down the corridor, spotting a toilet to the left. I swing the door open, push my way into a cubicle with urgency, drop to my knees, and vomit ungraciously into the toilet bowl. My stomach twists and clenches, as sweat starts to drip down my brow. I retch and heave over the toilet, dropping my forehead to my arm until the feeling subsides. I pull four sheets of toilet roll and wipe the remnants of sick away from the curve of my lips. I squeeze my eyes briefly shut and take a deep calming breath, as I hear the creak of the door open and footsteps approaching slowly, almost cautiously.

"Raleigh?"

I hear a soft female voice and I recognise it as Peyton's.

"Raleigh? It's Peyton. Are you ok, hon?" she asks, concern laced in her voice. I rise to my feet, flush the toilet, and swing the cubicle door open. I approach the sink slowly, catching sight of my reflection in the mirror. I look like shit. My eyes are full of sorrow and desperation, hollow and rimmed red. Peyton stands back silently and regards me carefully for a few moments. I wash my hands and splash cold water on my pale face, as I turn to face her. The look she gives me in return isn't one of sympathy or pity, it's understanding. She's letting me know that she feels the same, that she's hurting too.

The mess of emotions bulldozing their way through my entire body causes the torrent of tears to break free once again and I'm sobbing, leaning against the sink for the support. Peyton steps forward and wraps me in her arms.

"Hey, I'm here, hon, I'm here, shhh. It's gonna be ok, shhh."

I take comfort in her arms and shake my head.

"I can't lose him, Peyton, I can't. I love him so much."

I let out a stifled sob, and she squeezes me tighter, enveloping me in her scent.

"I know, I know you do. Congratulations, by the way, that's fantastic news. We're so happy for you."

I pull away from her and wipe away my tears on Brody's vest.

"Is it? Is it really great news? Brody didn't seem to think so when he walked out on me after I told him."

I curse my hormones to hell, as I go from feeling so full of sorrow to boiling rage within seconds.

"I told him he was going to be a dad, and he left me! He fucking left me after I begged him not to, after I told him I needed him! I confessed I couldn't do it on my own and instead of talking to me, he screamed at me. Telling me how he can't be a dad, how he can't infect a baby with his poison. He told me the reason he's never settled down in a serious, long-term relationship before was because he hurts everyone he gets close to! Why the fuck would he say that to me, Peyton! Explain to me! WHY!" I yell, angrily swiping the tears away from my eyes and I know I'm being irrational, but I can't seem to help myself.

"Because Brody Hart is addicted to himself, that's why. I don't know how else I can explain. I get that you're angry. Believe me, I'm fucking angry at him too. But it takes two people to make a baby. He's not a bad person. He was probably just in shock. I'm not making excuses for him, not at all, but maybe try and see it from his point of view. I know I'm one to talk. I got pregnant after Sam and me had been dating for seven or eight months, and it all happened so fast. But Brody's not wired like the rest of us, so at least try and just consider his perspective. He lost his mum when he was a child, he had no one, it's a lot for him to take in."

As I listen to her explanation, I'm slowly getting to unravel and know the real Brody Hart and that's going to have to be enough, for now.

***

I'm not sure how much time passes, but we are joined by a doctor. The doctor is a tall, lean, balding, middle-aged man who introduces himself as Doctor Cooper.

"I'm Doctor Cooper. May I ask who is Mr. Hart's next of kin?" he asks and Lenny steps forward, squaring his shoulders with an air of authority.

"That would be me, doc," he says gruffly, desperately trying to hold it together and be the strong patriarch figure that Brody has come to rely on for so many years.

"Whatever you need to say, you can say it in front of them. They're as much his family as I am, and this young lady is his girlfriend."

The doctor nods curtly, clearing his throat, and smiles sympathetically in my direction.

"We found significant traces of cocaine in Mr. Hart's blood stream and his body went into cardiac arrest."

I can't hide my shock, as I take in the Doctor's words and I hear Sam and Lenny cursing softly. *He was high? I thought he had been clean ever since he met me? Did I drive him back to the drugs? Oh God, this is all my fault.*

"He has some significant internal bleeding, due to the point of impact, which we're certain that the handlebars of his bike caused. He's also suffered a basilar skull fracture, and that has resulted in excessive leakage of cerebrospinal fluid. We'll need to operate as a matter of urgency. We're prepping him for surgery now, to hopefully stop it and prevent any further damage. We have to tell you this, I'm afraid, but because of the extent of Brody's injuries, there's a considerable chance he might not make it through surgery."

I let out a strangled sob and Peyton sobs softly too. She squeezes my hand and wraps her arm around my shoulder.

"What would happen if he didn't have surgery?" Lenny asks pragmatically, squeezing the back of his neck and clearing his throat.

"He could potentially bleed to death, organ failure, or the oxygen to his red blood cells would be compromised. There's also a risk with any type of brain surgery that he could suffer brain damage or, worse case scenario, live the rest of his life in a permanent vegetative state."

Lenny nods, as if taking in the information he has just been told, and I get to my feet, unable to wrap my head around what the doctor has said.

"What are the chances that he's going to come through this?" I ask, my voice quivering with pure anguish. Lenny moves closer to me and wraps his strong arm around my shoulder.

"Don't do this to yourself, love."

He tries to placate me, but I shrug him off, a little more harshly than I intend to.

"No! I want to know! I have to know! There isn't just me to consider anymore."

I admit, as I move my hand to my stomach and Lenny is taken aback by my words.

"You're...pregnant? He's...h...he's going to be a dad?"

He looks stunned, and I nod as the doctor clears his throat, momentarily halting Lenny's line of questioning.

"As of now? It's fifty/fifty, but there is a probable chance that he might not make it. We're doing everything we can to keep him stable and comfortable, but it all rests on how his body copes with the surgery," he says matter-of-factly and I nod curtly, unable to speak, swallowing back the tennis ball sized lump that has formed in my throat.

"We're going to prep him and take him straight down to the operating theatre."

He gives us a grave smile, as he turns and strides off down the corridor.

"Congratulations, love." Lenny's gruff voice, full of grief, cuts through my muddled thoughts, as I give him a watery smile.

"Thank you," I reply softly and he looks as if he wants to say more, but he stops himself. I'm not religious, but in that moment I pray to anyone who will listen to bring him back to me. *Please let him make it through.*

***

Time all blends into one, as I'm staring aimlessly into nothingness, overthinking the night's events, and trying desperately to keep my eyes open. My thoughts are interrupted by the muted sound of the large flat screen TV mounted on the wall in the corner of the room.

"Rock band Rancid Vengeance's future in the music industry looks bleak and uncertain tonight, as rhythm guitarist and well documented lothario, Brody Hart, has been involved in a major road traffic accident. The extent of Hart's injuries are yet to be confirmed. However, a spokesperson for Rancid Vengeance has been contacted for further comment. Hart, thirty-four, out spoken and hailed the notorious bad boy of the band has recently been linked to troubled Hollywood starlet, Raleigh Storm, twenty-nine. The reason behind this horrifying incident is still unclear at this stage. We will keep you updated on any developments as this story unfolds."

Peyton squeezes my hand, and I swear I hear Sam mutter under his breath. "Fucking vultures!"

I swipe away a stray tear that has escaped from the corner of my eye, as my phone starts ringing, blasting out the familiar *Def Leppard Pour Some Sugar On Me*. I take it out of my pocket and see Liv's name flash up on the screen. I let go of Peyton's hand and stand up, as I swipe the screen to answer the call. She doesn't give me the chance to even say hello.

"OH MY GOD! RALEIGH! I've just seen the news. Are you ok? What's happened?" she says in a rush and I pace a little further down the corridor, momentarily stepping away from the rest of the group.

"He's been in a motorbike accident, he's...fuck, Liv, I can't lose him, I can't."

The dam holding my tears at bay seemingly shatters under the weight of the situation and I break down in uncontrollable tears yet again, sobbing for my broken man lying helpless in his hospital bed.

"Hey! Everything's going to be alright, he's gonna be just fine. Do you need me to come to the hospital? Just say the word, Jensen is in Monaco and I'm due to join him tomorrow, but I can be there in twenty minutes," she asks softly.

"It's fine, Liv, honestly. I'm here with Peyton, the boys and Brody's sober sponsor," I explain and there's a brief pause.

"Are you sure? If you need anything at all, you just call me, yeah? This can't be good for the baby."

I subconsciously place my hand on my stomach and stroke in gentle circles, as if to remind myself that he or she is still there.

"I'm sure, thank you. I know, tonight has been awful, we argued before he left. I told him I was pregnant, and he flipped out. He told me in no uncertain terms that he doesn't want to be a dad. This is all my fault! What am I going to do if I lose him, Liv? What if those were the last words I ever got to say to him?" I sob softly, trying desperately to get my tears under control.

"Shhh, you can't think like that, Rae, he's a fighter, he battered the absolute shit out of your fucking ex, so he's got my vote! He's going to be ok, I'm sure of it."

I smile a watery smile at Liv's reassuring words.

"He was probably just in shock, that's all, you've been together such a short amount of time, and now all of a sudden he's going to be a dad, that's got to be a shocker for anyone, babe! Maybe he thought you'd have more time to enjoy each other before introducing a baby into the mix."

I take in her words and conclude that she's right.

"The stupid thing is, I know you're right, but I can't help thinking there's another reason for it. Was he planning to break up with me? Was there someone else? I don't know, Liv, I get that his temper can be volatile at times and he's prone to mental shut downs, but this was a whole other level," I babble, spilling out every hidden thought I've managed to keep to myself.

"Whoa! Volatile temper? He hasn't hit you, has he? Because if he has, I swear to God he'll know about it! I've seen Dexter, I know how to fucking bury a body, Rae!" she says, her voice full of fire and tenacity.

"No! Nothing like that, of course he hasn't. After Carter, do you really think I'd go there for a second time? Not a fucking chance! I'm not that girl anymore, Liv, that girl..."

I shudder to think about the way I allowed Carter to manipulate me, how I allowed him to violate me. It makes me feel sick to my stomach. Brody has shown me nothing but love and true affection. *When he's not being an emotionless shell*. But I don't say those words out loud. *She wouldn't understand.*

"I know, I know."

I squeeze my eyes shut briefly and shake my head to the ceiling, trying to compose myself.

"They've taken him down to theatre for emergency surgery. He had internal bleeding, and he suffered a fractured skull. The doctor said he might not make it and that it was fifty/fifty. I can't lose him, I can't."

As I say those words, I suddenly feel exhausted, both mentally and physically. I straighten myself out and my shoulders sag in defeat, as I push the heel of my free hand into my eyes. I stand there for a few precious moments, willing the tears that threaten not to fall and I take a long deep exhale before I speak again.

"I can't do this alone, Liv, I can't. I don't know how to be without him. He's been the only constant in my life recently."

I can't keep the acerbic tone from my voice.

"Thanks, that means a lot that you think so highly of me, Raleigh." she scoffs bitterly and I feel my hackles instantly rise.

"Well, if you weren't so wrapped up in yourself, you would have realised that I was fucking struggling! After Carter raped me, I wasn't in a good place and I injured myself to the point I needed fucking stitches!"

I whisper hiss, hoping no one heard my angry tirade and I almost think she's hung up on me, until I hear her gasp.

"R...Rae, I...I don't know what to say! But you could have come to me! You could have talked to me if you were struggling! I'm here, I've always been here! Now I feel like shit for not being there for you. I'm so sorry, I've been so wrapped up in Jensen, planning the wedding and work, but that's no excuse."

Her voice sounds full of remorse and I instantly feel bad for shouting at her.

"I know, I'm sorry Liv, I didn't mean to go off at you. I'm exhausted and hormonal!" I chuckle softly.

"You had every right to yell at me. I've been a shitty friend, there's no excuse for it and I'm so sorry. You've got nothing to apologise for. I just want you to know I'm here for you, always."

I sigh. "I know, Liv, I know, look, I have to go, I'll call you tomorrow," I reassure her.

"Ok, call me immediately if anything changes. Love you lots, Rae. Mwah!"

I smile to myself.

"Right back at ya, Livvy."

I hang up the phone and I feel my stomach start to roil again as I'm joined by Peyton.

"Raleigh?"

She brushes my arm and I turn to her with watery eyes, the extent of the situation suddenly overwhelming me. My heart starts pounding in my chest and I start to feel light-headed. I stumble a little on my feet and Peyton tries to steady me.

"Hey, come and sit down. You look don't look too good, are you feeling ok?"

I try desperately to swallow down the vomit I can feel rising in my throat.

"Raleigh?"

My name is the last thing I hear, as I feel the floor sway beneath my feet before the darkness consumes me completely.

3

Raleigh

I blink slowly and reluctantly, the harsh fluorescents making it hard to focus on my surroundings. I find myself somewhere completely unfamiliar and a feeling of helplessness washes over me. *How did I get here? What happened?* Everything in the room is bathed in a dull, cream hue. My head is pounding, and my mouth feels dry, as my eyes dart around the room looking for something familiar. They land on Sam and Peyton, who are speaking in hushed tones in the corner of the room. Sam is sitting in the large beige leather chair, with Peyton sat across his lap. The familiar pang of jealousy rears its ugly head and I instantly feel bad for feeling that way when they've done nothing but support me since I met them.

"Hey sweetheart, how are you feeling?" he rasps.

"W...what happened?" I ask, and he clears his throat.

"You passed out in the corridor; you scared the shit out of us."

His husky voice is full of concern, as a tall, blonde female doctor enters the room holding a clipboard in her hand.

"Miss Storm?"

I nod, as she approaches the bed wearing dark trousers, a white lab coat and her hair pulled up in a neat chignon.

"Doctor Fallon Fontaine, how are you feeling?"

I squeeze my eyes shut, willing the marching band in my head to go away.

"My head hurts."

She flips the paper on her clipboard and scribbles something down.

"Totally normal, you passed out due to low blood pressure. We've examined you and you're approximately seven weeks pregnant. Fainting is extremely common in the first trimester."

She presents me with a sonogram picture, and I take the picture from her with shaky hands and glossy eyes. My heart feels almost too big for my chest and I'm bursting with such love for our baby. As I examine the scan picture, all I can see is a clear dark circular shape with two black blobs in the middle, but casting my eyes over it, it all seems very real, and I can't tear my eyes away. *It's really happening, it's real and I'm not dreaming.*

I've never really put much thought into having kids, but as soon as I saw the word *'pregnant'*, the happiness seemed to outweigh the fear. There was a tiny human growing inside me and there was nothing more incredible than that, it was a truly wonderful life-changing feeling. I knew I was going to go through with it, with or without Brody because I had already started to let myself wonder what he or she would look like. *Would they have my eyes? Would they have Brody's nose?* But Brody's reaction tainted my joy until now. Seeing our baby in black and white has made me realise that there's not just me anymore, it's us.

"You need to take it easy, but we won't need to keep you overnight," the doctor informs me, and I nod, as she turns to leave.

"Congratulations, babe, we're so happy for you!" Peyton's enthusiastic voice cuts through my thoughts and I find myself smiling a genuine smile.

"Thank you, I'm so grateful that you're here, I don't know what I would have done without you," I say honestly, as Sam leans in and kisses my forehead.

"Anytime, sweetheart. We're going to head home to freshen up. We need to check on the boys and get a few hours' sleep, but we'll be back soon."

I nod, as they both leave, leaving me alone with my thoughts. I gently rest my hand on my stomach and fall into a dreamless sleep.

***

It's been hours since Brody was taken to the operating theatre for surgery. The sun has come up and a new day has begun. I've been discharged after my fainting episode with a strict warning to take it easy and I'm back sitting in the waiting area with bated breath, waiting to hear whether he made it through. I feel better after a few hours' sleep. Sam and Peyton have gone home, along with Nancy. Jax and Lucas have gone on the hunt for coffee and Lenny is wearing a hole in the corridor floor, by pacing up and down. The doctor from earlier joins us in the corridor, taking in the scene unfolding. He clears his throat and I turn to face him, looking for any indication on his face of the news he's about to share.

"Brody is out of surgery; his head injury was worse than we first anticipated. He had several seizures during surgery and his particular injury often results in significant swelling of the brain. The swelling puts pressure on the brain, which can damage brain tissue. To limit long-term damage, we've put him an induced coma to allow his body to fully heal," the doctor explains and I let out a strangled sob. *This isn't happening.* Lenny puts his arm around me, to stop my knees from buckling underneath me and I cling to him, as the doctor continues.

"The next twenty-four to forty-eight hours are critical. He's currently unable to breathe on his own so we've put him on a ventilator. We need to keep a close eye on him, and he'll be monitored every half an hour."

Lenny unwraps his arm from around me and steps forward, swallowing a few times before he speaks.

"What are the chances that he's going to recover?" he asks and I'm not sure I'm ready to hear the answer.

"Recovery is a gradual process, and we won't know more until he comes off the ventilator and he starts breathing on his own. However, that being said, the length of the coma is one of the most accurate predictors of the severity of long-term symptoms. The longer the coma, the greater the likelihood of physical disability, although sometimes that's only a guide. But like I said, the next twenty-four to forty-eight hours are critical. He's not out of the woods yet."

As I listen to the doctors words, it all of a sudden becomes too much. My heart physically aches, and I scream from the crippling pain that has lodged itself in my chest and I turn, rushing down the corridor trying to get as far away from this shit show as possible.

I follow the signs to the Intensive Care Unit, my heart beat quickening with each step I take, and I soon find myself stepping over the threshold and into the stark, dimly lit, sterile hospital room. An unwelcome feeling of hopelessness washes over me, as he lies there looking so pale and peaceful. There are wires coming from all directions, and the dull beep of the machines fills the room. I'm propelled towards him like a magnet, the nurse attaching an IV to his arm and smiles kindly, as she registers my presence.

"Hello, love, can I help?" she asks curiously, as I take her in. She is a short woman, plump, and looks to be in her late fifties. She has skin the colour of dark mocha, friendly, hazel eyes, and a warm infectious smile. Her dark greying hair is tied up in a neat bun.

"I'm his girlfriend, can I sit with him?" I ask with a sniff. She smiles warmly and nods.

"I shouldn't because you're not immediate family, but I won't tell if you don't, petal," she says with a wink.

"He's one of those dishy rockers, not the first time these boys have been here."

I find myself smiling at her friendly nature, instantly liking her. She pulls out the cream leather chair, gesturing for me to sit. I move closer and take my seat next to his bed.

"Talk to him, he can hear you. Tell him about your day. I'm sure he'd love to hear it," she says softly, giving my arm a reassuring brush.

"I'll leave you to it, love, I'm just doing my rounds, but there's someone at the nurses station if you need anything."

She leaves us to it, and I glance dejectedly up to the ceiling. I blink back the tears and take a moment to really take him in, realising just how lucky I am. The angular slope of his nose, his sharp cheekbones, the dimple in his chin, the defined set of his biceps and his collection of tattoos that depict his journey so far. *He is truly gorgeous, but he doesn't seem to know it.* His beauty is marred by the presence of a deep cut on his forehead with stitches holding it together, a nasty cut on his lip, his face is pretty banged up, but it doesn't take away from the magnificence of his good looks.

I can't seem to tear my eyes away from his the shaved section of his head and the large angry, red incision held together with stitches, lots of stitches. The wound runs from his hairline to the back of his head and it breaks my heart a little more seeing him so weak and damaged. I look around the hospital room and it is as devoid of beauty as I am of hope. Right now, I feel that all hope might be lost.

4

Raleigh

The hospital room seems barren, clinical and sterile. The room is bathed in a yellow tint, giving off a false sense of warmth when it was anything but warm. The pungent smell of the disinfectant invades my nostrils, causing my stomach to roil, as I take his hand in mine and stroke gentle circles with the pad of my thumb.

"I need you to wake up, Brody. Please wake up," I plead, as I take out the sonogram of our baby, looking at it with watery eyes.

"I'm seven weeks pregnant, we can't do this without you. I need to hear you call me kitten; I need you to look at me with those intense silver eyes of yours. I'm falling apart without you, Brody. I know you were in shock; believe me, I am too and I'm fucking terrified I won't be able to do this on my own. But this little person growing inside of me is relying on me to be strong. But right now, I don't think I have the strength, not without you."

I sob, squeezing his limp lifeless hand, as I'm startled by someone clearing their throat. I turn to see Lenny hovering in the doorway.

"Want some company, love?"

I nod and he steps into the room. I take him in, his grey slicked back hair looking more than a little exhausted and dishevelled. His blue eyes are pained as they land on Brody's lifeless form. He pulls up a chair with a noisy scrape and sighs heavily, dropping down into the chair.

"Who would do this to you, son?" he says wearily, as I try to piece together the extent of their relationship. The way Lenny talks, he's more than just a sober sponsor, their connection goes deeper. He's more of a father figure, someone who tries to keep Brody on the straight and narrow. From Lenny's reaction upon hearing of Brody's accident, it's obvious he cares about him deeply. He loves him like a son, something Brody was missing in his formative years.

"I'm going to kick his arse when he wakes up, little shit." he grinds out gruffly, breaking the silence, as an unwelcome feeling of helplessness washes over me.

"Every time he's visited me since he's been with you, it's like a light's been switched on. He might not want to admit it, but he loves you... deep down I know it. Brody's past isn't a fairy tale with a happy ending, it's dark and it's tragic. I wish to God I'd met him sooner, I wish I could have taken him away from that life and given him the love he deserves."

The devastation in Lenny's voice is apparent and my heart breaks for this kind-hearted old man, who's done nothing but love Brody and show him what a real parent is like. They might not be blood, but Lenny is as much Brody's dad in every way possible. I find myself reaching over to him and taking his hand in mine, as he turns to me and smiles softly.

"Don't go telling him I got all soppy and sentimental over him! He'll never let me forget it!"

He wipes a tear from his eye and we both laugh.

"Congratulations by the way, I had no idea."

My smile falters and I shake my head. "He walked out on me when I told him. He freaked out, saying over and over how he didn't want to infect our baby with his poison. How he couldn't be someone's dad. If I hadn't told him, he wouldn't be in here now. This is all my fault."

I burst into tears again, cursing my hormones to hell.

"You can't think like that, love. Brody's very self-destructive. He jeopardises his own happiness. He's got abandonment issues, but he's not incapable of love. Nor is he incapable of being a dad. It takes two to make a baby, he's as much responsible as you are, you're both adults."

I swipe angrily at my tears and shake my head.

"I can't do this without him, Lenny, I can't."

He squeezes my hand in a gesture of comfort and support.

"I know, love. Why don't you go home and get some proper rest. You're exhausted, and you passed out earlier. Your body is telling you to rest. It's not just you now, you have to focus on that baby in your belly too. Get some sleep, freshen up, and as soon as you're ready to come back, I'll send one of the boys to come and get you. Obviously, we'll call if there's any change," he says sternly, his voice full of authority. I look at him through desolate eyes and my shoulders sag.

"What if he wakes up? I need to be here," I state, trying to sound equally as stern, but instead I just sound exhausted and defeated.

"Go home. That's an order. You need to rest. Sam's back and waiting to take you," he gives me a look only a father could give his child and I smirk.

"So bossy!" I joke and he laughs throatily, as I stand up from my place at his bedside.

"You have no idea! Now, go!" He swats me away. I lean over Brody and place a tender kiss on his forehead.

"I'll be back soon, handsome. Love you." I whisper, as I leave the room. As I exit, Sam is leaning against the wall outside the door with his hand casually tucked in the pocket of his jeans, deep in thought. He registers my presence and pushes off the wall, his tall frame eclipsing mine.

"Ready?" he rasps, offering me his arm. I link my arm through his and we make our way through the maze of corridors. We eventually make it to the large waiting area, where one of Rancid Vengeances' bodyguards, Trey, is waiting. He looks uncomfortable folded into the chair that looks too small for his big body to fit in.

Trey stands to his full height from his position on the overstuffed chair in Reception.

"Yeah don't even think about stepping out of that door without me," he says coolly and Sam cocks his pierced eyebrow, as I see between fifteen and twenty paparazzi outside the building.

"Fucks sake," Sam curses, as Trey laughs putting his earpiece in place and pulling his sunglasses down to shield his eyes. He touches his ear and turns to Sam, there is a wordless interaction between the two of them as Sam nods curtly.

"On the move. Yep, you got it, boss. It's just Sam and Raleigh. Stay close," he says shortly and sharply. I move close to him, as him and Sam sandwich me between them, shielding me as we exit the building. I am blinded by the wild flashing of the flashbulbs and a crowd of enthusiastic photographers and journalists. The cat calls and the cacophony of chatter amongst them.

"Raleigh! Raleigh! Is it true that Brody's accident wasn't an accident?" One particularly over-enthusiastic reporter shouts and I'm struck dumb at the question. I freeze on the spot, my blood running cold at the thought of someone hurting Brody deliberately. It makes my stomach turn and I open and close my mouth, but Sam gently grips the top of my arm, shaking me from my private reverie. He mouths '*Are you ok?*' and I nod my answer robotically. There is a car idling at the curb and Trey opens the door to the waiting black Bentley. He puts his arm out to stop the vultures surging forward and clears a path for us to get into the car. Once I'm in the somewhat quiet confines of the car, I allow the enormity of the situation to the forefront of my mind. Sam pulls up the privacy screen, as the car starts to pull away into the flow of traffic. I drop my head into my hands and I sob for my beautifully wounded soldier.

Brody

I hear the sound of a muffled voice speaking in a hushed tone, it sounds distinctly female. The voice seems familiar and unfamiliar all at the same time. I feel like I'm in the midst of a thick, heavy fog. Everything around me is unclear, I can't focus on anything and no matter how hard I try, I can't open my eyes.

"I need you to wake up, Brody. Please wake up."

Her voice is thick with emotion and whoever she is she's upset.

"I'm seven weeks pregnant, we can't do this without you. I need to hear you call me kitten; I need you to look at me with those intense silver eyes of yours. I'm falling apart without you, Brody. I know you were in shock; believe me, I am too and I'm fucking terrified I won't be able to do this on my own. But this little person growing inside of me is relying on me to be strong. But right now, I don't think I have the strength, not without you."

Who is she? Do I know her? I don't understand what she's telling me. I'm not seeing anyone, I'm young, free and single, she has to be talking to or about someone else. I haven't got anyone pregnant, at least if I have, I'm not aware of it. She squeezes my hand I want to squeeze it back. I want to reassure this stranger, that everything is going is going to be ok, but my limbs won't co-operate and every part of my body hurts. *What the fuck happened? Why am I here? Is this a bad dream?* All of these thoughts barrel through my brain and my head feels like it's going to explode. *Did I hit my head?*

I hear another voice, but my brain won't allow me to focus on it. An overwhelming feeling of helplessness steamrolls its way through my consciousness, as the sound of dull beeps filters through my foggy brain. Pain shoots through my body and inside I'm roaring out in pain, but no matter how loud I yell, no one can hear me. Just when the pain was at its worst, it dissipated and the searing agony was replaced with a numb, floaty feeling. The distant sound of soft female sobs penetrates through my mind and the hushed conversation is back.

"I can't do this without him, Lenny, I can't."

Who's Lenny? Why can't I recognise their voices?

"I know, love. Why don't you go home and get some proper rest. You're exhausted, and you passed out earlier. Your body is telling you to rest. It's not just you now, you have to focus on that baby in your belly too. Get some sleep, freshen up and as soon as you're ready to come back, I'll send one of the boys to come and get you. Obviously, we'll call if there's any change."

His voice full of authority and it feels like some parts of my brain are doors that are currently locked and the reset button has been pushed. *Why is he asking her about her baby? Do they know each other?* He speaks to her as if he knows her.

I try to listen carefully to what they are saying, but everything is muffled and unclear as I give in to the blackness.

5

Brody
Past

I smell the pungent scent of burning rubber and I hear the dull sound of sirens. I can vaguely hear muffled voices speaking in hushed tones, I don't know who the voices belong to and I'm unaware of my surroundings. Everything around me is unclear, all I am aware of is that every part of my body hurts. My limbs feel heavy and I almost feel like I'm in the midst of a fucking acid trip. I'm floating and I can't open my eyes. My voice feels like it's trapped, locked away somewhere deep within me. I want to scream, I want to shout. Why the fuck can't I see? Where am I? A metallic smell permeates my nostrils and I feel a warm wetness somewhere on my body, but I can't seem to locate where. Am I bleeding? Am I dead? Is this what the end feels like? What the fuck is going on? Where's my bike?

I can sense someone approach, I can feel someone lift the visor on my helmet and grip my shoulders, shaking me gently. Ouch, careful, that fucking hurts, you wanker.

"Hello? Can you hear me? Can you open your eyes for me?"

I feel a feather light touch on my wrist, as I can hear the dull cacophony of idle chatter around me. A coldness settles deep in my bones. Why is it so fucking cold?

"Male, mid-thirties, he's unconscious and unresponsive. His pulse is weak, but he's breathing."

I hear the buzz and crackle of what sounds like a police radio.

"We need to cordon off the road and move everybody back! MOVE BACK NOW!" I hear a male voice shout, as my eyelids send a message to my brain and flutter open. A prolonged groan emits involuntarily from deep within me and I have a million questions on the tip of my tongue, but I don't vocalise any of them. I feel the presence of someone next to me.

"Hello? Can you hear me, can you tell me your name?"

A soft female voice breaks through the thick fog, as her face comes into view. She has a warm brown eyes and a friendly smile, she is of Asian descent. Her hair is pulled up into a high ponytail on top of her head and she is wearing a green paramedic uniform. I groan low in my throat and I go to move, yelling out loud, as a pain rips through every part of me.

"Please, don't move, you've been in an accident. You're in shock, but I need you to start by telling me your name, sweetheart."

She coaxes again softly, as I try to focus on my surroundings I see a dark figure in my peripheral vision, bringing down a sickle and I hear the scrape of metal across the asphalt. My whole world suddenly in slow motion. My head spins and I jerk at the sound, which sets my teeth on edge and causes an unbearable pain to barrel through my body. I look again and the figure has disappeared. Fuck me, that must have been some strong coke.The young woman beside me looks at me sympathetically and expectantly. Oh shit, she asked me my name.

"B...Brody."

My voice is hoarse and doesn't sound like my own, as fragmented memories of Raleigh's beautiful sorrow-filled face assault my still fuzzy brain.

"Raleigh, Raleigh, baby, I'm so fucking sorry."

I mutter incoherently, wondering if she heard me.

"Brody, nice to meet you, I'm Nicole. I need you to stay calm and nice and still for me. Do you think you can do that?"

Panic settles in my gut and an excruciating pain tears through my entire body. I'm in agony and I don't know why. Fuck me, I'm in so much pain right now.

"Brody, I need you to tell me where it hurts, can you do that for me?"

I can't focus on anything other than the pain barrelling through my broken body and a sharp pain ricocheting through my skull. It feels like my head is going to explode.

"IT FUCKING HURTS! MAKE IT STOP! PLEASE MAKE IT STOP!" I roar, tears bursting from my eyes and I'm suddenly terrified. I don't want to die, not now, not like this.

"It's going to be ok, I'm gonna make it stop, but I need you to be really calm for me, yeah?"

She shines a light in my eyes and it only heightens the pain. She catches the attention of someone in my peripheral vision and speaks in hushed tones.

"That's Brody Hart from Rancid Vengeance, we need to get his helmet off, now."

That's all I manage to make out, as I feel a second presence at my side.

"Hello Brody, I'm Debbie. You're doing brilliant. I'm going to help Nicole get your helmet off, so we can see you better, is that ok?"

I hum, trying desperately to focus on something other than the fucking torturous agony barrelling through my skull. Nicole reaches over, loosens my chin strap, and unbuckles it.

"You're doing great, sweetheart."

Debbie smiles, as they both work together to pull off my helmet. The cool night breeze tickles my face.

"He wasn't wearing leathers. He's got a fractured skull so we need to get him to a hospital, fast."

My chest starts to tighten, as I hear those words. What the actual fucking fuck? Lightning fast, I grab Nicole's hand in mine.

"N...Ni...Nicole, I can't breathe, I ca...can't, please, pl...ease, don't let me die. Please...I...don't want to die, not here, not tonight."

I plead, my breath coming in short, sharp bursts and the last thing I hear, as I succumb to the blackness, is Nicole's soft voice telling me everything is going to be ok.

Raleigh
Present

As I allow myself to focus on the chapters of our story so far, I came to the stark realisation that from now on, there would be only two chapters of my life, before Brody Hart and after Brody Hart. It's difficult for me to remember who I was before he breezed into my life, with his quick wit and his tattoos. *Oh, so many tattoos.* I could spend hours tracing the lines, deciphering the meaning of each intricate design and it still wouldn't be enough.

He is such a complex, complicated, multi-faceted, damaged human being, but he was mine. I belonged to him and he belonged to me in every way possible. Brody normally hides behind a mask, he hides behind his alter ego, Snake, and when we're alone, he momentarily lets that mask slip. I sometimes wonder if I'm the only person who has seen that side of him. He plays up to the fact he's the joker of the band and he doesn't take himself too seriously. In turn, no one else takes him seriously either, and that makes my heart hurt for him. He's so talented in his own right, but he's overshadowed by Sam's good looks, Jax's effortless flair and Lucas' cool persona.

People can sit and judge him, analyse him, they can lie him down on a psychiatrist's couch and still no one would get inside Brody's head. He's a part-time bad boy, crossed with a part-time gentle lover. From day to day, minute to minute, hour to hour, I never know which side of him I am going to be graced with. His head and his feelings are a locked door, even to those close to him. I've never seen inside his head, he never lets me in, not really. Trying to get anything out of him is trying to get blood out of a stone. I've seen rare glimpses of the man I know he's capable of being, but for some unknown reason he doesn't want me to see that side of him.

I know he's filled with issues I have yet to explore, and it didn't matter that he couldn't say those three words that I longed to hear out loud. That didn't matter at all, because all I've ever wanted is to be someone's one and only and I know without a shadow of a doubt, that I was his. My little brother, Jagger, was always the golden boy, and I had learned to live with that over the years. When I met Brody, he was the first man to treat me like I wasn't second best and the moment our eyes locked, I knew my life would never be the same again.

I have never been one to compare my life to others, but the only thing I have ever wanted is to be loved. In our short relationship, he's become the other half of my heart. He's the man I live and breathe for, the man I love so much I feel like I might burst. Brody Hart had turned me into a stronger, braver version of myself. He made me realise that I didn't need to apologise for the person I had become because of him and he made me believe that I was worthy of being loved.

My thoughts are interrupted by the low sound of the news on the radio in Sam's truck.

Brody "Snake" Hart, one quarter of popular rock band Rancid Vengeance, has been involved in a horrific hit-and-run accident. Notorious bad boy of the band has hit headlines in recent weeks for his blossoming romance with troubled Hollywood movie actress Raleigh Storm. Storm, twenty-nine, is currently starring in 'Rocked', directed by controversial British movie director, Damien Valentine. Hart, thirty-four, was identified as the victim at the scene and rushed to a nearby hospital. Sources close to the band say, "he's in a critical, but stable condition." Police are urging the driver of the other vehicle to come forward and are encouraging witnesses to contact their local constabulary with vital evidence. A spokesperson for Rancid Vengeance has been contacted for an official statement. However, the extent of his injuries are said to be severe and potentially life-threatening...

I don't get to hear the rest, as Sam crashes his fist violently through the centre console, the sound echoing around the confined space of the truck. He swerves aggressively to avoid an oncoming car and screeches to a halt at the side of the road. He frantically bashes his fists brutally on the steering wheel and roars at the top of his lungs, visibly trembling.

"Sam?" I say softly, glancing at the ruined screen. His breathing is laboured, his chest heaving, as he turns to face me.

"I...I'm so sorry, sweetheart, I...didn't mean to frighten you," he says huskily, his voice full of pain and remorse. I shake my head, dismissing him.

"I hate that our lives are there for everyone to judge, we're human as well! They don't seem to fucking get it! We have feelings and emotions too! I'm so fucking angry at him!" he barks, and I gently lay my hand on his thick, tattooed bicep.

"The fame gets a little too much for me sometimes, I get it, I really do. More than most." I murmur. "And believe me, no one is more fucking angry at him than me, right now. How could he do this to us, Sam? And how could someone just leave him there lying in the road?"

My voice is thick with unshed tears and I will them not to spill down my cheeks, as I take a steadying breath.

"When I thought I'd lost Peyton, I was in a dark place. I drank down the grief like it was the finest red wine. After a while, I stopped being able to tell the difference between pleasure and pain, between good and bad, between right and wrong. The lines became blurred, and I'd wake up every morning either hungover, or next to a woman that wasn't her, sometimes both. What I'm trying to say is, grief does strange irrational things to people. It makes you act out of character. I was a total fucking mess, and I kept it bottled up inside until it was too late. I'll never be able to take that back, but if I could rewind time and do things differently, I would in a fucking heartbeat. If you ever need to talk, no matter day or night, I'm here for you. Me, Peyton, and the rest of the boys. You're part of our family now, whether Brody cares to admit it or not, you're one of us."

A tear rolls down my cheek at his kind words and I curse my hormones to hell for reacting so emotionally.

"I'm sorry I lost it back there, I just get so fucking frustrated. Our lives aren't our own, we live in a world of half-truths and sensationalised lies. For fourteen years we've put up with people thinking they know us, thinking they're our best friends, when in reality they don't really know us at all. In the beginning, Brody surrounded himself with the hangers on, people who would take advantage of him and his kind nature. He let them because he didn't know any better. He grew up relying on his own wits, relying on only himself. None of us knew the true extent of his childhood, not really, he let us see what he wanted us to see. It was all a façade, an act, when really he was going home to an empty fridge and he was all alone."

I listen raptly to Sam tell Brody's story and my heart breaks for him. *No child should grow up like that.*

"This baby, I want it to be a second chance for him, for both of us. To right the wrongs of our pasts, to right our parents' wrongs, but he rejected us like we meant nothing."

I subconsciously place my hand on my stomach, dropping my gaze from his.

"Don't give up on him, sweetheart," Sam says gruffly, his voice full of emotion and I shake my head.

"I won't," I whisper. With those words, Sam starts the engine, pulling smoothly away from the curb. His words hanging in the air and in that moment, I vow to keep my promise.

6

Raleigh

I'd forgotten what it's like to just sit back and do nothing. I've always been so busy with work, going to the gym and I'm lucky that I have such an active social life. I also don't cope well with boredom, which is why I'm scrubbing Brody's kitchen within in an inch of its life. It's become a lot more difficult in the past few weeks, as my bump has slowly gotten bigger. In reality the kitchen doesn't need to be cleaned, but it occupies my mind and gives me something else to do other than worry myself into an early grave.

Brody came off the ventilator after two days. He was breathing on his own but was still unresponsive. I have temporarily moved into Brody's mansion in Chislehurst. I couldn't bring myself to go back to my apartment in Kensington. I feel close to him here, surrounded by all of his things. All around me are pictures of him, looking larger than life, grinning like an idiot. I close my eyes often and let my mind fill with his voice, I can hear him teasing me, and telling me all the wicked things he wants to do to me when we're alone like he's there in the room with me. I spend endless days sitting hopelessly by his bedside willing him to open his eyes. I spend sleepless nights crying hot, endless tears, emotional pain emanating from every pore. The grief ebbing and flowing, as if he's already dead. I'm exhausted, both physically and mentally.

I have my music blasting and I'm wailing along to Five Finger Death Punch Remember Everything, when I'm interrupted by the doorbell ringing. *Who could that be? I'm not expecting anyone.* I pull off my rubber gloves and call out to Alexa to stop the music. I head bare foot into the open living space, approaching the door apprehensively. With each step, my heartbeat starts to quicken. *Relax Storm, Jace is in the security cabin, watching the CCTV, it's his job to protect us. If he saw anyone suspicious even approaching the gates, he wouldn't let them anywhere near us, not without our say so. You're safe.* I open the door cautiously and I'm more than a little taken aback, as I am greeted by my mum, dad, and my little brother. *Fuck my life, this is the last thing I need.*

***

I let out the breath I didn't know I was holding, as I take in all three of them. I stand there for a few moments, my mouth agape, looking from my mum to my dad and then to my little brother, who is paying no attention to the scene playing out in front of him. Choosing instead to remain engrossed in the game on his Nintendo Switch.

"Well, aren't you going to invite us in, darling?" she says sweetly. *Who is this woman and what the fuck has she done with my mum?* Last time we spoke she dropped the nuclear bomb on me that Carter had been paying my therapy bills, we've hardly spoken since that day.

"Mum, dad! What are you doing here?" I try to sound enthusiastic, but fail miserably. My dad catches the look on my face and laughs sardonically, as he moves forward, engulfing me in one of his famous bear hugs. *God, I've missed him.* The emotion becoming almost too much for my hormonal body to deal with. I swallow back the golf ball sized lump in my throat, as I cling to him as if he is a lifeline.

"It's good to see you too, kiddo."

I pull away momentarily and flash him a smile, willing myself not to burst into tears. My dad looking as handsome as ever, his blonde hair, peppered with grey at his temples, his blue eyes warm. I invite them in, kicking the door shut behind them.

"We came as soon as we heard about that young man of yours, awful business," My mum adds. *Who is this compassionate creature and what the fuck have they done with my mum? She's been replaced with a clone.* I take her in, her ice blonde hair cut into a sharp long bob, framing her heart-shaped face with amethyst eyes, identical to mine. She has Michael Kors sunglasses perched on top of her head, she is wearing a loose silk black blouse, tied at her slender neck. Her long legs encased in dark blue Gucci skinny jeans and wearing a pair of sky high black patent Christian Louboutin heels. Her Louis Vuitton overnight bag hanging from her arm. Avril Storm is nothing if not stylish outside of the court room, making her look younger than her fifty years.

"Aren't you going to give your mum a hug?"

I smile awkwardly and hug her; she takes me in her arms, holding me close to her.

"Have you put on weight?"

There's my mum, I wondered how long it would be until she started with her judgmental comments. I pull away from her, as she holds me at arm's length, studying me closely. Her eyes widen when they land on my baby bump. She gasps in shock, slapping her perfectly manicured hand over her mouth.

"Raleigh Storm!" she shrieks and I roll my eyes.

"Stop with the ostentatious, over-the-top bullshit, mum! Yes, I'm pregnant! You're one to talk, you were pregnant with me by the time you were twenty one! I've got what...eight years on you!" I retort heatedly, feeling more than a little angry at her reaction.

"Exactly how did you know I was here anyway?" I ask curiously, changing the subject, looking from my mum to my dad, who has his head dropped into his hands. *That isn't a good sign.*

"Carter called us, sweetie. He said he was worried about you. He...expressed his concern for you after the rock stars accident," my mum says nonchalantly, not an ounce of concern in her cold voice and my hackles start to rise. I can't fucking believe what I'm hearing. *Fucking Carter.*

"He's got no fucking right to stick his nose into my business! And his name is Brody! If you've come to gloat then you can turn around and go back the way you came! Because I haven't got the time or the energy to deal with your bullshit!" I raise my voice a few decibels, as my brother Jagger momentarily looks up from his game.

"Nice pad, sis, what's the wi-fi password?" he asks with a bored tone to his voice, and he looks as if he would rather be anywhere else than here right now. I roll my eyes and take a deep steadying breath.

"For fucks sake!" I grumble, throwing my hands in the air in absolute despair, my day taking a turn for the worse. I put my hand to my head and briefly squeeze my eyes shut, desperately trying to find the strength and resilience I need to deal with Avril Storm and her over-the-top, Karen-like ways.

"So, how far along are you?" she asks studying me carefully and I turn to face her, trying to appear more confident than I feel.

"Around three months, give or take," I explain and she nods.

"Still early days then. Early enough for something to be done about it?" she asks matter-of-factly, gesturing toward me and I can't believe what I'm fucking hearing. *Is she for real right now?*

"How fucking dare you! You know what, just get out!" I yell, my resolve seemingly snapping. My dad moves between me and my mum, who is paying no attention to me at all. Her face expressionless from all the fucking botox.

"Raleigh, sweetheart, calm down. It can't be good for the baby," he tries to placate me, in his soothing voice, but I shrug him off.

"No! No, I won't fucking calm down, dad! Are you seriously going to let her speak to me like that? Or are you in the doghouse again?" I spit sardonically, as he hangs his head in shame and I laugh bitterly. *Really?*

"What is it this time? Another woman?" he puffs out a breath, dropping his gaze guiltily to the floor.

"For fucks sake!" I mutter and my mum starts to drag Jagger towards the door.

"Come on, Jagger, I know where we're not wanted! Your sister clearly doesn't want us here!" She whines dramatically, taking out a handkerchief from her pocket and dabs at the non-existent tears. My brother still refusing to look up from his game.

"Are you coming, Vinnie?" she asks my dad, and my dad looks from her to me.

"Well, we've come all this way, so I'd like to spend some time with our daughter," my dad states, and it's not a request. Her eyes flash as if she is about to say something, but she thinks better of it. She yells in frustration and just storms out with Jagger trailing behind her, slamming the door behind them. *Fucking typical.*

"Why don't you just leave her, dad?" I ask, after I make us both some lemon tea and we settle on the sofa for a long overdue catch up. He shakes his head and I sigh.

"It's not that easy, sweetheart, I wish it were."

I scoff, narrowing my eyes on him. He looks tired and washed out, I've never seen my dad look this way before, he's always so put together. "It's as easy as you make it."

I reach for his hand and he lets me, as he smiles softly, noticing he isn't wearing his wedding ring, but I choose not to say anything.

"When did you get so wise beyond your years?"

I laugh. "I got it from you obviously!" I quip, as I blow on the hot liquid and take a sip of my tea.

"You love him, don't you? This rock star?"

I feel the familiar burn of tears behind my eyes and nod.

"More than anything, I'm terrified I'm going to lose him, dad. He's been in a coma for weeks."

He squeezes my hand reassuringly, as I feel hot tears roll down my cheeks.

"I can't lose him, dad, I can't. I just want him to wake up. I've never felt this way about anyone before, not even Carter."

As I say those words, I surrender to the grief that I tried so hard to keep hidden. I cry gut-wrenching, soul destroying sobs of utter, despair. I cling to my dad, as he hushes me, and I feel like I am five years old again. My dad holds me for the longest time, until my wracking sobs have subsided.

When I was growing up, my dad was my hero. Our bond was unbreakable, he was my light when I couldn't see the path ahead. His fierce protectiveness, his larger-than-life personality and his over-the-top optimism is what kept me going. He was my staunch, unwavering defender... my rock. He always made sure I knew I wasn't the centre of the universe, but I was the centre of his. My relationship with my mum was never the greatest. She had high expectations, and I never met any of them. In her eyes I wasn't the perfect daughter, but to my dad I was. He championed me from the side-lines, and I always knew I was loved because he told me often. Vince Storm has always been the strong yet gentle patriarch holding our family together over the years. Him and my mum have been in a loveless marriage for the longest time, yet he refuses to leave her, choosing to seek solace in the arms of numerous other women, with no regard for his wife's feelings. *Not that she has any.*

I hear him let out a sigh and kiss me on top of my head tenderly.

"How about I cook for my best girl? I can cook Chicken parmigiana; it was always your favourite growing up."

Hearing him mention my favourite food chicken parmigiana, my stomach starts to growl, reminding me I haven't eaten today. I smile up at him and nod.

"Yes, please."

He chuckles softly, as I think back to the last time I had my favourite dish, which feels like a lifetime ago. I didn't realise how much I was craving comfort food cooked by my dad and in that moment, I feel a little more optimistic that everything is going to work out just fine.

7

Raleigh

Days turned into weeks, weeks turned into months and Summer had turned to Autumn. He had been in a coma for three months and I was now five months pregnant, my bump growing every day. By now, my pregnancy was public knowledge, fodder for the press to feast on. Speculation on whether the baby was Brody's, or the product of a rekindled romance with Carter, was all the reporters seemed to ask me about. What they didn't know was, I was pregnant with twins. Believe me, no one was more shocked than me, when I found out, with Liv by my side.

Raleigh
Past

Brody has been in a coma for coming up to two months. There's been no significant change and as the days go on, I seem to be losing a little more hope with each day that passes that he's going to recover. As my pregnancy was continuing, my clothes seems to appear a little tighter, the contours of my body seemed somehow more rounded and feminine. I love the experience of being pregnant, my stomach slowly swelling by the day, feeling the gentle movements of the baby inside me. Early on in my pregnancy I felt a sense of motherhood almost instantly. As soon as I saw those two blue lines, I was already someones' mum. I already felt so much love I felt like I could burst. I was growing a literal human inside me and there was nothing more beautiful than that. It would be the greatest privilege and the greatest accomplishment and I was more than ready for the challenge.

Today is the day I have my ultrasound check up, Liv has been with me every step of the way and she's been my rock throughout. I don't know what I would have done without her these past few weeks. The nurse, Chrissie, squeezes the gel on my stomach, and I flinch as the coldness makes contact with my stomach.

She presses the device against my lower abdomen, and I feel like I need the toilet, after I drank almost a litre of water beforehand. Everything pales into significance, as I turn my head to see the screen and hear the tympanic heartbeat of our baby from the ultrasound wand. The rhythm strong and steady, as my eyes start to well with happy tears and Liv grips my hand tight.

"That's your baby, Rae!" she squeals excitedly and I giggle at her enthusiasm. My heart swells with such love for the baby I haven't met yet.

The doctor presses a few buttons and frowns as she moves the probe back and forth across my stomach.

"Is something wrong?" I ask apprehensively, suddenly terrified that something's wrong and I feel a fear I have never felt before. My stomach instantly knotting and I squeeze Liv's hand tighter, as the nurse moves to the left and a beaming grin spreads across her face.

"Congratulations Raleigh, you're expecting twins!"

My eyes widen at her statement and Liv practically screams with delight.

"Twins?" My mouth drops open and I let the words sink in. Twins had never crossed my mind, not in a million years, but as I watch Chrissie move the probe back and forth across my stomach, hearing their heartbeats in perfect sync, suddenly makes it real. I swallow back the lump that has lodged itself in my throat.

"I can't tell the sex yet, but we're going to keep a close eye on you, and we should definitely be able to determine the genders by the next scan date."

She reassures me and Liv laughs, squealing excitedly.

"You definitely don't do things by halves, Rae! TWINS! OH MY FUCKING GOD!"

She bounces from one foot to another, and I find myself grinning right along with her. I can't believe it either, as I swipe a stray tear that has tracked its way down my cheek.

"Hey, it's going to be alright, you know? You're going to be the best mum in the world and those babies are going to be the luckiest kids in the world having you as their mum and me as the cool aunt!"

We both laugh and in that moment, I'm eternally grateful for her support.

***

I find myself staring down at my scan picture, as I'm sitting at Brody's bedside, still in a state of shock, trying to come to terms with the fact we're having twins.

"You're going to be a daddy of twins, babe," I choke out, feeling so emotional that I'm experiencing all this alone without him by my side.

"Twins, who would have thought it? I need you to wake up. I need you now more than ever, please."

I clutch his hand, resting my head on the edge of his bed and I cry. My eyes red rimmed and puffy, I've been crying a lot lately; my hormones are all over the place.

"Please come back to me. I can't do this without you, please, Brody. Wake up, please wake up, I need those glittering silver eyes of yours. I'm barely functioning without you," I plead and as the days go by, I'm losing all hope, resigned to the fact I'll be raising our babies as a single mother.

Raleigh
Present

I've been by his bedside every day for three months solid, without fail. I've taken an indefinite hiatus from my acting career, deciding to focus on a healthy pregnancy and being there for the man I love more than life itself. I'm sitting in my usual spot at his bedside, as my breath catches in my throat. *I will not fucking cry; I feel like I've spent the last three months crying.* As the days have gone on, I've grown to accept the fact that he may not wake up, that he may never recover from his accident. Three months ago, a few days after his surgery, he was moved to Weymouth Street Hospital, a private hospital situated between Harley Street and Marylebone High Street in the heart of Central London. The doctors specialise in brain injuries and the hospital he was transferred from, put him in a medically induced coma to allow his brain to fully heal. After several attempts to bring him out of it, his body protested. With Lenny's permission as his next of kin, they are allowing him to come out of it on his own. I hold his lifeless hand in mine and pray to whoever may be listening, to bring him back to me.

"Go home, sweetheart," Sam's familiar rasp startles me from my thoughts.

"You're exhausted. Go home, get some sleep, some food, a shower and a change of clothes. It's not good for those babies, they can sense if you're stressed."

He smiles softly and I stroke my swollen stomach to remind myself that they're still there.

"Jax is waiting outside to take you home in my truck. Go home, it's not a request, it's an order, sweetheart. He'd kick my arse for not looking after you, so please, just go. I'll sit with him and I'll call immediately if there's any change, I promise."

I nod, and he kisses my forehead.

"Good girl, Jax is waiting. Cole will escort you out, there's paps everywhere, fucking wankers," Sam curses low in his throat. As I go to let go of Brody's hand and kiss his forehead, silently begging him to come back to me, I feel a slight squeeze of my fingers. It was barely there, but I definitely felt it.

"Brody, baby, it's me, can you hear me?" I say softly, and he squeezes my fingers again. I look to Sam and he wraps his arm around me for support.

"Brody?" I repeat, and his eyelids begin to flutter.

"Brody, it's Raleigh. I'm here, baby, it's me," I try to reassure him, while trying to hold back the sob that's threatening to escape. He lets out a hoarse groan and his eyes struggle to focus on the all too bright lights attacking his eyes. He rips his hand away from mine and starts to tear the wires from his body, kicking and flailing wildly. The noise he makes rocks me to the core, as an alarm sounds. The loud, squawking noise puts my nerves on edge, as the door swings open. Within seconds, the room is filled with doctors and nurses crowding around Brody's bed, trying to calm him, and shining lights in his eyes. Sam and me quietly leave the room and we are greeted by Lenny.

"What's wrong, love, you look like you've seen a ghost," He says with concern in his voice.

"He's awake."

The relief in my voice is evident and for the first time in three months, I smile a genuine smile and I'm hopeful that this is the start of something new.

8

Brody

I attempt to focus on the unfamiliar environment I seem to find myself in and my heartbeat starts to accelerate. I squint in a bid to sharpen the blurred images before me. My clothes feel scratchy, the strong smell of antiseptic assaulting my nostrils, causing my stomach to roil. The room silent, except for the dull beep of machines and something feels...off. I'm terrified that I went on a bender and ended up in rehab again. I don't know this room, but it looks like a hospital, a nice one, it makes me feel safe. The lights aren't harsh, there are clean sheets and flowers decorating the side table. I turn my head and that's when I see her—my Raleigh, my beautiful, stunning girlfriend. Her exquisite features tarnished with apprehension and unease.

"Hey," I say hoarsely, as I struggle to recall the last thing I remember.

"Hey yourself," her voice flat and devoid of emotion, as she leans over giving me some water through a straw, to soothe my dehydrated throat.

"Where am I? What happened?" I question, with more than a hint of unease and confusion to my voice. She reaches for my hand and I relish in the comfort it brings me, as she wraps her soft, warm hand around mine.

"You're in hospital, babe. You were in an accident," she explains, her voice steady and my stomach drops. All of a sudden, I'm struck by the fact that I might have hurt someone.

"D...did...I...hurt someone?"

My voice trembles, as I say those words, and she shakes her head. I can tell she's struggling to keep the tears at bay.

"No, you didn't hurt anyone."

The relief that washes over me is almost overwhelming.

"What happened? I...I can't remember anything," I say with absolute terror in my voice, and she kisses the back of my hand in a gesture of silent reassurance.

"It's going to be alright; I promise. You suffered a fractured skull; some temporary short-term memory loss is normal. It's just your body's way of healing itself."

She declares robotically, almost as if she's practiced it and my blood runs cold. *Fractured skull? What the fuck?* I swallow, as I try to wrap my head around her words.

"What happened?" I ask apprehensively, almost scared of the answer. She closes her eyes briefly and takes a deep, steadying breath before she starts to speak.

"You were in a motorbike accident, you took a corner too fast and crashed into an oncoming car, which failed to stop in time. It was a hit and run, they still haven't caught the driver. You were found unconscious in the middle of the road, covered in blood. You suffered a fractured skull, a broken wrist, fractured tibia and fibula, and a broken collar bone."

I lift my hand up to wipe a tear from her eye. She's wary of my touch, as she sniffs.

"I thought I'd lost you, Brody. You had some internal bleeding and swelling on the brain, you suffered several seizures during surgery, the doctors didn't know if you'd make it."

As she speaks, I struggle to take in what she's just told me. *A motorbike accident?* I've *never* had a motorbike accident in all the years I've been riding.

"I...I've never had an accident, *ever*. I..." I stop speaking and as she shifts in her chair, I spot a visible baby bump. *What the fucking fuck?* She follows my eyes and attempts to cover it with the loose hoody, which I recognise as one of mine.

"What the fuck?"

I curse softly. Instantly regretting it, as the bitter sting of rejection is clear in her beautiful face. She rearranges the baggy hoody she's wearing, pulling the sleeves over her hands, and folding her arms protectively over her stomach. I narrow my eyes on her and she avoids my close scrutiny. I struggle to remember the last thing I said to her. *I can't remember, why the fuck can't I remember?*

"Brody, please, don't."

The hint of desperation in her voice, pierces me in the chest and I feel my heart slam violently against my ribcage. I want to say more, but my words get trapped somewhere in my throat and our moment is interrupted by Sam entering the room.

"Welcome back, man!" he rasps, as he pats my shoulder, looking between me and Raleigh with a quirk of his pierced eyebrow.

"Goodto have you back in the land of the living, mate" he says genuinely, his beaming, dimpled grin infectious and I find myself smiling right along with him.

"It'll take more than a motorbike accident to finish me off. I'm like the cat with nine lives!" I joke and we both laugh.

"I'm pretty sure those nine lives ran out years ago!"

His smile turns serious in a matter of seconds and he runs his hand savagely through his dark hair.

"Don't ever fucking do that to us again, you cocksucker," he says with a clenched jaw, his voice full of intense anger.

"What the fuck were you even thinking?" he raises his voice a few decibels louder and I can't comprehend what I put them all through. *I'm a selfish prick.*

"Actually don't answer that because you clearly weren't fucking thinking! You were clean for six months!"

My stomach turns, as I struggle to remember. *Was I high? By the look on his face the answer is yes. Fuck my life.* I have the sense drop my gaze down to the bed and suddenly the loose cotton on the scratchy sheet is the most interesting fucking thing I've ever seen.

"Are you even fucking listening to me?"

At that moment, that no amount of apologising or grovelling is going to make this even remotely better, so I don't say anything at all.

"You know what? Fuck this and fuck you, Hart!"

He roars, throwing his arms up in the air in absolute despair and storms out.

Fucking wonderful.

***

I try desperately to remember conversations from before the accident; my mind feelsoddly fragmented, and I can't seem to latch on to one single thought or memory. Nothing from before is clear, it all seems so hazy. An overwhelming feeling of hopelessness washes over me and the frustration I feel, drowns me where I lay.

"How far along are you?" I ask curiously, clearing my sore throat and she seems hesitant to answer my question.

"Five months," her voice falters and the look on my face must say it all, as she pushes her chair back from me, the scrape of the legs across the floor setting my teeth on edge.

"Five months, wow," I whisper, as she reaches into her bag, pulling out a scan photo.

"You're going to be a dad," I swallow hard, not sure how to feel about it. My mind working at a snail's pace, struggling to take in her words. *I'm going to be a dad.*

"Say something."

She turns the scan picture towards me and as my eyes glance over it, I open and close my mouth, trying desperately to find the words I know she wants to hear.

"We're having twins, a boy and a girl."

My eyes widen, dumbstruck at the revelation. *Twins? What the fuck?*

"Hang on, how fucking long have I been here?"

I rub furiously at my temples, my voice full of confusion and obvious irritation, as she pauses briefly, to try to gauge my mood.

"You've been in a coma for three months."

My eyes widen in pure shock. *Three months are you fucking shitting me?* I'm struck dumb. *A lot could have happened in that time.*

"What?" I swallow harshly, as I try to comprehend what she's just told me, and I can't seem to wrap my head around it. *Who bought me here? How? Where?* Out of impulse, my hand travels to the back of my head, running over a deep, raised laceration.

"What happened in those three months? What about the band? Your movie?" I ask in a rush, the series of questions interrupted as she flashes me a smile. For the first time since I woke up, I see my girl for the first time. *The girl I fell hopelessly in love with.*

"There's my favourite smile."

She smiles again, and I swear, my heart feels like it's about to jump out of my chest.

"The boys are fine. Sam's been writing for the new album, he's been collaborating with Jett Powers from Skarlett Ribbon and writing a column for a music magazine. He's been spending a lot of time with Peyton and the boys... she had another miscarriage. Jax has been spending time with Thea. He's been doing some guest judging on a panel of a talent show and it's early days, but he's met someone. As for Lucas, well he's been photographing, he's started writing a memoir to help people, specifically kids, who have dealt with grief and abuse. They didn't feel it was right to carry on touring without you, so they postponed the tour indefinitely, to focus on being there if you woke up. As for my movie, Rocked made over one hundred and seventy million in the opening weekend. It's been nominated for a Bafta and there's a good chance of could go on to be nominated for an Oscar. Damien was so pleased with my work, he's asked me to star in another one of his films, the sequel to Rocked."

I can't comprehend the amount of time that has passed and the things that have happened, the things I've missed out on while I've been unconscious.

"*Wow!* That's fucking amazing! I'm so proud of you, kitten."

I take her hand in mine and kiss her knuckles tenderly, sensing that she's been craving my touch. She closes her eyes briefly and relishes my touch.

"I've spent every day by your bedside, praying you'd wake up. I've wanted this for so long. Now I've finally got it, I don't know what to do, or how to feel."

A sob escapes from her lips and she snatches her hand away from me.

"I can't, I can't do this!" she bursts into tears and I find myself at a loss of what to do to make it better.

"Raleigh, please, don't cry. Tell me what I can do," I plead softly and she shakes her head vehemently.

"I just need some time. I'm sorry, I can't, I'm so sorry," She gets up from her chair and rushes out of the room without a word, leaving me speechless.

I'm not alone for long when Lenny enters the room, suited and booted. Three buttons on his pale blue shirt are undone, revealing a smattering of white chest hair, he is wearing a thick gold chain around his neck and his grey hair is slicked back.

"Looking good, old man, who you trying to impress! Please tell me you've not been trying to chat up the nurses!" I joke and he laughs throatily.

"Good to have you back with us, boy, you gave us all a fright, you little shit!" he chastises, giving me a sobering look.

"Not you as well," I sigh out loud, my voice weary and full of mild annoyance.

"What happened with Raleigh? Did you use one of your awful chat up lines?" Lenny says wryly and I shake my head, pressing my fingers to my temples.

"I don't know, she was filling me in on all the things I've missed out on, then she just burst into tears and ran out on me. What did I do, Len? I can't remember."

Emotions barrel through me and I squeeze my eyes shut to quell the tears. Lenny walks further into the room and takes a seat next to my bed.

"I can't remember what happened, Len, what have I done? Why can't I remember? Did I hurt someone? What isn't she telling me? Why won't she tell me?" I repeat panicked, my hands trembling as I run them through my hair. *Fuck, it feels so long.*

"You had a motorbike accident, son, you were high. You were doing so well, why would you want to undo all that?"

The disappointment in his voice is evident, and it makes me feel like shit.

"I...I don't know! WHY THE FUCK CAN'T I REMEMBER?" I raise my voice and my heartbeat starts to quicken.

"Calm down, you need to stay calm, son. It isn't good for your brain injury," he placates softly, placing his hand on my forearm and I quickly snatch it away. I see the look of hurt in Lenny's eyes, but he disguises it with a cough.

"FUCK MY BRAIN INJURY! AND I AM FUCKIN' CALM!"

I drop my head into my hands and every part of my body feels so out of control.

"Who bought me here? How did I get here?" I ask, feeling agitated and tugging at my hair.

"You were found in the middle of the road, son, you were in pretty bad shape." Lenny explains.

"What won't you fucking tell me? I want the truth not some generic bullshit you've had three months to conjure up!" I retort bitterly and he lets out a laboured sigh.

"YOU OF ALL PEOPLE, LEN! WHAT THE FUCK ARE YOU HIDING FROM ME!" I bark and I'm trembling, but I'm not sure if it's rage, or something else entirely different. I'm in the midst of a meltdown, as two police officers enter the room. *Fuck my life.*

9

Brody

The two police officers are standing near the door, both in plain clothes, wearing matching black suits. They both nod curtly in my direction and I stare blankly at them, not really registering why they're here.

"Mr. Hart, this is Detective Maddox and I'm Detective Fellows, we'd like to ask you a few questions regarding the motorbike incident that occurred on the twelfth of July."

Lenny stands up and squares his shoulders.

"Look, the boy's just woke up from three months in a coma, for fucks sake. Is this really necessary? And shouldn't you be focussing on catching the prick that caused the accident in the first place?"

Lenny interjects, his voice full of disdain. He has a particular hatred for men of the law, even more so since I found out he used to be a copper over thirty years ago.

"It is absolutely necessary, since we were reliably informed that Mr. Hart was under the influence of a class A substance at the time of the accident," Detective Fellows snaps bitterly and almost sarcastically, his face twisting in clear repulsion.

"Could you tell us what happened at the time of the accident?" Detective Maddox asks, and I shake my head.

"I can't remember," I whisper weakly, feeling pathetic, squeezing my eyes shut, willing something, anything to come back to me about that day.

"According to CCTV footage from the traffic cameras, you were driving recklessly and aggressively. Drug driving seriously impairs your judgement, and it's a criminal offence to drive with illegal drugs in your system. You could face prosecution and a potential driving ban," Detective Fellows counters and it feels more like good cop, bad cop, as I look from one to the other.

"I don't remember, but I know I wasn't fucking driving dangerously!" I try to sound more confident than I feel right now, and he regards me with obvious disgust.

"Mr. Hart, could you please refrain from swearing?"

I let out a laboured breath, trying to rein in my growing temper, but I find myself failing miserably. *This is fucking bull shit!*

"Can I ask, if you can't remember, how do you know you weren't driving dangerously?" Detective Maddox asks almost mockingly, and I squeeze my eyes shut, desperate for the memories that I know are there to come back to me.

"I've been riding since I was seventeen, I've never been in an accident, I..." my words are suddenly robbed from me. My tongue feels almost too big for my mouth and unexpectedly, my head feels like it's going to explode. It is the kind of headache that makes my head throb and I close my eyes, trying to fight the nausea that threatens to choke me. I roar out in agony, as it thrums behind my temples, I can feel the rhythm of my blood pulsing somewhere in my head. The vice-like grip that feels like an elastic band squeezing and constricting my skull. I start to see flashing lights, almost blinding me, as my vision starts to blur, and I hear Lenny calling my name. His voice sounding like he's underwater.

"Brody, son, Brody, can you hear me?" Lenny's gravelly voice filled with panic and concern.

"YOU, AND YOU, GET THE FUCK OUT! NOW!" he barks at the Officers, pushing a button and an alarm starts sounding. I tug at my hair, agitated.

"LEN! MAKE IT STOP! PLEASE, PLEASE MAKE IT STOP!" My voice full of fear, as I feel warm liquid trickling down my nose, nausea settling somewhere in my gut and I succumb to the darkness once again.

Raleigh

I head to the lush green, perfectly landscaped grounds at the back of hospital and drop my arse down to the wooden bench defeatedly. I shift my gaze to the grass and allow the fat tears of utter hopeless despair spill down my cheeks. I enjoy the precious few moments of silence, as I wrap my arms around myself protectively. In those few moments, I allow my mind to wander. Ever since I was a little girl, I've chased the picket fence life, the knight on the white horse to come riding in and sweep me off my feet. I had almost given up on the fantasy until I met Brody, seeing him a shadow of his former self lying in that hospital bed, his memories robbed from him is breaking my already fragile heart.

As I allow myself to come to terms with the extent of his injuries, I can't comprehend or wrap my head around the fact that he's so familiar, yet so different, all at the same time. The doctor warned us he could wake up totally different to the way we remembered him. But I wasn't quite prepared for this and I'm not sure how to move forward from it, not right now. I want to take care of him, but the overwhelming fear settles itself somewhere deep within me like a lead weight bearing down on me. All I want to do is cry, but I have to be strong for him. I take a deep breath, ready to go back inside, when I look up to see Sam's tall, muscular frame jogging towards me. He comes to a halt in front of me, he hasn't even broken a sweat. I follow his thick jean-clad legs up to his face.

"You need to come back inside. He had a seizure, and he's been rushed for an emergency MRI scan," he says a little too calmly. My stomach drops and I automatically place my hand where I know our babies are growing.

"W-what happened? He was fine!" I stutter incredulously and Sam shakes his head, as he runs his tattooed hand through his soft, raven black spikes.

"The police turned up; they were questioning him about the accident. He got agitated because he couldn't remember. The next thing I hear shouting and Lenny screaming for help."

I'm on my feet in a second, the blood rushing to my head and momentarily knocking me off balance. Sam steadies me and he offers me his arm for support, I take it without question.

"You good, sweetheart?"

I swallow a few times and nod, feeling a little dazed at the turn of events. It takes a few minutes for my brain to send a message to my legs and I turn to follow Sam back into the hospital, bracing myself for the storm to come.

Brody

A few days later, after I suffered a seizure due to frontal lobe damage, I was met with strict instructions from the doctors to rest, which meant no visitors. It gave me some time to get my head around the true extent of my injuries and the consequences of my reckless actions. *What the fuck was I thinking?* It had taken three days for me to finally be up to accepting visitors and my thoughts are interrupted by someone softly clearing their throat. As I look up, my eyes land on the last person I expected to be here. Lorna Lavelle. I desperately try to remember the last time I saw her, but all I know is she looks even more stunning than I remember. Her hair is cut into a sleek, dark brown long bob, it's no longer the vivid red I remember. She's wearing a leopard print playsuit and white Converse, which compliments her skin tone. As I silently take her in, I struggle to remember the last conversation I had with her. Trying to remember, feels as if I'm following a trail of breadcrumbs and it just ends, so I stop. I slam the heel of my hand into my forehead, relishing the sudden sharp pain, as I roar with frustration. She takes a few cautious steps back from me, swiping the tears away from her eyes.

"I promised myself I wouldn't cry," she says in her familiar Northern brogue, laughing bitterly.

"It's good to see you," I declare tenderly and she sniffs.

"I wanted to come sooner...I should have come sooner, I'm so sorry," her voice faltering and I shake my head.

"You've got nothing to apologise for, what matters is that you're here now," I reassure her, as she moves closer to the bed, dropping down onto the navy armchair next to my bed, placing her bag at her feet.

"I'm finally going to leave him, Brody. It's you...it's always been you; it took me almost losing you to admit to myself that it's you I'm in love with. It's you I want to spend my life with."

I look up into her aquamarine eyes and see the woman I was once so in love with. I'm rendered speechless at her admission and apparent declaration of love. She reaches over to stroke my cheek lovingly and I lean into her touch, relishing in her soft warmth like a desperate dog starved for attention. But it's short lived, as I unexpectedly come to a harsh realisation.

"You've got no idea how long I've waited to hear you say those words, but it's too late, L."

The pained look she gives me in return almost shatters my resolve.

"What? Isn't it enough that I'm willing to leave my marriage for you? It's taken me four fucking years to come to the conclusion that I haven't been in love with Stefan for a long time. I was just too scared to admit it to myself, let alone you. What I felt for you scared the shit out of me, surely you understand that?"

I close my eyes briefly, desperately trying to find the words to explain.

"My brain might be fucking scrambled egg right now, but how can you say those words after the way I've treated you? If I really cared about you at all, I could have gotten you away from him years ago. Instead, I let him use you as a punch bag, I let him lay his fucking hands on you! I could have stopped him, I could have beat him within an inch of his sorry fucking life. I could have given you money and paid for you to have a new life away from him. I let him continue to hurt you because I was fucking terrified that our sordid little affair would be exposed! All I cared about was my reputation! How selfish does that make me? How can you sit there and still want me? Why would you want to be with someone like me? Someone who willingly allowed you to stay with a fucking wife beater! What sort of person does that make me?"

The sudden, stark realisation sucker punches me right in the gut and my stomach roils, causing me to instantly feel nauseous.

"Why are you saying this, Brody? Why would you say that to me? I'm willing to give up everything for you! It's taken me almost fucking losing you to realise that it's you I wanted to fall asleep next to and wake up next to. I want you in every way possible, in every way that matters. I chose to stay with him, even after he beat me, even after he forced me to have sex with him, I chose to stay in that situation because I was too fucking weak to leave him!" she declares and the thought of him forcing himself on her makes me hate him even more. The familiar boiling rage rising to the surface and my jaw tightens.

"Lorna, I..." I stutter, opening and closing my mouth like a complete fucking loser. *Smooth, Hart, real smooth.* "I'm so fucking sorry, I can't be the man you need, L. I'm sorry I wasn't the man you needed, I could have taken you away from that life, it could have been so different for us, but I was a fucking coward and I'll never be able to apologise enough."

She is about to speak again when we're interrupted by Raleigh entering the room. Her bump looks more prominent today, and she looks glowing, almost ethereal. I feel like even more of a prick, as she stands in the doorway taking in our interaction for a few moments. She looks from Lorna to me, narrowing her eyes suspiciously. *Fuck me.*

"What's going on? Who are you?" she directs her question calmly to Lorna. Lorna's eyes bug out of her head and she practically leaps up from her chair, knocking it back with force.

"Brody?" Raleigh says incredulously and I can't speak, I'm rendered mute. Lorna attempts to rush out of the room, but Raleigh blocks the doorway, halting her from leaving.

"Have we met before? You look really familiar?"

Lorna shakes her head, dropping her gaze to the floor, avoiding all eye contact. She practically shoves Raleigh out of the way and leaves without another word. *Well shit.*

10

Raleigh

As I watch the mystery woman who looks oddly familiar leave the room, my stomach in knots. The moment I walked in the room and I watched his face pale, as he looked up at me.

"Who was she?" I say impatiently, aware it my voice sounds accusatory. His Adam's apple bobs, as I move further into the room.

"No one," he says with an almost bored tone to his voice.

"Liar," I spit venomously, feeling every ounce of rational thought leave my body almost instantly.

"Have you fucked her?"

He winces at my crass tone, but doesn't say anything, his mouth forming a straight line.

"Don't fucking lie to me, Brody!"

He continues to stay silent, and I immediately know I'm right. *Fucking hell, I feel sick.*

"Oh my fucking God!" I shriek and I don't care that I'm shrieking. He's been fucking another woman behind my back, after I spent three months by his bedside praying he would wake up. *How could he do this to me? To us?* I move my hand protectively to my stomach and I can't stop the angry tears rolling down my cheeks.

"How long?" I sob, as he briefly closes his eyes.

"It doesn't matter," his voice void of emotion and I can't believe what I'm hearing.

"Of course it fucking matters! It matters to me!" I sob, but he doesn't deserve my tears.

"Answer the fucking question, Brody, or so help me God! HOW FUCKING LONG?"

I feel so betrayed right now and I don't know if I'll ever be able to forgive him.

"Four years," he murmurs and my stomach starts its familiar roil.

Four years? What the actual fuck? I let out a whimper and my heart feels like it's been shattered into a million pieces.

"Has anything you've ever said to me been the truth? All this time you've been fucking her behind my back!" I raise my voice a few decibels louder than appropriate for a plush private hospital, but I don't give a shit right now. He's ripped my heart out and presented it to me on a silver platter.

"It's not like that! It was never like that! Don't ever think that!" he says defensively.

"What is it like then? What am I supposed to think? Tell me! Fucking enlighten me!" I snap, feeling every modicum of decency draining from me. I suddenly feel exhausted and I'm still struggling to wrap my head around the enormity of his betrayal. That's when I think back to a previous conversation we had before his accident.

Raleigh
Past

"What's going on in that pretty head of yours, kitten?"

We had just had sex, and I was relishing in some post-coital cuddling, as he climbs into bed and pulls me to his side, wrapping his arm around me. I rest my head on his pec and snuggle into him.

"Why did you end up in rehab?" I ask him curiously.

It was a thought that has been bothering me for a while. I always had a sneaky suspicion that he wasn't entirely truthful about the real reason he was in rehab. He idly traces shapes up and down my arm and as I ask him that question, he momentarily stops.

"You already know why I was in rehab," he replies defensively.

"I know, but I always had a feeling that you weren't being entirely truthful about the real reason," I admit candidly.

"I know you were a drug addict; you were the stereotypical rocker in rehab. You were literally a fucking walking cliché!" I joke and he chuckles softly.

"That's me, the walking cliché! Yeah, I was a massive drug addict, I couldn't function unless I had some chemical or another running through my veins. I...wasn't in a good place back then, I was a mess. The path I was on I was going to be dead before I hit thirty-five, I didn't want to be that person anymore. The truth is, the drugs were the main reason I was there, but the other reason was a woman, amongst other things," he answers vaguely, with a shrug and I stiffen as he says those words.

A woman? Well, Brody Hart, you continue to surprise me at every turn, I definitely wasn't expecting that.

"Don't be jealous, kitten, it doesn't suit you. You asked me for the truth, and I gave you the truth. I was in rehab because I was fucked up in more ways than one, I was in a dark place. I was battling a drug addiction and the woman I thought I was in love with, rejected me like I meant nothing. I felt like I was that scared, messed up kid, who was rejected by his mother all over again. She made me feel things I've never felt before, but she was never mine to begin with."

His voice is thick with emotion and I've never seen this side of him before. Maybe this could be a turning point for us?

"What do you mean, she was never yours to begin with?" I ask, more than a little confused by his statement.

"She was married, babe. I was the other man, and that made me feel so fucking ashamed. I was sleeping with another woman who would ultimately go home and share a bed with someone who wasn't me and that made me feel fucking sick to my stomach."

He unwraps his arm from around me and I feel him distancing himself from me.

"What was her name?" I ask meekly and don't know why I need to know the answer to that question. He perches himself on the edge of the bed and runs his hand through his short hair.

"It's not important."

And with those words, the conversation is over.

Raleigh
Present

I am snapped back to the present, shocked at the sudden revelation. The thought fresh and at the forefront of my mind.

"She's the married woman you were sleeping with? The one that sent you to rehab?"

He can't look me in the eye, and I know I'm right.

"I never meant for any of this to happen, is that what you want to hear?"

I laugh bitterly, as I drop down onto the navy chair next to his bed.

"I don't know what I wanted to hear; when we met, I was under no illusion that you were the perfect man. I'd been warned off men like you my whole life, even Damien Valentine warned me! How fucking stupid could I be? In my head you were my Mr. Right, you were selfless. You put me first, I was no longer second best, no man had ever treated me like that before."

I try hard to make sure my voice is steady, and I see something that resembles shame cross his face.

"I'm still that man! Don't you get it? Do you think I'm enjoying this? Do you think I enjoy hurting you? I'm sorry, I don't know what else I can say."

My thoughts are barrelling through my head at a million miles an hour.

"Do you love her?"

I don't know why I want to know the answer, but he immediately drops his head into his hands. *Oh God, this isn't happening.*

"I don't know what you want me to say, Raleigh!"

I slam my hand down on the armrest of the chair, the sound echoing around the room.

"I want you to tell me the fucking truth for once in your life! Do you love her?"

I annunciate the last four words, as he sinks his teeth into his bottom lip. His eyes glaze over, and he nods his head.

"Yes! I fucking loved her! Is that what you want to hear?" he snaps and my heart slams against my rib cage and I let out a strangled sob.

"I FUCKING HATE YOU!" I scream and he has the sense to balk at my obvious hatred towards him. I get up from the chair and start attacking him. I claw at his chest, punch and slap him with everything I have. I scratch my nails down his face and he doesn't stop me. After a few minutes of letting out the hatred and pent up aggression towards him, I suddenly feel exhausted, emotionally, mentally and physically.

"I can't fucking do this."

I step back from his hospital bed, as if I have been burned and rush out of the room.

11

Brody

I know it was wrong after all this time and I hold my hands up, but I fucking swear I never meant to hurt her. *Not intentionally.* I'd give my right arm to take back the look in her eyes when she figured out I had been having sex with Lorna, it broke my heart and I'll never be able to undo that. After everything we went through to be together, the fights, the tears, the arguments, and the crazy, sweaty, angry make up sex, the highs, the lows, and everything in between. We've been dating for just under a year and I stuck my dick in a woman that wasn't my girlfriend. Even though it had been going on for four years, way before we met, I can't justify my actions. The consequences of that have just potentially ruined fucking everything. No matter how many times I say sorry, no matter how many times I promise it'll never happen again, I know she won't forgive me. She's headstrong and stubborn. One moment of madness and I'll never be able to take it back. I was thinking with the little head in my pants instead of the big head on my shoulders. *I'm such a fucking idiot.* Watching the pain in her eyes was probably one of the worse things I have ever seen. The look of pure heartbreak as I let her claw and punch me. I deserved every single slap, every single punch and every single ounce of pain she gave me. Watching her lose it so completely felt like a thousand knives piercing my skin. As I try to wrap my damaged brain around the extent of my actions, I roar at the top of my lungs and that's when the tears come. Soul destroying sobs of despair and the thought at the forefront of my frontal lobe is, I don't know how to make this fucking right.

***

I spend long days on my own feeling sorry for myself, stuck in my own head, refusing to see anyone, refusing anyone who came to visit and sending them away. My mind still oddly disconnected and muddled. I had significant gaps, but now it was offering me snippets of conversations and small fragments of information that wasn't there before. It was like I was watching a compilation of my memories from the last ten years. I could clearly remember the things from years ago with crystal clear clarity, but I couldn't remember the more recent things and that terrified me the most. The temporary amnesia is a roadblock of sorts and it wasn't romantic like the movies, I just felt lost and incapable of dealing with the intensity of the emotions charging through my body.

My mood is bleak and I can't seem to focus on anything, so I lay back on my pillows in an attempt to rid my mind of the dark, wayward thoughts that reside there. I close my eyes and drift off to sleep.

***

"Brody, I'm pregnant."

...

"S...say something for fucks sake."

...

"I'm not a fucking idiot, Raleigh. We've never gone bareback, Jesus Fucking Christ!"

...

"Don't you fucking dare, Raleigh. Don't ever try and lay that shit on me! My mum was a selfish fucking cunt, who didn't give two shits about me! I'd never ever do that to my child! I'm not going to get the opportunity, because I don't want anything to do with that...thing inside of you!"

...

"After everything I just said, you lay that on me! No, no, I can't, I can't do this. I fucking won't do this."

...

I jerk awake, my eyes flying open. I'm back in the bright hospital room, disturbed and upset at the fragmented memories plaguing my broken mind. I feel sick, my stomach roiling at my abhorrent behaviour, I'll never be able to take that back and that is the thought at the forefront of my brain, as I try to rid myself of the desperate need to get high.

***

As the days go on, the doctors are happy with my progress after long exhausting hours in physical and occupational therapy. My body is getting stronger by the day and my mind is still disjointed and full of blank spaces, but I'm hoping I can go home soon. I can't wait to get back to some sense of normality and get back on the road with the boys. I'm watching endless re-runs of Friends, aware I've seen them all before, but it feels like the first time all over again. The doctor walks in and she is a middle-aged female called Doctor Amal Stewart. She is short with skin the colour of chocolate, short black hair, peppered with grey. She greets me with a warm smile.

"Good Morning, Brody, how are you feeling this morning?"

I nod and flash her a cheeky grin.

"Yeah, I'm good, thank you."

She nods curtly, checks my chart, and examines me thoroughly. When she is finished, she stands at the foot of the bed.

"I don't see why you can't go home today. You need to keep up with the exercises, attend regular narcotics anonymous meetings, take it easy and come in for frequent appointments. I'm strongly advising you to steer clear of alcohol, drugs and caffeine for the time being," she says with a stern tone to her voice, and I nod in agreement.

"I'll prepare your discharge notes."

She smiles and leaves. I am so relieved that I can finally go home, so I can begin to put this situation behind me and move on.

***

Sam and Jamie-Leigh have packed up all my stuff in preparation for me to go home. Jamie-Leigh presses a kiss to my forehead, and I smile tenderly, as Sam picks up my sports bag.

"Are you ready, darling?" Jay asks and I nod, as she wraps her arm around me. We collect my medication from the pharmacy on the way out, flanked by three of our security team Kai, Trey and Jace, they help me into the car. We make our way out onto the busy London street and as I step out onto the street, I am blinded by flashbulbs and a crowd of enthusiastic fans, photographers, and journalists. I feel myself start to panic, as my heartbeat starts to quicken. Kai clears a path to the car idling at the curb and opens the car door.

"Brody, over here."

There are shouts from different directions, and I am suddenly overwhelmed by the attention.

"SNAKE! OH MY GOD! SNAKE!"

I hear the familiar screams from our fans, which makes me smile and I give them a wave, as I climb into the car. The door slams shut, and I am glad for the silence. I am unusually quiet on the long journey back to my place, grateful for Jay's idle chatter. My racing thoughts are interrupted by the sound of a news report on the radio.

"Brody Hart from rock band Rancid Vengeance, has today left Weymouth Street Private Hospital. Hart, 34, was the victim of a horrific road traffic accident in July and his injuries were said to be life-threatening. Snake, as he is known to his die-hard fans, has since had a long road to recovery after suffering a severe brain injury, among other undisclosed injuries. He looked a shadow of his former self as he left hospital, waving to the crowd of adoring fans. Sources say that 'He's lucky to be alive.' The reason behind this major incident is still unclear. However, our sources say Hart suffered a relapse after years of battling a harrowing cocaine addiction. In recent months, guitarist extraordinaire and winner of Guitar Magazine's Guitarist of the year for six years running, has been in the press for his blossoming romance with Hollywood starlet of the moment, Raleigh Storm. Storm, 30 is said to be pregnant with Hart's child, but this is yet to be confirmed. We will keep you updated on any developments, as this story continues to unfold."

I hear Sam growl from his seat next to me and clear my throat.

"How is she?"

Sam half turns to me and shakes his head, his face looking grave.

"She's not good at all, man. She's moved back to her apartment in Kensington."

I drop my head into my hands. "This is all such a fucking mess, I don't know what to do, Sam," I admit. Ever since the accident, my emotions are all over the place and I start to sob hard. I sob for all the mistakes I had made, I sob for Raleigh, I sob for our babies, I sob for all the regrets and everything that is wrong in my life. I am left wondering; *will I ever be able to repair this horrible fucking mess?* Right now, I don't have an answer and that's what scares me the most.

12

Raleigh

I've learned the hard way that sometimes the person you'd take a bullet for is the one behind the trigger. I have spent the past week in hell. I just want the dull, permanent ache in my chest to go away. I want to feel something other than...betrayal. I still hadn't managed to wrap my head around why he would do something like this to me, to us? I stroke my stomach, feeling the familiar strong kicks of our babies growing inside me. I want to do something other than cry. Every time I thought about him with...her, I felt sick to my stomach at the thought of her hands on something that was mine. *Did she know about me? Of course she did, the shame that plagued her face when she looked at me. Did she even care?* My heart hurts and I feel nothing but utter humiliation. He had spent four years sleeping with that woman, was she the one he was in love with? It didn't bear thinking about, I couldn't allow myself to think such thoughts, not right now at least. I had to focus on a healthy pregnancy and being strong for our children, who are yet to come into the world.

For the past week, I have shut myself off from the world and distanced myself from Sam, Peyton, and the rest of Rancid Vengeance. It makes me feel shitty, but I can't help but wonder if they knew about the other woman the whole time? *Were they part of the lie?* They have been friends for over twenty years, how could they not know? That thought makes my stomach roil and I feel the familiar bile rise in my throat. I fucking hate him, I hate him for making me feel like this. I hate him for making me feel so fucking worthless and in that moment, I fell apart so completely. It was the most beautiful moment ever, because right there, I realised I could put the pieces back together the way I wanted them to be, and it didn't include Brody Hart.

***

I'm reading through some movie scripts when when my phone starts ringing, I check who's calling. I don't recognise the number, but I answer apprehensively anyway.

"Hello?" a female clears her throat on the other end.

"Erm...hi, this is Lorna, Lorna Lavelle, I'm..."

I cut her off before she continues. "Brody's mistress, yeah I know who you are. What do you want and why the fuck are you even calling me? How did you get this number?" I say with obvious disdain and I know I'm being rude, but I can't seem to help myself where she's concerned.

"I just wanted to know if you were ok. I know it must have come as a shock and I know it's cheeky of me to ask, but I wanted to meet with you."

What the actual fucking fuck? Is she actually for real? Shock doesn't even cover it.

"Shock? Are you for real? Why would you even ask to meet me? I've got nothing to fucking say to you! Well, nothing kind at least."

I feel my hackles rise at her blatant impertinence.

"I feel like I need to explain."

I laugh bitterly. "Explain? What's there to explain? The fact you've been fucking my boyfriend for four years? Or the fact that you were found out?"

She pauses briefly.

"Look, it's not his fault and I know I'm the last person you want to talk to or even see, but please, I feel like we need to talk woman to woman."

I let out a sarcastic bark of laughter. "Do you want to compare notes? Braid each others' hair? I've got nothing to say to you like I said."

She lets out a sigh. I feel my temper boiling with each second that passes and with that, I stab angrily at the screen and hang up the phone without saying goodbye.

13

Brody

Since I was discharged from hospital a week ago, I had fallen into a deep depression. I had also taken comfort in the coldness of a void and taken solace shutting myself off from the world. I wanted to be left alone to wallow in my own self-pity. I wasn't seeking a happier version of me; I was just seeking a less broken version of myself. When I woke up from a three-month coma, I started to see the true darkness that settled itself deep inside me, and soon, there were no more colours left in my world, just black clouds, and shadows of the life I had before. There was sorrow where there should have been joy, that I was going to be someone's dad, I couldn't see anything beyond that.

My brain was broken, temporarily damaged, and I felt a fear that I'd never felt before because I didn't have a time frame of how long it would last. I still couldn't fully remember how to do simple tasks; I couldn't remember the lyrics, or the chords to songs we had sung and played for fourteen plus years. I couldn't feel what I was supposed to feel for my girl, who had sat so patiently waiting for three months. She had given up so much to make sure she was there, every day without fail and she didn't deserve that, not one bit. She deserved the world that I was incapable of giving her and she found out that I had committed the ultimate betrayal by having sex with another woman. Not only was she another woman, but she was a married woman who I had a four year affair with. My secret had been exposed, and I fucking hated myself for it.

The annoying beep of the answer machine signalling I had a message from Sam, caused a dull throb in my skull. All I wanted to do was pull the covers over my head and hide away from the world outside. I close my eyes, ready to drift off back to sleep, when I hear a loud pounding on the door. *For fucks sake.*

"HART! I KNOW YOU'RE IN THERE, YOU PRICK! OPEN THE FUCKING DOOR, OR I'M GONNA BREAK IT DOWN!" Sam's husky, booming voice echoes through the house, breaking the silence.

"HART! OPEN THIS MOTHERFUCKING DOOR, OR SO HELP ME GOD!"

I turn over and groan at the sound of the intrusion to my otherwise peaceful bubble. A few seconds later, I hear the distinct sound of a foot connecting with the door, the splintering of the wood piercing my eardrums and sending the door hurtling against the wall with a deafening thud. *Fuck my life, this isn't going to end well. Why won't they just get the hint and leave me the fuck alone!* I hear the sound of several sets of footsteps getting closer and closer, until my bedroom door swings open.

"For fucks sake!" Sam mutters, as the protection of my duvet cover is flung away from my body and I'm faced with the judgemental wrath of Sam, Jax, Lucas and Lenny looming over me like the fucking Four Horsemen of the Apocalypse.

"Dude! It fucking reeks in here!" Lucas states, as he flings the curtains open and pushes the window open, daylight flooding the room. The pounding instantly starts thrumming in my head, temporarily blinding me.

"*Jesus fucking Christ*, boy," Lenny says gruffly and the disappointment in his voice makes me feel a sense of shame that I've never felt before. For the first time in my life, I feel vulnerable and with that thought, I burst into uncontrollable floods of tears and I don't know if I'll ever be able to stop.

Raleigh

"He's in a bad way, sweetheart, he needs you," Sam rasps and I laugh bitterly.

"Funny, he didn't need me when he was sticking his cock in another woman," I state snarkily, I can't help myself. *It all still feels too raw right now.*

"I get that you're angry, but he's refusing to talk to anyone. He's refusing his meds, he's refusing to go to his NA meetings, and he's refusing to attend his therapy sessions. I don't know what else to do, I'm worried about him, we all are."

The emotion in Sam's voice is evident, and it makes my heart hurt. I want Brody to suffer and feel the same heartache that I do right now, but I have to be the better person. I have to see him at some point, he's still the father of our children.

"Ok, fine, I'll see him," I sigh defeatedly down the phone.

"Great, I can have one of our security team come and pick you up in an hour?" he says, with a little more optimism in his husky voice.

"I can make my own way there; I can be there in an hour," I state matter-of-factly, feeling suddenly defiant and wanting to do it on my own terms. He hums his agreement and there is a brief pause.

"Raleigh?" Sam clears his throat and breaks the uncomfortable silence.

"Yeah?" my voice small.

"Thank you, honestly, thank you."

I smile to myself.

"I'm doing this for you and for our children. I haven't forgiven him and I don't know if I ever will. Not after everything he's done. After everything he's put us through, why the fuck do you still put up with him, after all this time, Sam?" I ask, genuinely interested at why they keep giving him chance after chance.

"Because he's our family, and he's got no one else. because deep down, he's still that scared ten-year-old boy who found his mum dead. I know he can't use that as an excuse forever, but it's all I've got. I don't know how else I can explain, sweetheart. Ever since he's been released from hospital, he's shut himself away, he's hidden from the world, because he's terrified his brain damage is going to be permanent. He still can't remember lyrics, he still can't play his guitar and I think that's what's scared him the most. That he can't remember how to do the one thing that keeps him grounded, the one thing he loves."

Listening to Sam explain, my heart slams against my ribcage and despite my current feelings for Brody, I have to put that aside and be there for him, if not as a lover, then at least as a friend.

***

A few hours later, Cliff and I pull up outside Brody's. His house is extravagant, but looks very elegant from the outside. The looming, grey brick farmhouse, with large sash windows and a large rectangular gravel driveway. The door is swung open before I knock and I find myself smiling, as I'm greeted by Peyton. She throws her arms around me and I'm instantly enveloped in her calming scent of Calvin Klein Deep Euphoria.

"Raleigh! It's so good to see you, babe!" she says enthusiastically and I laugh, happy to see the woman who became a close friend when I went on tour with Rancid Vengeance. She accepted me as one of her own and I have found a lifelong friend.

"Good to see you too, girl!" I offer brightly, as I pull away from her and take her in. She looks gorgeous as always, her dark hair with purple and electric pink flashes is perfectly tousled on one side and shaved on the other side. She is wearing a red and white checkered shirt, tied at her tanned, flat midriff, her belly button piercing glinting in the light, she is also wearing blue cropped, skinny, ripped jeans, and a pair of red Converse.

"You look fantastic! You're glowing! Come, come in!" she compliments, inviting me in and I step inside the familiar, opulent hallway, with white marble flooring. I follow her into the large, cosy lounge and that's when I spot him. He looks so different to the way he did a few weeks ago. He is sitting in his recliner, wearing blue, white and black checkered pyjama bottoms and a v-neck black t-shirt. His feet are bare, and his dark hair is flat and longer, as it falls haphazardly into his eyes. He has grown a short beard and his silver eyes look vacant and lifeless, as they lock with mine. I clear my throat, breaking the awkward silence between us.

"Hey."

He drops his gaze from mine and goes to stand.

"Don't stand on my account, it's fine."

It hurts to see him looking so fragile, his movements are slow and he looks so weak. His muscles aren't as prominent, and his face looks pale and gaunt. Peyton observes our exchange warily, glancing down at her smartwatch.

"Please, sit, I need to get to the shop. Seb's opening up a new shop in New York and I've got back-to-back appointments. But if you need anything in the meantime, the security guys are in the control room and Linda, our housekeeper will be here in an hour. I'll leave you to it."

She kisses me on the cheek, kisses Brody on his forehead and whispers something in his ear. He looks up at her, smiling warmly as she turns to leave. I drop down heavily onto the large navy sectional, U-shaped sofa, suddenly feeling exhausted and completely unprepared for what's to come.

Brody

I feel all sorts of edgy and anxious, as I observe her watching me carefully. I feel the tremors start in my hands and I hope to fuck she doesn't notice. I'm not ready to lose her, I know I've hurt her, but I want to make it up to her. I'll spend the rest of my life making it up to her if that's what it takes. I have to make amends; I need her to forgive me for all I've done and for all I put her through.

"I'm sorry," I mutter throatily, at a loss of what else to say. She laughs bitterly, fidgeting almost uncomfortably in her seat.

"Wow! That's it? That's all you've got?" she snaps. *This is going fucking brilliantly, well done, Hart. Dickhead.*

"I came here today because I thought you might have at least had something new to say. But it's the same old Brody bullshit I've heard a million times before! Have you ever stopped, and fucking asked me what I want?" she yells and I have the sense to recoil at her obvious rage.

"Actually don't answer that question! You say you care about me, but you can't even say I love you out loud and you sure as hell don't act like it! You've never once asked me how my day was, what my favourite colour is, anything that even remotely shows that you care to get to know me beyond the sex."

It breaks my heart to hear her say those words.

"I'm sorry," I say again, my voice full of remorse and obvious sincerity. As I look into her turbulent amethyst eyes, all I feel is a sense of overwhelming fucking shame and the look she gives me in return all but destroys me. I wish I weren't the reason she looks at me with such intense hatred and bitter disappointment.

"You always say you're sorry, then you go and break my fucking heart again. I'm so done with that, Brody! I didn't fall for you, you fucking tripped me! It was inevitable that I fell for the unreachable rockstar and I hate myself for feeling like this. I hate that I *let* you make me feel this way! I fucking hate you! I spent three solid months at your bedside praying you'd wake up, praying you'd come back to me. I'm carrying your babies, for fucks sake and you were sleeping with another woman the entire time! How could I have been so stupid!" she says with an uncontrolled, intense, seething fury I never knew she possessed. I swallow past the lump that has lodged itself in my throat and I will myself not to sob like a fucking baby.

"I'm done with caring about people who don't care about me" she says coldly, with zero emotion. "I'm starting with you, it's fucking over between us, Brody. I can't do this, I don't think I can forgive you, not this time, you've gone too far."

I struggle to get to my feet, but with maximum effort, I manage to shuffle the short space between us and drop down heavily next to her. I reach over to stroke her tear-stained cheek and she lets me. She leans into my touch and I place my other hand on her swollen stomach. Her pained amethyst eyes meet mine, and I try my hardest to remember them and commit them to memory, because I knew through no fault of my own, after today it would be a long time before I see her again.

I press my forehead to hers and move both of my hands to cup her face.

"Brody." My name falls from her lips like a prayer, and I gently press my lips to hers. I expect her to stop me and push me away, but she doesn't, she lets me kiss her. She tastes exactly as I remembered and the feel of her soft plump lips against mine after all this time, feels like heaven. She coaxes me to deepen the kiss and I introduce my tongue, our tongues perform a sensual dance, as she teases and caresses my mouth. I worship her mouth with mine and I feel my cock stir in my pyjama bottoms, as she cups my erection. She's breathing heavily into my mouth, as I grip the nape of her neck with my hand.

"Kitten, tell me to stop. Please, make me stop," I plead, but she answers by rubbing my cock urgently through my trousers.

"I don't want you to stop. Oh God, please, please don't stop. Don't you dare fucking stop," she pants, as I move my hand down to her aching centre.

I feel the heat radiating from her, as I rub her pussy in gentle circles through her clothes. I groan loudly, as she slips her hand inside my pyjama bottoms and grips my steel erection in her hand.

"*Fuck,*" I curse low in my throat, as she starts to move her hand up and down my hard shaft. *Jesus fucking Christ, I've missed her hands on me, it's been so long.*

"Do you like that?" she pants seductively and I nod, unable to speak. I sink my teeth into my bottom lip and throw my head back in pure ecstasy. She pulls my erection free from the confines of my trousers and moves her head into my lap. She sinks her mouth onto my cock and starts with slow licks from the top to the base. She teases the head with her tongue, as she moves up and down.

"*Fuck,* Raleigh, you're gonna make me come," I grind out, growling low in my throat. I feel her the wet heat of her mouth slide down my entire length, as she takes me to the hilt.

"OH FUCCKKK!" I yell, as she cups my balls with her hand. I growl primally, as she flicks my piercing with her expert tongue. I can feel my cock twitching with its pending release.

"*Jesus fuckin' Christ,* that feels so good, kitten, I've missed you so much," she continues sucking and I grip the back of her head, as I fist her hair between my fingers and tug gently.

"*Shit! Fuck! Bollocks!* I'm going to come, I'm going to come so hard, Raleigh," I pant almost urgently, as she stops sucking, releasing my cock from her mouth with a pop. She wipes her mouth on the back of her hand, with a satisfied, almost evil grin on her beautiful face. *What the fuck?* She gets to her feet, her bump protruding in front of her. She tousles her hair, blows me a kiss and flashes me a wink, as she turns and walks out leaving me a fraught, desperate fucking mess on the sofa. *Fuck my life.*

14

Raleigh

I feel almost empowered and extremely satisfied, as I swing the door open to leave Brody's mansion. I leave to the sound of him yelling my name, as I slam it behind me and carefully take the stone steps one at a time down to the gravelled driveway. Cliff sees me approaching his slate grey Range Rover Evoque and his face drops when he sees my expression.

"Everything ok, sweetheart? Have I got to go in there and kick his arse?"

I laugh at his reaction, Cliff is usually a quiet, serious, protective, but stoic man and he has become a father figure to me over the years. I shake my head and walk up to him, kiss him on the cheek and get in the car to the sound of him chuckling softly to himself. He gets in the car and starts up the engine. Brody's frail figure puffing out his cheeks as if he has just run a marathon is the last thing I see before we pull away and make our journey home.

***

"So, you sucked him off and just as he was about to nut, you just stopped and left?" Liv bursts into hysterical laughter, I nod and grin proudly.

"High five, girl! *Fucking prick!*" she high fives me and I laugh along with her, grateful for her company. We are both in our lounge wear, not a scrap of make-up between us. Her blonde hair is messily piled up on top of her head, but she still looks as gorgeous as ever. I look the complete opposite; I feel like a fucking beached whale, and I stopped being able to see my feet a few weeks ago.

"I would loved to have seen the look on his face!" she takes a long gulp of her wine and points her manicured finger at me, as I look at her glass longingly. I lick my lips, wishing I could drown my sorrows in the exact same way.

"I'd be lying if I said I didn't feel anything for him, Liv. I wish I fucking didn't, it just hurts, ya know? How could I not have not noticed the signs? How could I have missed the fact that he was sleeping with another woman behind my back for our entire relationship?" I say incredulously, feeling my lip trembling and the familiar lump forming in my throat.

"*Fuck him,* Rae! *Fuck him!* He's not worth your tears!" she squeals, angry on my behalf, as my phone starts dancing on the table, it's him again. I've had thirty two missed calls, sixteen text messages and seven voicemails from him since I ran out on him yesterday. I haven't listened to or read any of them. A stray tear rolls down my cheek and I swipe it angrily away, annoyed at myself that I'm allowing him to make me feel this way.

"I have focus on being strong for my babies, but it's not easy. I shouldn't be experiencing this on my own! We should be going to ante-natal classes and experiencing being first-time parents together! I fucking hate him for that! I despise him! I want him to suffer! I'm so angry, Liv!"

At that moment, I curse my hormones to hell for making me go from ugly crying to molten rage in two seconds flat. She shifts closer to me, envelopes me in her arms and I break down so completely, I'm not sure if I'll ever come back from it.

Brody

"I know I don't have the right to ask you to forgive me and I'm not sure if you're even listening to these messages, but you're everything I hate and love about myself, all at the same time. You're...fuck...I'm struggling to find the words, Raleigh. Ever since the accident, I've got a second shot at righting everything I did wrong, and I don't want to fuck it up. But it seems that's all I'm doing and I'm so fucking sorry. I'm not very good at putting my feelings into words. But never doubt my love for you, it's the only thing I'm sure of. I know I haven't been able to admit it out loud before, but I fucking love you, so, so much."

My voice breaks and this is totally new to me. My emotions are heightened and all I want to do right now is break down in floods of tears.

During the weeks that passed, I found myself getting stronger every day. I am attending my hospital appointments and with the go-ahead from the Doctor, I started working out again. I am attending regular Narcotics Anonymous meetings and once per week sessions with Rick. I am going back on the road with the boys. In a few months, we are embarking on a sixty two date UK and European tour. The *"Vengeance – I'm not Dead"* tour sold out in eleven minutes, breaking our records. I felt good for the first time since the accident, my memories were slowly returning, and I was healing with each day that went by. I hadn't heard from Raleigh or seen her since she pleasured me and left me hanging that day, but she was never far from my thoughts. I had thrown myself back in to exercising, writing songs for the new album, and rehearsing with the boys in preparation for our tour that starts in less than two months. I occupied my mind writing, reading, experimenting with melodies, and reteaching myself the songs I had temporarily forgotten, anything that would help take my mind off missing the woman I was sure I wanted to spend the rest of my life with. I needed her like Sam needed Peyton, like Jax needed Zeppelin. I had to get her to hear me out somehow and I was determined to be a good boyfriend and a good father to our twins.

I had spent the previous weeks coming to terms with the fact I was going to be a dad. I had never really contemplated wanting kids before, as I didn't want to infect my child with the poison that ran through my veins, but I was more determined than ever not to let that happen and right the wrongs of my past. I wanted to prove to Raleigh and to the babies that grew inside her that I was capable of being the best father I can be. If that's what it took, I would spend the rest of my life proving it to all three of them and that thought alone, was what had gotten me through the past few weeks. It had to be enough, for now at least.

After a dull and silent journey, I find myself outside Rick Delaney's London office, in the heart of Greenwich for my weekly session. I'm flanked by Kai, one of our bodyguards and a photographer practically shoves a camera in my face, catching me off guard and my heartbeat starts to quicken, as Kai ushers him away from me. I smile my thanks and make my way into the plush building, wanting to be anywhere but here. The receptionist greets me in her usual overly friendly manner and Rick steps out of his office. He is average height with mid-brown, almost ginger hair, and brown eyes. His wearing black jeans, brown Timberlands, and a green and black plaid shirt, open at the collar.

"Good to see you, as always, Brody, mate," he says in his familiar Mancunian accent.

I greet him wordlessly with a curt nod of my head and step into his office. He closes the door with a click, and I sit down on the sofa, raking my hand through my unkempt hair. Rick observes me with his usual caution, as if I'm an animal about to attack and picks up his navy leather notebook, flipping it open. He clears his throat, leans back in his chair, and begins to speak.

"So, do you want to tell me what's been happening since our previous session?"

I cross my long legs at the ankle and remain silent for long moments, reluctant to answer his question. He observes me briefly and starts to scribble in his notebook, before looking back up at me.

"Is there a reason you're reluctant to answer the question, Brody?" he asks, carefully trying to gauge my mood, as he clicks his pen in quick succession.

"I fucked up," I answer with a bored and uninterested tone to my voice, as he picks up his pen and starts to write. The scratch of the pen against the paper sets my teeth on edge and I start to feel all kinds of agitated. The dull throb in my head back with a vengeance.

"Do you care to elaborate?"

I lean back in the chair.

"Have you ever done something so bad you feel irredeemable?" I ask and he sets his pen down, stroking his chin as he contemplates my question.

"I think we've all done things we're not proud of at some point in our lives," he answers and I laugh.

"So, you're going with your usual generic bullshit?"

I'm unable to keep the bitter sarcasm from my voice. *Fuck, I need to get high.* I don't want to feel this ache in my chest, I don't want to feel broken and so completely hopeless. I want to block out every thought of *her*, I want to go back to before the accident when everything was normal.

"Have you ever felt so useless that you think the world would be better off without you in it?" I say darkly, my mind automatically going to a place I'd rather not be. "Have you ever heard the woman you love tell you she hates you? Has your brain ever been so completely fucking scrambled that you can't remember lyrics, or important conversations you've had? Have you ever felt so out of your depth that you want to get so fucking high you don't ever want to come back from it?"

I babble, I can feel myself getting anxious and the desperate craving for a hit is so powerful, my hands start to shake. I haven't felt this way since before the accident and the feeling overwhelms me.

"Raleigh left me because I've been having sex with another woman for four years," I blurt out and he coughs, trying and failing to hide his obvious shock and nods. I laugh bitterly at his reaction, leaning forward to brace my elbows on my knees.

"I told you I'd fucked up! I hate myself for doing that to her! Why would I do that to her? I've asked myself that question a lot lately, but you know the fucked up thing? I haven't got an answer!"

I drop my head into my hands and feel myself slowly spiralling out of control, as if I am looking from the outside in.

"Do you think it's because you sabotage your own happiness? Because you feel like you don't deserve it?" Rick states and I take a few minutes to think about his question.

Do I sabotage my own happiness? The answer to that is yes. I've knowingly and repeatedly pursued a woman in a committed relationship. I avoid emotional pain at all costs and people always expect the worst from me so I play up to the fact and disappoint them anyway. I am my own worst enemy, failing to see the positives and focusing on the negative aspects. I could use the excuse that it all stems back to my childhood, but that would be an absolute fucking cop out. At that moment, I come to the blinding realisation that Rick is right, as much as it fucking pains me to admit it.

"I've spent my whole fucking life waiting for the other shoe to drop. Maybe I do sabotage my own happiness because I don't deserve it! I've gotten so off my tits on drugs over the years, I've done things..." I stop myself from continuing that sentence, as I'm instantly transported back to the night I got locked in the dressing room by J.D.

Johnnie 'J.D.' Diamond was our manager, and he had an unhealthy obsession with Sam. He had signed us to his record label 'Diamond Records' when we were young, naïve twenty-year-old boys who had no clue about the music industry. He kidnapped Peyton, along with Sam's sister, Savannah. They manipulated us all and destroyed our lives, as we knew it.

He made the boys think I was so high I couldn't perform, but that was so far from the truth.

Brody
Past

I'm so fucking buzzed after the bottle of Jack I downed and those cheeky lines of coke I've just snorted. My adrenaline is pumping; my blood is singing, and I feel like I could run a marathon without breaking a sweat! I'm rubbing my forefinger underneath my nose, and I sniff, as I walk down the corridor of the venue we're performing at tonight with a spring in my step. I can't remember the name; they all look the same and blend into one just lately. I haven't had a day off in months, I'm due a huge fucking blow out. I bump into J.D. and he grabs my arm, gripping it tightly.

"Are you high?"

He looks me in the eyes, and I try to look anywhere but at him. Fuck me, who let the fun police in?

"Jesus fucking Christ, you are! Get your shit together, Brody! For God's sake! Those boys don't deserve you dragging them down! If it were up to me I'd have sacked you a long time ago!" he barks and his words don't register, as I hold my hands up defensively, desperately trying not to burst into a fit of hysterical laughter.

"Consider my shit together, Sir!" I shout wryly in his face, while saluting and snatching my arm away from him.

Fuck me, I'm nowhere near high or drunk enough to deal with his bullshit. Pretentious prick. I continue my journey down the corridor and push my way into the toilet, ignoring someone calling my name. I push all of the doors of the toilet cubicles open with my boot, checking there is no one else in here. When I am satisfied I'm alone, I go into a cubicle, pull the seat down and drop down heavily on to it. I reach into the pocket of my jeans, take out my bank card and my bag of cocaine. I pull out my phone, pour the snow onto the screen, the strong, pungent smell of petrol permeating my nostrils. I make quick work of making two neat lines and I begin to salivate, as I roll up a fifty and quickly hoover both up my nose, sniffing hard. Fucking hell there is nothing like the feeling of pure elation, as the coke starts to work its way through my system. My heartbeat starts to quicken, as I tip my head back briefly, a sick feeling settles in my stomach and as quick as it comes on, it's gone. I pinch my nose and get to my feet. I move my head from side to side, cracking my neck.

I've been taking coke for so long now, I've forgotten what it's like to function like a normal human being without it coursing through my veins. My nostrils tingle and the back of my throat feels numb. I feel so full of energy I could bounce off the fucking walls! I unlock the toilet door and walk towards the mirror, meeting my reflection. My face is sweaty, and my pupils are like fucking saucers! I slap my cheek with my palm and a feeling of inner tranquillity and calmness washes over me. I exit the toilet and begin my walk down the corridor back to the dressing room. My whole body feels weightless. My senses are on high alert, my smell, my taste, and my receptors firing on all cylinders. My heart is pounding,

and I feel like Superman! Fuck Kryptonite! Fuck Lois Lane! Fuck Lex Luthor!
I can shoot lasers out of my eyes; I can fucking fly and I wear a motherfucking
cape! I grin to myself as I swing the door to the dressing room open. J.D. regards
me with disdain, standing in the middle of the room with his hands on his
hips. He is a tall, lean man with a slightly tanned complexion, black hair
in an old-fashioned side parting, dark-brown eyes, and black-rimmed glasses.
Everything about him creeps me out. Fucking weirdo.

"Jesus fucking Christ!" he mutters, as Sam enters the room and I swear to
Christ J.D. looks at him as if he's dinner. I regard them both with narrow eyes
and sniff hard.

"Are you high?" J.D. spits and I burst out laughing.

"Is the Pope a catholic?" I answer wryly and he shakes his head, furiously
chewing on a piece of gum. The euphoric feeling I felt just five minutes has turned
to a dull buzz. I sniff again and bounce from one foot to the other. Jesus fucking
Christ, if I'm going to have to deal with this prick I need another line, or three.
Sam leaves the room and the voice on the tannoy informs us that it's five minutes
to showtime. I go to push past J.D. and he grabs my arm.

"If you fuck this up..."

I snatch my arm away from him and cock my eyebrow. Is this idiot for real?

"You'll what? Sack me? You haven't got the fucking balls, mate!" I snap and
slam the door to the dressing room toilet behind me. I reach into the pocket of
my jeans and take out what I need. I pull out my phone, pour the coke onto the
screen, making two sets of two neat lines this time, roll up the fifty, and snort. I
place my hand onto the wall to steady myself, feeling the usual fleeting sickness
in my stomach. I feel like I've had ten cups of coffee! Fucking bring on the gig!
The familiar pre-gig nerves are nowhere to be seen, as I open the door back into
the dressing room. The room is empty, I pick up my guitar and go to the open the
door. I shake the door handle for a few seconds, the door must be stuck.

"Hello?"

I start to pound on the door.

"HELLO! IS SOMEONE THERE?"

I rattle the handle, but it won't budge.

"I'm in here! Let me out!" I shout, but I'm met with silence when I hear the
familiar roar of the crowd and the pound of Lucas' drum from the auditorium.
I hear footsteps outside the door and knock.

"Hello? Who's there? The door locked, can you let me out?" I ask with a sniff trying to remain calm.

"Those boys don't need you bringing them down, you junkie piece of shit! They've gone on stage without you, I told them you were too high to perform!" J.D. laughs bitterly.

"This isn't fucking funny, J.D.!" I yell, as he continues to laugh.

"Oh, it's fucking hilarious! Sammy, it's for his own good!" he says mockingly and I shake the door handle vigorously.

"LET ME OUT, J.D.! OR SO HELP ME GOD!"

He laughs like a hyena and it grates on every fucking nerve in my body. Jesus Christ, this bloke is a fucking sociopath! "Or what?"

As soon as this door is opened, I swear I'm going to fucking punch his teeth down his throat until he's choking.

"OPEN THIS FUCKING DOOR, J.D.!"

I shake the handle again, my mind racing just as fast as my heart, an unsettled feeling lodging itself in the pit of my stomach.

"I know you're in love with Sam, you sick piece of shit!" I blurt out and he stops laughing.

"DON'T YOU DARE SPEAK HIS NAME! YOU KNOW FUCKING NOTHING!" he yells, his voice hard but full of panic at the same time. I take a deep breath, pressing my head to the cool, smooth wood of the door, squeezing my eyes shut briefly. Dread engulfs my body, as a flashback of myself as a child, locked in my bedroom, tears rolling down my seven-year-old face, listening to my mum's latest boyfriend beating the shit out of her. The memory was so vivid, I claw at the door trying to get to her.

"Leave her alone! Get your fucking hands off her!" I whisper softly to myself, as a tremor shakes my body, causing my teeth to chatter.

"You're fucking pathetic!" J.D. spits, his voice full of hatred. My legs feel weak, as I spin around, out of control and trapped inside my head. The memory clinging to me, as I slide down the door and onto the floor. Well fuck me.

Brody

Present

I'm jolted back to the present by the sound of Rick clearing his throat, as he glances at his Apple watch, his pen hovering over the page in his notebook.

"We've touched upon your relationships briefly with the rest of the boys in the band, Peyton and Raleigh in our previous sessions, do you want to enlighten me on the relationship with the woman you've been sleeping with?"

He watches me prudently, as I squeeze my eyes shut and all I see is *her*. Lorna fucking Lavelle. Her hair wrapped around my fist, her long legs entwined with mine, the intensity in her aquamarine eyes, the way she smiles and the way her skin feels pressed against mine. *Fuck. I have no business still wanting her, but I can't seem to help myself.*

"No, not really," I answer aloofly, my eyes darting around the room.

"What good would talking about it do? It won't change anything! She's my weakness, my fucking Achilles heel, she's the forbidden fruit. I have no business wanting her, but I can't help myself! I should have walked away as soon as I found out she was married, but by that point I was already falling for her, I was in deep and there was no way out!"

He picks up his pen and seems to think better of it, as he sets it down again. I get up from my chair and start to pace the room, feeling more than a little anxious.

"Is there a reason why talking about this is making you feel agitated?" Rick asks coolly and I go over to the floor to ceiling window that offers a panoramic view across the city, the pounding in my head becoming unbearable.

"I couldn't keep my fucking dick in my pants because I wanted what I couldn't have. I messed around with someone else's wife; I have to deal with the consequences."

I breathe in through my nose and out through my mouth trying to quell the need to drown myself in a mountain of white powder. Rick pauses briefly, as he regards me intently.

"Is it because she rejected you and it reminded you of the way your mother rejected you?"

He states and I clench my jaw tightly, feeling myself become more and more overwrought and twitchy with each moment that passes. I am clucking for a fix and the vein in my neck starts to pulse wildly.

"You know nothing."

My voice is flat, as Rick observes me carefully.

"So many people are focused on traumatic childhoods being the root cause of mental and physical illnesses, but I don't believe that for a second. It just shines a light on it, it doesn't diagnose, or even solve the issue."

He explains and I gnaw on my thumbnail, feeling my hand begin to tremble. The pain in my head intensifying with each moment that passes. I press my lips together, reluctant to continue talking about Lorna. Rick nods curtly, as if realising that subject is closed for now.

"Ok, do you want to tell me about the accident? You seemed hesitant to give me the full details in our previous sessions? Before the crash, I felt we were making real progress after the P.T.S.D. diagnosis."

I turn around to face him, dropping my head slightly. *I'd almost forgotten about that.*

"Do you know what it feels like? Do you? It's all happening right in front of your eyes, over and over again. You want to close your eyes and hide from it, your body is still here, your mind is still there. There's three doors you can go through; one to get away from it, two to relive it and three to face it head on. You're just frozen to the spot, and you don't know which one to open. It's gotten to the point where my nightmares are bleeding into my daily life, sometimes I can't even differentiate whether I'm awake or asleep. So don't fucking sit there and pretend like you know what I'm going through because you have no idea what it's like to see something you know you couldn't prevent on a loop, over and over again."

My heart starts to pound a frantic tattoo in my chest and I'm back underneath that church pew again. I can hear the piercing sound of gunshots and me softly reassuring Ruby, as I see the life slowly fading from her brown eyes. I shake my head to rid myself of the horrific memory and the sudden urge to run overwhelms me. *I can't do this, I can't.* I shake my head vehemently.

"I can't fucking do this. I can't be here. I can't," I mutter in a rush, as I turn and sprint out of the room without looking back. *Fuck it all to hell.*

***

I haven't slept in six days…could be seven, or ten, my days have no clear beginning or end, they all seemed to blend into one. For days, I've been in a permanent state of oblivion, starting and finishing my days with endless lines of coke, pills and anything else I could lay my hands on. When I'm off my pickle on drugs, I don't see the look of disgust on Raleigh's face, as she spat words of hatred at me. I don't see Ruby pleading with me to save her and I don't see Lorna declaring her undying love for me, I don't feel anything at all and I relish the silence that it brings.

After my session with Rick, I called Kev, he supplied me with what I needed and took me back to his plush apartment in Canary Wharf. I'm unaware of my surroundings and I can't remember the last time I ate. I'm still wearing the same clothes I was wearing days ago and I'm sweating profusely. *Why is it so fucking hot in here?* I'm lying on the floor after sniffing enough coke to put a rhino on its arse when unexpectedly, I feel a sharp kick to my ribs.

"Fuck off!" I shout, my voice thick with exhaustion, I feel it again and I crack one eye open, looking up at the mountain of a man hovering above me. *Sam fucking Newbolt.*

"We've been looking for you for six fucking days!" he rasps, raising his voice, but I don't say anything. I roll onto my back and stare up at the crisp white ceiling, willing him to just go away. He moves into my line of sight and the look in his eyes is positively murderous, as he hauls me to my feet, cursing low in his throat. I stumble into him, and he grabs my t-shirt by the shoulder, yanking me forward, pushing me against the wall and pinning me to it with his forearm.

"GET YOUR FUCKING SHIT TOGETHER, HART! FOR FUCKS SAKE! I SHOULD KNOCK YOU ON YOUR ARSE, YOU PRICK!" he yells, his voice sounding far away. I can't seem to focus on anything, as my head flops forward and I succumb to the blackness.

15

Raleigh

I head quietly down to the basement, and I can hear masculine grunts and loud rock music pulsing through the speakers. I recognise the song as *Wash it All Away by Five Finger Death Punch.* As I step closer to where the sound is coming from, Brody comes into view. He looks so different from the last time I saw him; his dark hair is no longer the unkempt, dishevelled mess from a few weeks ago. It is neatly styled into a side swept undercut, he has at least a weeks' worth of stubble on his face and the scar that stretches from his hairline to round the back of his head is visible from a distance. He is doing pull-ups in the doorjamb, shirtless and glistening with sweat. His muscles are prominent and bulging, the veins in his arms thick. His waist is visibly leaner, and his jaw line looks a little more chiselled. I lick my lips at the sight of him in all his tattooed, muscled glory. He looks delicious, a far cry from the weak, fragile, pale man I saw just weeks ago. I stand still just observing him for the longest time and wonder how the fuck we got to this point. He looks surprised, as he turns his head and spots me gawking at him. *Subtle, Storm, real subtle.*

"Hey," he drawls lazily, as he jumps down from the bar and landing lithely on his feet.

"Hope I'm not interrupting? Linda let me in," I ask shyly and he smiles, as he wipes his face on a nearby towel.

"Course not, don't ever think that. It's good to see you and I must remind Linda not to let strange women into my house!" he jokes and flashes me a grin that makes his face light up. It's so boyish and child-like, a hidden dimple appears on his sweaty cheek. He wraps the towel around his neck, and we stand there in silence just staring at each other for what seems like an eternity.

"I listened to your messages."

I break the silence and I hear him gasp at my revelation. He finally admitted out loud that he loves me in an answer machine message. Despite my own protests, I gave in to the temptation and curiosity and listened to the messages he left. It took me a while to build up the courage to listen, but as soon as I heard him say those words, I couldn't stay away any longer. He steps closer to me and I can feel the tension radiating between us. The scent of Dior Sauvage mixed with sweat, and all things Brody invade my nostrils. His intense, stormy silver eyes are back with a vengeance, as they lock with mine. He moves closer to me and I can feel his hot breath tickling my cheek, as he wraps me in his strong muscular arms. I cling to his sweat glistened biceps for dear life and breathe him in as if it is the first and last time. My heart beat pounds in my chest like a harsh drum beat.

"Brody," I whisper, as he nuzzles his face into my neck.

"*Fuck,* I've missed you so much," he declares and I briefly pull away to look up at him. *Jesus Christ, is it possible that he actually looks hotter than I've ever seen him?* His muscles are huge and would give Sam's a run for their money, his shoulders are broad, and his thighs are thick and powerful. His tattoos stand out against the light bronze of his tanned skin. We stand there both mute, just looking at each other. He tilts his head and crushes his lips against mine, the unexpected feel of his lips teasing mine causes a rush of heat between my legs. He pulls away briefly, resting his forehead on mine and cupping my face in his large, tattooed hands.

"I'm so fucking sorry," he voice trembles, as he squeezes his eyes shut. When he opens them they are glossy and filled with such emotion it makes my heart slam against my rib cage.

"The last thing I wanted to do was hurt you, Raleigh, I know I fucked up, but I'll spend my life making it up to you if I have to."

I swallow past the lump in my throat and stroke his stubbled face.

"I don't know if I'll ever be able to forgive you, but I want to try," I admit honestly and he nods, as he reaches over and traces from my cheek to my collar bone with a feather-light touch. I feel the all too familiar heat between my thighs. Being pregnant, I am so horny all the time, and seeing Brody for the first time in weeks, I crave his body like a drug. His silver eyes are glittering, and I can feel his urgent need for me emanating from him in waves because it matches my own. He moves closer and presses his lips to mine, I moan softly into his mouth. His tongue seductively dancing with mine, lazy and unhurried. I feel his hand snake down my ribs, across my swollen stomach and I silently plead with him, to take me right there on the padded floor of his state-of-the-art home gym.

Our breaths are ragged, and perfectly in sync, as I feel his heart pounding in his hard chest. He moves his hand from my stomach and moves up to cup my tender, engorged breast. I gasp as he pulls the cup of my bra down and his thumb strokes my sensitive nipple into a hard-erect bud. I wrap my arms around his neck and encourage him to go further. I can feel the slick heat pooling between my legs. A fierce ache begins to blossom within me, and I need him to take it away. He pulls me closer to him until I can feel his erection solid between us.

"I need you, Brody."

My voice doesn't sound like my own, as I beg him with my eyes to take me to bed and worship me like only he can.

"I need the words, kitten, let me hear you say them out loud," he says low and seductively.

"I need you to take me to bed and fuck me like you used to," I say assertively, almost desperately. With those words, he lifts me up and carries me up the stairs to his bedroom and I am anticipating all the delicious things he's going to do to me.

16

Brody

I lay her down on my bed and it's a race to see who can get undressed the fastest. We're both naked in record time and I crawl up the bed, settling between her thighs. She looks gorgeous, her baby bump protruding in front of her. Her pale lilac, almost blonde, hair perfectly mussed and her amethyst eyes utterly captivating me and holding me hostage. I can't look away, as she wordlessly demands my attention. I move up her body and kiss her deeply, her hot, velvet tongue duelling with mine. We can't get enough of each other, she claws at my biceps, as if she can't get close enough. I break our kiss and move back down between her thighs.

"Spread your legs, kitten, I'm going to worship you now."

I sweep my finger through her moist slit and she writhes, cupping her breast in her hand.

"Mmm," she moans out loud and bites down on her plump bottom lip. I push my long finger inside her, moving in and out, increasing the momentum with each plunge of my finger.

"*Fuck*, you're so wet for me," I growl, my erection so hard it's almost painful. I introduce a second finger, as her breaths become urgent, and she arches her back.

"Oh God! Brody! *Fuck*! That feels so good!" she screams out.

"That's it, I want you to come for me, kitten. Come hard all over my fingers."

She moves her hand from her breast and starts to grip and bunch the sheets in desperation.

"*Fucking hell*, that's so hot. I can feel you throbbing around my fingers, you're close."

I increase the pace, as she starts panting and almost whimpering. I contemplate taking her right to the edge and leaving her hanging in exactly the same way as she did to me weeks ago, but I think better of it. *She's pregnant and hormonal, she might beat the shit out of me!*

"Look at me, kitten; I want to watch you come. I want to watch you fall apart as I bring you to orgasm."

My voice is demanding and her amethyst eyes lock with my silver ones. Her eyes are filled with lust and something else I can't put my finger on, but I don't dwell on that thought.

"Good girl, let go. Give it up for me, Raleigh."

It's all it takes for her orgasm to tear through her like a raging thunder storm. She screams loudly, as I squeeze every last drop of pleasure from her.

"*Jesus Christ,* I've missed this," I admit, as she flashes a lazy grin and I'm a total goner.

"I need you to fuck me, Brody."

I kneel between her creamy thighs as I fist my cock a few times and she doesn't take her eyes off me when my hard cock finds her entrance. I push in gently, aware it's been a while, but she encourages me with her eyes. I shove forward into her slick channel and she cries out.

"OH GOD!"

I bury myself deeper inside her and the feel of her velvet walls around my cock. It's been so long; I just remain still for a brief moment. I look down at her beneath me and she looks so beautiful. Her short hair has grown out into a bob and the lilac of her hair has faded, her natural blonde roots showing through. She writhes beneath me, snapping me from my momentary reverie.

"Move," she says impatiently, arching herself up towards me. I reward her with a sharp swivel of my hips, and she moans loudly, as I build up a punishing pace.

"Oh fuck, Brody!"

My thrusts become slower and unhurried, as I hold myself back for fear of hurting her and our babies. I don't just want to fuck; I want to make love to her. I want to show her that I'm capable of so much more than the selfish prick she remembered from all those months ago.

"Does that feel good, baby?"

She hums her approval, as I move in and out at a painfully slow pace, with each measured plunge, I feel the flutters of her orgasm. Her inner muscles ripple around my stiffness.

"Fuck, I can feel you, you're close. Come for me, Raleigh. Let me hear you scream for me."

She lets out an ear-piercing scream, as she explodes around my throbbing cock.

"OH GOD! BRODY! I'M COMING! OH FUCK! I'M COMING!"

My orgasm isn't far behind and I throw my head back, finding my release and yelling her name in garbled ecstasy.

It takes a few minutes for our laboured breaths to return to normal, then I pull out and lie down next to her, tucking her under my arm. I pull her close to me and she rests her cheek on my pec. We lie in silence for long moments. I trace idle shapes on the back of her neck, and I think she's fallen asleep until she shifts and places my hand on her stomach. Her belly ripples and I feel soft flutters against my hand. She giggles girlishly, as she looks up at my widening eyes. I'm rendered speechless as I continue to feel our babies kicking and moving inside her. I shift her gently from beneath my arm and settle myself between her legs, resting my cheek on her growing tummy.

"Hey, I'm your daddy. I can't wait to meet you both."

We continue to lie there for the longest time. She doesn't need to know I went on a bender and went missing for six days. After going cold turkey with the help of Lenny and the boys, and attending almost daily NA meetings, I felt good for the first time in weeks. I was content with having my girl back where she belongs. *Right now, life is pretty fucking perfect.*

17

Raleigh

As the weeks continued to go by, I could feel myself slipping away, the familiar dark part of me overshadowing the bright side. Ever since his accident, I've been struggling to maintain a grip on the me I was before. Ever since we re-connected, Brody has been the man I had wished him to be all those months ago. He's attentive, he's open about his feelings now and it's refreshing, but I can't help but think that things are a little too perfect. He's been throwing himself into work, rehearsing for his upcoming tour with Rancid Vengeance, in between recording a new album and I was going over several scripts I had been sent by various different directors who wanted me to be in their movies.

I was now over six months pregnant, and my pregnancy had been smooth sailing so far. Brody and I are lying in bed at his house after a marathon sex session, when curiosity gets the better of me and I push pause on the movie we are watching.

"What was her name?"

Referring to the woman he had spent the last four years having an affair with. *I can't help myself; I know I already know after she called me, but I want to hear it from him.* He sighs softly.

"She's not important. Not anymore," he states nonchalantly.

"I don't buy that, not for one fucking second. She had to mean something to you, you were sleeping with her for four years!" I say incredulously, pushing him for an answer.

"What good would it do? What relevance is she to you, to us?" he argues. I don't want to cause an argument, but I suddenly feel an overwhelming urge to know more about it, about her. Maybe then I can start to understand why, why he was so fascinated by her.

"I know you loved her," I declare matter-of-factly, and he drops his head into his hands, cursing softly to himself.

"Ok, if that's what you want, don't say I didn't warn you."

I nod, giving his hand a reassuring squeeze.

"Her name is Lorna, Lorna Lavelle. She was my weakness. She had been since the day I met her. I know you probably don't want to hear it, but we had a deep connection, and it went beyond the sex, for me at least."

It stings listening to hear him talk about another woman that way, but I asked him, I wanted to know more about this woman.

"We met at a Burlesque club. It was your stereotypical insta-attraction, I was drawn to her. We would sneak away to hotels, stealing moments where we could. I begged her to leave her husband. Her husband beats her, yet she refused to leave him. I thought I could save her, fix her, and take her away from that life, but what I didn't realise is that my world is far more fucked up than hers. My world of debauchery and rock n' roll, my world is filled with women and even though I knew deep down that she would never be mine, I kept going back for more, time and time again. I kept going back for more. I was a glutton for punishment. I was no better than her constantly going back to her husband every time he beat her within an inch of her life, like an abused puppy. I knew it wasn't healthy, but I couldn't help myself. I'm so fucking sorry, Raleigh, I'm so sorry I put you through that."

The pain in his voice is evident, and he pulls me closer to him, tucking me into his side. He kisses me on top of my head and in that moment, it all becomes clear. He loved her so completely, but that love was never reciprocated by Lorna and I understand how that must have messed him up.

"My love for her crushed me, I knew our relationship was toxic from the very fucking beginning, but I kept trying to justify it to myself. I'm ashamed of the person I became because of her. I hit the self-destruct button, and I didn't have to guts to admit it to anyone, let alone myself. I ended up in rehab after Sam's wedding because she told me she was pregnant with my baby and she miscarried because her husband pushed her down the stairs. "

I gasp audibly at his revelation and the raw emotion in his voice makes me want to burst into tears. That alone would fuck anyone up.

"I've never told anyone that, not even Sam, or the boys. I knew I should have ended him as soon as she told me, but instead I went on a seventy-two hour bender. I don't remember anything about any of it, except it was Sam and Cole that found me. Apart from that, all I know is I took a fuck load of drugs; a literal cocktail, you name it, it was running through my veins. I just wanted to block it out, I wanted to drown in oblivion. I didn't want to remember that some fucking low-life, wife beating prick had robbed us of our baby. I wanted to be numb to it all. I was selfish. Instead of taking her away from that life that night, I buried my head in the sand and I fucking hate myself for it"

He lifts me from his from his chest and swings his long legs out of bed, dropping his head into his hands. Just as I thought I was getting somewhere, I can feel him shutting down on me and at that moment, we're back at square one.

Brody

Fuck me, I can't do this. I can't. I sit up, swing my legs out of bed and drop my head into my hands.

"Brody?"

Her concerned voice filters through my foggy brain and it breaks my heart, but I can't let her see me like this. I run my trembling hands through my hair and as soon as my feet hit the floor, I practically sprint out of the room to the sound of her calling my name.

I rush to the bathroom and briefly hang on to the door frame with my head down, desperately trying to steady myself and panting like a fucking race horse. *Shit, shit, shit.* I push the bathroom door open and lock it behind me. My heart is pounding in my chest and I drop down heavily onto the closed toilet lid. I purged the sordid details of mine and Lorna's four year affair and it created a fresh need to get high, after my bender a few short weeks ago. I didn't need a reason to cave in, I just needed a reason not to and right now, I couldn't think of a reason why not. I know the doctors specifically told me not to use again after the accident, but that didn't stop me. I was doing well with my NA meetings, but I can't seem to help myself. It was a physical need and I couldn't stop it from taking over my entire being.

I get to my feet, lift up the toilet tank cover and take out the familiar small black toiletry bag that I stashed when I moved in. I set about taking the clear bag with the white powder inside and make two lines with the credit card on the marble vanity unit. I sniff hard and squeeze my eyes shut, enjoying the silence for a few moments as the cocaine works itself into my system. I grip the rim of the porcelain sink and try to steady my hands.

"This is the last fucking time, Hart," I whisper to myself, as I lift my head up, catching my reflection in the mirror and there is blood trickling from my nose. I swipe it away and wash it off my hand in the sink, I'm transfixed on the crimson of my blood mixed with the water swirling down the drain. The buzz I feel is like nothing I've felt in weeks, but the feeling of joyous rapture is short lived, when there is a swift rap on the door. *Fuck my life.*

"Brody? Is everything ok in there?" her concerned voice filters through my foggy brain, as she rattles the door handle.

"Brody, why is the door locked? I thought we were finally getting somewhere?" she states with an exasperated tone to her voice, and I scrub my hands down my face. *Fuck me, I don't need this shit right now.*

"We were...we are...I'm fine honestly. Look, go to bed, I'll be out in a sec."

I tip the remaining contents of the clear bag into the toilet bowl. I flush them away, returning the toiletry bag back to its hiding place and carefully replace the toilet tank cover. Maybe tonight was a turning point and by flushing the rest of my stash down the toilet, I had just proved to myself that my decade long love affair with cocaine was over, at least for now.

***

A few days pass and after my minor relapse, I feel more determined than ever to kick my drug habit once and for all, after being in its clutches for well over fifteen years. I'm at my weekly Narcotics Anonymous meeting at Kedlestone Walk Community Centre in Bethnal Green with Lenny. After I told him about my relapse, the bitter disappointment on his face, as he looked at me made me feel so fucking shitty and I instantly regretted my actions.

"Right, who would like to start tonight?" the group leader Tina asks brightly, chewing gum and blowing a bubble with a loud pop. She is wearing a long, dark orange and khaki green skirt, a white vest top and her dark blonde dreadlocked hair secured in an orange and yellow bandana. She looks like she got dressed in the dark in an Oxfam shop. Lenny nudges me with his folded arm and narrows his eyes on me. I roll my eyes and mutter *'for fucks sake'* under my breath and reluctantly raise my hand, all eyes of everyone in the room turning on me.

"Brody! Good to see you again, darlin'!" she says in her prominent East London accent and beams at me. *She's way too fucking happy to be an NA group leader.* She used to be a crack addict, until she discovered veganism and took up yoga, she has been clean for twelve years. I flash her a grin and she melts on the spot. *You've still got it, Hart.*

"What would you like to share with the group?"

I clear my throat, unsure of how to admit out loud, or even begin to explain what happened.

"I had a relapse three nights ago," I admit, my voice full of regret, as I hang my head in absolute shame. I conveniently leave out the events of a few weeks ago. *No one needs to know about that.*

"It's nothing to be ashamed of, mate, it's happened to us all at some point," Jez reassures me. I look up at him and he offers me a soft sympathetic and reassuring smile. Jez is Tina's fiancé, he also used to be an addict. He was a heroin addict until he met Tina. They helped each other through their darkest times and fell in love along the way.

"I'm not proud of it. Me and my girlfriend had a particularly rough conversation...I cheated on her. Not my finest fucking hour. I slept with my ex behind her back, and I couldn't handle the feelings it bought to the surface. I've never been good at expressing my feelings, or really sharing my feelings with anyone. I snorted some coke, I hated myself as soon as I did it. It just made me feel nothing, so I flushed the rest of my stash after that."

I let out the breath I didn't realise I was holding. Tina looks at me, smiling warmly and almost proudly. "Thank you for sharing that with us, Brody, I'm proud of you for flushing the rest of your stash. That proves you want to get clean. That's a huge achievement and a big step for you."

The rest of the group start to give me a round of applause and I feel my face flush. I can perform to crowds of thousands of fans, but having the attention solely focussed on me unnerves me and makes me feel particularly awkward.

"Is there anything specific about the conversation that caused you to relapse?" Tina asks curiously and I pause for a few moments, reluctant to share the real reason.

"Take your time, hon," she reassures me softly, as I take a breath and begin to speak.

"I had a four year affair with a married woman. She was the first woman I fell in love with, which is why it's been so hard for me to admit my true feelings to my current girlfriend. It's caused a lot of conflict and a lot of arguments between us, but since my accident, things have improved immensely. I don't deal with emotions in the way normal people do. I told her something that I've never told anyone before and it...it fucked me up big time."

I turn to Lenny and he looks at me questioningly. I shake my head in warning and he nods curtly, a silent understanding between the two of us.

"Go on, we're all friends here. There's no judgement, man," Jez encourages, as he pushes his black-rimmed glasses further up his nose.

"My ex, she was pregnant with my baby, and she miscarried because her husband pushed her down the stairs."

There is a collective gasp from everyone in the room and at that moment, my feelings completely and totally overwhelm me. My heart starts to pound and I feel beads of sweat begin to form on my brow. I let out a laboured breath, as my chest starts to tighten. *Oh fuck, not now, not here.*

"I...I'm sorry," I mutter, gasping for breath, as I get up from my chair, it scrapes across the floor, setting my teeth on edge and I sprint out of the room without another word.

I rush down the long corridor and manage to make it into the men's toilets, before I sink down to my knees and vomit violently and unceremoniously into the bowl. I rest my head briefly on my forearm and tear off some toilet paper to wipe my mouth. I manage to get to my feet and flush the toilet, when I hear the sound of the door creak noisily open. I hear footsteps clicking across the tiled floor.

"Son?" Lenny's gruff voice echoes and I swing the cubicle door open. The look he gives me is one of pure, quiet concern and I shift my gaze to the floor, uneasy at being under such close scrutiny.

"Why didn't you mention any of this before? I could have been there for you!" he admonishes softly, as I walk over to the sink and wash my hands.

"What good would that have done, Len? You knew me back then, I was a fucking mess! I blamed myself for the whole thing! He hurt her, he murdered our baby, and it was all my fault! I couldn't wrap my head around it and it fucking crushed me! He took that away from us! Things could have been so different," I raise my voice a few decibels louder and I desperate try to hold back the sob that is threatening to escape.

"I went on that seventy-two hour bender. I didn't care if I lived or died. I fucking hated myself at that point and I just wanted the pain to stop. I wanted it all to stop."

With those words, I give in to the debilitating grief and the dam breaks, as I sob hard and uncontrollably.

Raleigh

A miracle happened last night. Brody actually slept for the whole night. He stirred once, but that was only so he could snuggle up closer to me and wrap himself around me like a vine. I woke up this morning too hot and my bladder protesting. I try to awkwardly peel myself away from him, but every time I get close, he groans sleepily and wraps me back in his arms. I chuckle softly to myself, as I try for a third time, he pulls my back to his front and his solid morning erection digs into the base of my spine.

"Mmm," he hums.

"Babe, I need to pee!" I giggle, as I bat his octopus limbs away from me.

"I'm comfy," he grumbles sleepily, as I swing my legs out of bed.

"I'll be right back," I reassure him and head to the bathroom to relieve myself. As I step back into the bedroom, he's sprawled on his back and snoring softly. I shake my head and smile to myself, as I pad out of the room and quietly down the stairs. I enjoy the peace and serene calm before the day officially starts. The area is so calm and quiet away from the hustle and bustle of the busy city. The only sound I can hear as I enter the kitchen, are the birds singing their early morning song. I switch on the kettle and set about making myself a steaming cup of herbal tea, missing my morning hit of caffeine terribly.

I'm not sure how much time passes, but I'm lost in thought, when I hear a soft chuckle from behind me. I turn to see Brody standing in the kitchen, fresh from his morning shower. His hair still damp, wearing a plain white t-shirt, which showcases his sculpted, tattooed muscles, a pair of loose black jogging bottoms, which hang low on his hips and his feet are bare. I lick my lips at the sight of him and I stand there for a few moments admiring the view.

"Morning, kitten. Enjoying the view?" he asks with an amused tone to his voice and I hum my appreciation when the intercom starts buzzing. Brody sighs, as he moves to answer it and as soon as he answers, all the colour drains from his face and I'm left wondering what now.

18

Brody

I pick up the phone connected to the intercom at the security gate and I'm met with the panicked voice of Jace, one of our security team. He doesn't bother with a greeting, he just gets straight to the point.

"Brody, I've got a woman at the gate. She's asking for you and she doesn't look good at all, mate," he says in his familiar Irish lilt. I'm about to speak when I hear an ear-piercing scream.

"Brody! Please help! He's lost the plot, he knows! Please! You've got to help me!"

The distinct sound of Lorna screaming, causes my stomach to drop, as I hear her frantic pleas.

"Let her through," I say in a clipped, impatient tone and hang up the phone, not bothering to say goodbye, or wait for a reply.

"Brody? What's wrong, babe?" Raleigh asks softly and I shake my head. I know if I speak, I won't be able to hide the alarm in my voice. I rush towards the door in a blind panic and within seconds, there is a loud pounding on the door. The sight that greets me will haunt me for the rest of my fucking life. Standing on my door step is Lorna, her left eye is black, she can barely open it. She is covered in blood, she has a cut above her eyebrow and a split lip. She also has a set of angry, purple finger marks around her neck, her clothes are torn and she can barely stand up straight, as she clutches her side. As I swing the door open, she stumbles through the door and practically collapses into my arms. I catch her before she hits thefloor, and she sobs hysterically into my chest, as her legs give out from under her.

I lift her up and carry her into the main vestibule of the house, kicking the door shut with my bare foot.

"Brody. I'm sorry, I'm so sorry," she sobs, as I hold her in my arms, shushing her softly. I take her into the kitchen and sit down on the marbled floor, with her cradled in my lap. I hear footsteps approaching and look up at Raleigh, her amethyst eyes full of fire and rage.

"Brody, is that...her?" Raleigh states with clear disdain to her voice, as she places her hands on her hips. *Fuck my life, I don't need this shit.*

"What the fuck is she doing here?" she spits, raising her voice louder than necessary, but the words die on her lips as she catches sight of a bloody Lorna. The sight of her beaten and broken body causes my heart to stutter in my chest, a lump forming in my throat and I can't speak. *This is all your fucking fault, Hart, you caused this. How could you think there wouldn't be consequences?* I push that thought to the back of my mind, as I feel the familiar dull throb start at the base of my skull.

"Lorna?"

She looks up at me with frightened, desolate eyes and she looks like a scared animal.

"I need you to tell me what happened, sweetheart."

She clings to me as if her life depends on it and I can feel Raleigh's eyes boring into us, observing our interaction carefully. Her hair is matted and has dried blood in it, I push her hair away from her face and she flinches violently.

"It's ok, it's going to be alright, it's just me, I'm here. Shhh, I've got you, shhh. You're safe," I placate her softly. I don't voice the next thought that enters my head because I won't be responsible for my actions. *Please God no, tell me he hasn't.*

"I need you to talk to me, L. I can't help if you don't tell me what happened."

I squeeze her a little tighter to me, my muscular biceps bunching and flexing, as I try to soothe her. She winces and the sob that follows causes me physical pain. I'm trembling, but I don't know if it is with rage, or because I'm terrified of what she's about to tell me. The thought of Stefan fucking Lavelle hurting a hair on her head is making me feel physically violent, but I keep my temper in check for her sake. *This is where Rick's advice comes in, 10,9,8,7,6,5,4,3,2,1,0.*

"You're scaring me, Lorna, you need to start talking, or I'm gonna fucking end him like I should have done in the first place."

The conviction in my voice is evident, as she looks up at me like a deer caught in headlights.

"Y...you c...can't. H...he knows...about us."

Her eyes are wide, her voice small and shaky. I kiss the top of her head and stroke her hair tenderly.

"He can't hurt you anymore, L, not while I'm around. What did he do? Did he...?"

I can't bring myself to finish that sentence, but the relief floods through me, as she shakes her head no and my shoulders sag in relief. She takes a breath, as if to ready herself to tell me what happened, clinging to me like a toddler clings to its mother.

"He followed me to the hospital that day. He was already suspicious, and he went through my phone. It's not the first time, but that confirmed it for him. I'd been so careful and I thought I'd deleted our last messages. He found every single one saved on the iCloud and he found my diary too under the floorboards. He knows every sordid little detail about us. I'm sorry, I'm so sorry."

She sobs and it takes her a few minutes to compose herself to tell me the rest.

"When he found out, he grabbed me by my hair and told me he knew everything. He then proceeded to tell me what a worthless, cheating whore I was. I don't really remember much after that, he slammed me against the wall and I hit my head. He's unhinged, Brody, he's gone off the fucking chain! I think he broke my ribs and dislocated my shoulder. I'm terrified of what he's going to do next. I didn't know who else to come to."

The fear in her voice is clear, and it sets my nerves on edge, as she steals a look at Raleigh. Raleigh's face softens, as they silently take each other in.

"I'll go and find the first aid kit," Raleigh adds and I smile my thanks, as she leaves the room.

"I don't know how I managed to get away from him, I just knew I had to because if I stayed he would have killed me, I know he would. I have no doubt in my mind that's what he was going to do. He scared me, Brody."

Her woeful, sombre aquamarine eyes lock with mine and after a few moments, she goes lax against me. She is shaking fiercely in my arms, as I cling to her tightly. The dam holding her sorrow in, seemingly breaks and she starts to sob soul destroying, gut-wrenching sobs. It breaks my heart to see her this way and I can't help but blame myself. *This is all my fucking fault.* I have to make it right, I have to make sure he never does this to her again.

I lift her up and she cries out in pain. My heart slams against my rib cage at the sound.

"*Shit!* I'm sorry, I'm sorry."

I shush her and sit her down on a bar stool at the slate grey marble breakfast island.

"I'll be right back, don't go anywhere."

I flash her a reassuring wink and she nods. I turn and leave the kitchen in search of Raleigh. I find her in the downstairs bathroom, retrieving a first aid kit from the storage cupboard under the sink. I'm about to mutter my apologies, when she moves in front of me and places her finger on my lips, shaking her head.

"Don't apologise, just do whatever you have to do," she says with utter conviction and in that moment, I couldn't love her more.

19

Brody

As I crack my eyes open, the pain explodes in my temples and I wonder where I am. I'm disoriented, my vision is somewhat blurred, but I look up and see Lorna sitting opposite me. I try to rub my face to clear the cobwebs a bit, but I soon realise I can't move my hands. *Why the fuck can't I move my hands?* As I struggle, I hear Lorna softly sobbing and suddenly I feel rough, scratchy ropes around my wrists, I also notice that my legs aren't tied. Then I remember the manic drive back to Lorna's house, planning what I was going to do to that prick of a husband, with Lorna quietly beside me. I had lied and told her that we were going to get her things and that I was merely there to make sure he behaved himself. In reality, I could feel the solid brass knuckles in the pocket of my jogging bottoms. *That dickhead wouldn't know what fucking hit him.* I was absolutely fucking seething that he laid his hands on her. I wanted to tear off his arms and beat him with the wet ends.

The regular mid-terraced house in Maidstone, looked quiet when we pulled up to the curb, there were no lights on from the outside and no car on the drive. I was truly crushed at the thought that he wasn't there. I told her to wait in the car while I checked, took her keys and cautiously approached the front door.

Now, I'm sat here tied to a fucking chair and I have no fucking idea how both of us got here. I suddenly notice that Lorna looks worse than she did earlier. She has dried blood on her face, her nose is bleeding and her lip has been split open again. She has what looks like fresh marks on her face, arms and the top of her chest.

"Brody, wake up. Please, wake up."

I hear absolute terror in Lorna's voice.

"Lorna? What the fuck is going on?" I barely manage to rasp. *Fuck me, my head is throbbing so bad.*

"It's Stefan, he's completely lost it. I've never seen him like this before."

As she says those words, Stefan enters the room looking oddly cheerful. After four years of sleeping with Lorna, we never had sex at her house, we always met up at hotels, so I had never even seen a picture of him. He's taller than I imagined, with a dark Hawaiian complexion. He is clean shaven, extremely muscular with dark brown eyes and curly black hair, which flows past his broad shoulders.

"Good morning, lovebirds," he says in a strange sing-song voice. As he speaks, I see a long carving knife glistening in his hand and my heart beat starts to quicken. *What the actual fuck?*

"And what should we carve first today then? Hmmmmmmm?" he hums, swishing the knife through the air in a sweeping motion like he's fucking Zorro.

"Chicken or beef?"

He looks from me to Lorna, as he says those words and he points the knife, all while whispering *"Eeny, meeny, miny, mo"* repeatedly. *Fuck me, this guy has lost his fucking marbles.*

"Stefan, please, let us go. I'm sorry," Lorna pleads, as I manage to focus properly for the first time and I stare straight into dull, lifeless brown eyes, completely void of any emotion. *Fuck me, he looks insane.*

"Run little chicken, scamper away and bring back the big angry bull. IT'S STEAK NIIIIIIIIIIIIIIGHT!"

As he says this, he starts animatedly running on the spot. *Fucking lunatic.* Unexpectedly and completely out of nowhere, he slashes the knife down my forearm, lightning fast, cutting so deep I see blood start to ooze out of the open wound. I attempt to twist and contort my body out of the way, but in quick succession, he stabs me in my left side, the dark crimson instantly saturating the material of my white t-shirt. The pain hits me and I scream out in absolute agony.

"You mental cunt! I'm gonna rip you apart, piece by piece and dance on your fucking guts," I yell loudly with more confidence than I actually feel, while vehemently struggling against my restraints. He just laughs and moves closer to Lorna, casually backhanding her hard enough so the chair rocks back on its legs.

"Now, now angry bull, be careful what you say. It will not bode well for our little chicky here, if you upset me," he says melodically and my shoulders sag in defeat.

"Ok, ok, I'm sorry," I plead with him, desperately trying to placate him.

"Look, mate just untie us, yeah? You and me can have a little man-to-man chat, no-one needs to get hurt," I try to reason with him.

"Get hurt?" he laughs, but sounds distraught at the same time.

"Did you think about hurting anyone, when you poked your big bull cock into MY FUCKING WIFE!" he barks and at the same time, his hand shoots up and down at an angle, slicing straight through Lorna's throat. I watch as the light fades from her aquamarine eyes and my heart splinters in my chest.

"NOOOOOOOOOOOOO!" I scream, as loud as I can, as Lorna gurgles and her lifeblood spurts out of her throat. The arterial spray pushing it with such force that it squirts all over the walls and drenches my face. It manages to land in my mouth and I gag on the warm, bitter, metallic taste.

My feet aren't tied to the chair and I manage to stand as best I can and charge straight at him. Like a fucking cat he prances out of the way, still laughing maniacally as he shouts "*Ole!*" Like a demented fucking matador.

I twist myself as I hit the floor and manage to land awkwardly on the chair, causing it to break beneath me. The rope loosens and I free my hands, but I keep my hands hidden from view. Stefan skips around the room and bends down, getting close to my face to taunt me.

"Ooopsie!" he puts his hand over his mouth, starts to laugh maniacally and resumes skipping around me. He is humming a tune which sounds distinctly like '*Ding, dong the witch is dead.*' Fuck me, this bloke really has lost the fucking plot. I turn my head and see Lorna's dead lifeless gaze staring back at me and I feel such hollow agony as the full realization of what just happened hits me like a fucking truck. *He fucking killed her.* He slit her throat like a piece of fucking cattle, I can hardly contain the white-hot, seething rage that erupts from my very soul. Then an inner peace washes over me and I'm as calm as a Hindu cow. I know what needs to be done. I stand slowly, and I feel a sharp pain just above my left hip. Stefan stabbed me, but I neither care or react as I slowly turn. I slip my hand into my pocket and into the brass knuckles. Stefan lurches towards me, knife aiming at my stomach like he wants to gut me like a fucking pig. I slap his hand away and in one smooth motion, I bring my right hand up with as much force as I can muster, the brass knuckles connect with his chin. A noise like a thunderclap echoes around the room and his head snaps back so violently, I think I may have broken his neck. He lifts off the ground and flies backwards, hitting the floor with a thud, like something from a cartoon. As he falls he drops the knife, and to my utter fucking horror it lands blade first in Lorna's leg, defiling her beautiful body.

Stefan groans, so I know he's not dead yet, more's the fucking pity. I feel blood trickling down my thigh and start to pool in my boot, but nothing matters anymore except this piece of human excrement, that's now mewling on the ground in front of me. He's lying on his front, so I use my foot and flip him over. His eyes have rolled back in his head, so he doesn't look demented anymore, just fucking pathetic. His jawline, which was straight is now at a peculiar angle, clearly broken. His eyes slowly focus on me, as his eyes meet mine, I see fear and maybe understanding of how absolutely fucked he is.

"Not humming anymore are you, you prick!" I say with a slight amusement in my voice.

"Bleeeeesh doe," he moans incoherently.

"Whats that, mate, I can't quite hear you," amusement still clear in my voice. *Why the fuck am I enjoying this? He just murdered Lorna.* As that thought crashes through my brain, I drop down onto his chest and hit him again, his cheekbone disintegrating under my fist. I hit him again and his eye socket crumbles and his eye rolls lazily out and just hangs on his temple. I think he tries to scream, but all I hear is garbled nonsense, as his arms flap uselessly up at me trying to stop what's coming. My fist slams into his nose, spraying blood over the carpet beneath his head, his hands stop flailing and the gurgling noise slowly stops. But I don't, it only encourages me to rain down blow after blow onto what's left of his hateful fucking face.

20

Raleigh

"Brody, it's me, again, answer your fucking phone! I'm worried about you, please let me know you're ok. Call me back as soon as you get this, love you."

I've been trying to call Brody since he left to go to Lorna's earlier on, it's been hours. My stomach is in knots and I feel sick with worry at his silence. I feel the familiar flutters of our babies kicking and I stroke my stomach softly.

"I feel you, jelly beans. Where's your daddy, huh?" I say to them. I look like a fucking beached whale, I'm six months pregnant, I'm exhausted all the time, and my back is fucking killing me. I haven't seen my feet for a while and I want to eat everything and anything in sight. I have been suffering from painful cramps for the past few hours since Brody left, and our babies are kicking the shit out of me every time they move around in my stomach. I'm desperate to meet them both now, but I'm terrified I'm going to let them down, or disappoint them in some way. I have been trying to occupy myself and not let my imagination run away with me, as I think of Brody with Lorna. The way he looked at her, the way he held her in his arms, I couldn't help the overwhelming feeling of jealousy that reared its ugly head watching the way they interacted with each other. He's in love with her, that much is obvious. I'm lost in thought, when a wave of crippling pain washes over my body. I've never felt pain like this before and I clutch my stomach, as the pain rips through me, I fight hard to regulate my breathing. A sharp cramp almost knocks me off my feet. *Oh fuck, this can't be happening.* It's too early! I choke on a sob, as I lean heavily on the kitchen island grappling desperately for my phone. I shakily dial Brody's number and it goes straight to voicemail. *For fucks sake!*

"B...Brody, it's me again. Please pick up the phone. I think the babies are coming."

The terror in my voice is evident, as I try to hold back the tears threatening my composure.

"Please, you have to come home. Wherever you are, please come home! I can't do this without you!"

I hang up and dial the next person, she answers on the second ring.

"Raleigh, hey!" Peyton greets me brightly, as a strangled sob escapes.

"Peyton, I think I'm in labour."

My voice small and filled with panic.

"I'll be there in five minutes," she says calmly and hangs up, as another overwhelming pain tears through my body, incapacitating me. I cry out and drop to my knees on the hard marbled floor. I'm not sure how much time passes, but I hear the sound of quick footsteps and I'm joined by Peyton and Sam.

"Raleigh! Oh my God!" Peyton says with concern in her voice, she sits down on the floor next to me and takes my hand in hers.

"It's going be alright, I promise. Sam, I need you to ring an ambulance."

He nods curtly, flashing me a reassuring smile.

"On it, angel." he rasps as he strides out, leaving me and Peyton alone.

"Where's Brody, babe?" she asks and I shake my head, unable to hold back the sobs any longer.

"Peyton, I'm scared, it's too early! They can't come yet, it's too early!"

She squeezes my hand. "I know, I know, but it's going to be alright. They've got yours and Brody's genes flowing through them. They're going to be just fine."

Another contraction rips through me and I scream out in pure agony, the pain excruciating. That's when the floor moves beneath my feet, my vision swims, and the last thing I see before darkness consumes me is Peyton's face full of worry.

Brody

I hit rock bottom when Sam found me in my bathroom, after I had overdosed and he gave me CPR, but that doesn't compare to how I feel right now, standing in Lorna's kitchen covered in hers and her husbands blood. I think I'm in shock. I can't move. I'm numb. the enormity of what just happened hits me full force and I roar out in absolute disbelief. *Lorna is dead and I've just murdered her husband in cold blood.* The overwhelming need to get high is at the forefront of my foggy brain and I can't think straight. *Come on, Hart, think, there are two dead bodies in the next room.* My hands are trembling, my heart is pounding, and I feel like I need to throw up. I take in a few deep, steadying breaths, *in...out, in...out,* and slap my cheek hard.

"Come on, Hart, get your fucking shit together!" I say to no one in particular, as I brace my hands on the kitchen countertop for a few moments, while I try to gather some composure. I take another deep exhale of breath, hoping it will provide me the equilibrium that I so desperately need. I pull my phone out of the pocket of my jeans and dial the number I need, it rings three times before it connects.

"Len, it's me," I try to sound steady and rational, but he laughs throatily as he hears the apprehensive tone in my voice.

"What sort of fucking trouble have you got yourself in this time, boy?" he asks, his voice laced with amusement.

"I need your help, something really fucking bad has happened."

I try to maintain some semblance of composure, but I feel my control slipping with every second that passes.

"What's happened, son?" he asks, his voice filled with a fatherly concern.

"Something really fucking bad, Len," I repeat again, my voice trembling and I'm bordering on fucking hysteria, as I begin my journey pacing the floor.

"Calm down, son, tell me what the problem is," he says, sounding impatient at my mindless rambling.

"Len, I don't know what to do. You've got to help me, please," I babble in a rush, my legs buckling underneath me, the weight of the situation crashes through every fibre of my being and I start to sob. I lean against the kitchen cupboard and catch my reflection in the glass door of the cooker, I look like shit and I'm covered in blood.

"BRODY! CALM THE FUCK DOWN AND TELL ME WHAT IS HAPPENING!" he yells, interrupting my meltdown.

"Calm the fuck down!" he growls again, snapping me back from the brink of insanity.

"You need to tell me what's happened, son, I can't help if you don't talk to me."

His voice is calmer this time and I squeeze my eyes shut briefly.

"They're both dead, Len," I say simply, all of the fight and bravado drained from my voice. *I'm fucking exhausted.*

"Right, text me the address and I'll be right there. There' are a few things I need to know first," he states, his voice cool and steady. Lenny used to be a man of the law, until he watched his partner get murdered in front of him and the bloke who did it got away with it due to insufficient evidence. Lenny tried in vein to save him and that sent him into a downward spiral and head first into a bottle of whiskey every night.

"Have you spoken to anyone else, anyone at all? Does anyone else know? Does anyone know where you are?"

I swipe the tears angrily away from my face and take a breath before I answer his questions.

"No, I haven't spoken to anyone, Raleigh knows I was taking Lorna to grab some things," I answer, as I think of my beloved Raleigh.

"Good, that's good, did anyone see you go inside? Are there any witnesses?"

I try to push the image of the knife slicing across Lorna's delicate throat to the back of my mind.

"I don't think so," I say quietly and honestly.

"Ok, is there anything else I need to know?" he asks on a cough.

"It's really fucking messy, Len," I sniff, as I move the phone away from my ear to put him on speaker phone. I text the address to him with a trembling hand and send it. I hear a beep and a few clicks before he speaks again.

"Sit tight and try not to touch anything, I'll be there as quick as I can and Brody?"

"Yeah?" my voice small and almost childlike.

"Try not to get yourself in any more fucking trouble."

With those words, he hangs up.

***

It felt like an eternity, but it was only been about fifteen minutes. I hear a sharp rap on the door and I jolt nervously at the sound, as I scramble hastily to my feet. I peek around the door frame and see a dark, looming shadow in the frosted glass of the front door, my heart beating a frantic tattoo.

"Son, it's me," Lenny confirms gruffly. I open the door hesitantly, careful not to show my face to the neighbours. As my eyes land on Lenny, I've never been so fucking scared or relieved in my life. He pulls his suit jacket together and fastens the buttons, squaring his shoulders and taking a deep breath.

"Well, don't just fucking stand there like a spare prick at a wedding." he says wryly, as he steps inside he takes careful steps and peeks around the doorway into the living area, cursing under his breath.

"Fuck me, boy, what have you gotten yourself into?"

I drop my head into my hands and I know the question was rhetorical, but I still can't bring myself to give him a fucking answer. Lenny squeezes my shoulder in a gesture of reassurance.

"Are you going to tell me what happened?" he asks, as softly as he can muster.

"Lorna turned up at my house. She was a fucking mess, Len. Her piece of shit husband beat her, again. He found out about us."

I put my hand to my head, as I think about the state she was in.

"I bet that went down well with Raleigh."

Lenny quirks his eyebrow and I sigh heavily.

"About as well as a fucking fart in a lift," I say sardonically and Lenny laughs.

"He found out about us and beat her within an inch of her life. She had nowhere else to go. Raleigh really wasn't happy, which is understandable, but as soon as she saw what sort of state she was in, she understood. I cleaned her up and bought her back here, I can't remember what happened when we arrived. All I know is that I came to, and I was tied to a chair. Lorna sat opposite me and her fucking nutjob husband was dancing around like a lunatic."

I press my lips together, as I remember what happened next and steel myself to say the words out loud.

"He slit her throat in front of me, Len, he killed her." My voice falters and I squeeze my eyes shut to suppress the image from my exhausted brain.

"There was so much fucking blood...I...I flipped, I'd failed her in the four years we were sleeping together, but I knew I couldn't let her down again. I couldn't let him get away with it. It wasn't revenge, it wasn't like that, not at all. It was...my way of redeeming the way I treated her over the years. I don't know, but I hit him with a pair of brass knuckles and I just kept hitting him over and over and over again. I wanted him to fucking pay for taking her life like it meant nothing, he slit her throat like she was some sort of fucking animal. She didn't deserve that, how could he still be breathing after that?"

The words spill from my mouth like verbal diarrhea and Lenny listens carefully and intently to me recount the horror of the last few hours. He moves closer to me, his eyes meeting mine and grips me by the nape of my neck.

"You know you've got two choices, don't you, son? And I'll support you one hundred per cent which ever one you decide."

I swallow past the tennis ball sized lump in my throat, as I allow the weight of his words to settle in my brain. He's right, I have two choices; call the police and face the consequences, or let Lenny clean up my mess and make it all go away. *Right now, I have no idea what it's going to be.*

Raleigh

"Answer your fucking phone, you prick! Where are you! Raleigh's been rushed to hospital, get your fucking arse to the Portland Hospital as soon as you get this and call me back!"

Sam's gravelly voice is the first thing I hear when my eyes flicker open. I lift my hand to shield my eyes from the harsh artificial light and try to focus on my surroundings. My body feels unusually hot, as I feel a dampness on the back of my neck and I shift uncomfortably on the bed.

"Raleigh?" Liv's concerned voice filters through my foggy brain, as an overwhelming pain rips through my body. I scream out loud and she is at my side in an instant.

"It's ok, it's going to be just fine, I'm here and I'm not going anywhere," she soothes, taking my hand in hers.

"Where's Brody?" I ask, suddenly terrified at the prospect of giving birth without the man I love by my side. She strokes gentle circles on the back of my hand, as the pain begins to subside.

"Just so you know, I'm gonna cut off his fucking balls and feed them to him, one by fucking one if he misses this! He should be here!" she scolds, raising her voice a few decibels louder than what is acceptable.

"He's not answering his phone. He's gone radio silent. No one knows where he is," Liv explains after she spends a few moments to calm herself. Sam flashes me a wink from his position in the doorway.

"I promise you I'll find him and bring him straight here, sweetheart."

I smile, as he turns to leave with his arm slung around Peyton's shoulder. Another pain tears through me and a nurse enters the room.

"Raleigh, how are you feeling, my darling?" she asks softly, as she moves to the side of the bed, taking my vitals.

"You're in early labour, you've suffered a placental abruption. The placenta has separated itself from the inside of the womb wall and you were bleeding heavily when you were bought in. We're monitoring you closely, because you have an extremely high blood pressure, possibly bought on by extreme stress, which could also cause pre-eclampsia. There's a probable chance that we're going to have to perform a cesarean section in order for you to give birth safely. However, if we deem the abruption to be mild, the bleeding stops and both babies' heart rates are normal, you may be able to rest at home for the duration of your pregnancy," she explains and I struggle to take in what I am being told. *What the fuck?*

"As of right now, both of their heartbeats are strong and there's considerable movement from both of them, so that's a great sign," she smiles reassuringly and I swallow past the lump that has formed in my throat.

"Are they going to be ok?" I ask, more than a hint of fear in my voice.

"At the moment, both of them are healthy and doing just fine," she shifts her gaze to the screen to the left of the bed as the strong, steady sound of my babies heartbeats in sync with each other. The da-dum-da-dum, echoes loudly throughout the room and I can't hold back the sobs, as another contraction surges its way through my exhausted body.

"Liv! I can't do this! I can't! I can't do it, not without him!" I sob, my breaths coming in short, sharp pants. She squeezes my hand and presses her forehead to mine. Her blonde hair tickling my cheek.

"Listen to me, Raleigh Storm, you are the fucking strongest woman I know. No other person has been through what you've been through and come out the other end fighting, with their head held high and fucking proud! You're not on your own... you have Brody, me and Jensen, your family for what it's worth, and you have Sam, Peyton, Lenny, and the boys. I'm sure there's a reasonable excuse as to why he isn't here."

I shake my head.

"You don't understand, Liv! His ex turned up at his place, she was...fuck, Liv her husband had beaten her so badly," she gasps, as the pain gradually starts to dissipate.

"*Fuck!* Where did he go?" she asks, as she holds my hand in hers.

"He took her back to her place to get her some things, then he was taking her to her parents' house, I think. I don't know I can't remember!"

I struggle to remember the exact details of our conversation; it all feels so long ago now. He's been gone for hours.

"I couldn't just let him abandon her; she was a mess."

She curses under her breath, as I try to justify his actions to my best friend.

"Why the fuck are you still defending him? He cheated on you, Rae! He was having an affair with a married woman, for four fucking years! He could be balls deep in her again right now!" she whisper hisses and I snatch my hand away from hers, desperately trying to push the thought of him having sex with Lorna from my mind.

"Because I fucking love him, Liv! He might not be perfect, but he's...since the accident, he's different. He's not the unreachable, uncaring rock star he once was. He's changed."

I try to explain to her, but she laughs bitterly.

"Ha! Changed! Yeah, of course he has, he had a brain injury, not a fucking personality transplant! How fucking dumb are you! He's cheated once, and you forgave him. That gives him carte blanche to do it again, and again and again! How can you be so sure he won't do it again? When are you going to learn! You already let one man almost destroy you."

I recoil, as she spits harsh words of hate at me and in all the years I've known Liv. I've never seen her this angry, and she has never directed such blatant outrage in my direction before.

I'm about to rip her a new one, when a pain I've never felt before renders me speechless. I scream in absolute, raw agony. It feels like a period cramp but amplified and a million times more painful.

"Oh God! Please, Livvy, make it stop!" I cry out and shift uncomfortably on the bed, gripping her hand tightly in mine.

"I want Brody! Please, someone get Brody!" I babble almost incoherently, the terror blanketing every nerve in my body. I've never been more scared and all I want is the man I love to make it stop.

21

Brody

As I sit in the back of a police car, I give in to the overwhelming grief that is weighing down on my tired, exhausted body. Wailing sobs of despair wrack my body and I can't comprehend the destruction and devastation barrelling through me like a fucking steam roller. I can't think straight, my head is spinning and my thoughts are a barrage of rage, regret, and grief. I look down at my trembling hands covered in Stefan's blood and my stomach revolts fervently, as the events of the past few hours sprint through my mind. When I dialled nine, nine, nine, I knew I had to do what was right. I had to face the consequences of my reckless actions. The old me before the accident wouldn't have hesitated to let Lenny clean up my mess and make it all go away with one phone call. The new me on the other hand, wanted some sort of redemption for taking someone's life. I had to be punished for cutting someone's life short, no matter how deserved it was.

"Breaking news just coming in, Brody Hart from popular rock band Rancid Vengeance has been taken in for questioning in connection with an incident that left two as yet unidentified people dead. Hart, thirty-four is being held at Bexleyheath Police Station for further questioning. Forensics are gathering evidence at the scene to piece together what occurred in the hours leading up to the incident. We will keep you updated on any developments, as this story continues to unfold."

The drive to the police station and the events on our arrival are a blur. Fear settles like a lead weight in the pit of my stomach. I'm allowed one phone call and I call our solicitor Vance Stryker. Vance has been our solicitor for fourteen years; he is extremely good at his job and has become an ally and a trusted member of the Rancid Vengeance family.

I gave the Officer Vance's name at the front desk and the officer dials the number for me, while looking around the dismal, bleak, lifeless interview room wondering how the fuck I'm going to get out of this mess I've created.

"Vance Stryker," he answers in a clipped, business-like tone.

"Vance, it's Brody Hart," I say flatly.

"Ah, Brody, a little birdy told me you've been a naughty boy?"

Normally, I would laugh at his droll response, but I don't even chuckle. I'm about to speak again, when he interrupts me.

"It's all over the news, is it up to me to clean up your proverbial mess of sorts? Would that be an accurate and correct description of your sticky little dilemma?"

I rest my head on my forearm and squeeze my eyes briefly shut, willing the throbbing that has settled in my temples to go away.

"Yeah, pretty accurate. But it's not what it looks like, I swear. I'm at Bexleyheath Police station, how soon can you get here?" I ask with sheer panic in my voice.

"Right away. Do not answer any questions before I get there. If they ask you anything at all, just respond with no comment. When I get there, I need you tell me the facts and none of your usual bullshit, Hart."

I let out a long, audible sigh.

"Tell Lenny to call Raleigh and tell the boys I'm fucking sorry."

He hums his response, "See you soon, Hart."

I hang up devoid and defeated of all hope, for now at least.

***

Vance steps into the interview room with his briefcase at his side, looking larger than life and ever the professional. He is average height, dark hair with a receding hairline and balding on top. He is average build with dark hazel eyes. He has a weeks' worth of stubble across his face, which is trimmed neatly, and he is impeccably turned out as always in an expensive black suit.

"Hart."

He nods in greeting and turns to the tall police officer at the back of the room, who looks like he wants to be anywhere but here.

"May I have a moment with my client, please?" he asks, the officer agrees with a grunt and leaves, closing the door behind him with a click.

"I need the full story. The cold, hard facts. Don't leave anything out, not even the smallest detail and like I said on the phone, none of your usual bullshit," he says in his typically British accent. I scrub my hands down my face, looking down at the deep laceration on my arm. It hurts like hell, the blood around it has congealed and dried, but it looks like it still needs stitches. They've taken my clothes as evidence for forensics, so I am sitting at the table in an attractive flimsy, white paper suit.

"I just need you to fucking get me out of here, Vance."

I pinch my thumb and forefinger on the bridge of my nose, briefly closing my eyes. He takes a seat opposite me and takes a Dictaphone out of his briefcase. He lays it down on the table and presses the record button, as I begin to tell him my version of events.

I spend the next half an hour filling him on the events of the day, up until the moment I made the call to the police. His eyes widen, and he nods, taking in the information I have given him. He stops the recording and places the Dictaphone back in his briefcase.

"And there's definitely nothing else I should know?"

I shake my head and he nods, smiling his shark-like smile.

"Let me earn those big bucks you boys pay me," he winks, as he strides over to the door and calls out to the detective in charge. It's the same detective who questioned me after my motorbike accident, Detective Fellows. He's average height, with a bald head, steel-blue eyes, and a dark goatee beard. He gives me a look of pure contempt, as he stands there with his hands on his hips, his ill-fitting suit jacket stretching across his broad shoulders. He takes a seat opposite me, eyeing me with clear disdain.

"Are you going to charge my client, Detective?"

Vance states and the Detective smiles, which makes him look like he's straining for a shit.

"There's sufficient evidence from the crime scene tying Mr. Hart to the double murder. We can detain him for up to ninety-six hours."

Vance smirks and cocks his eyebrow.

"And exactly what evidence is there tying my client to the murders?"

Detective Fellows laughs bitterly, as Vance sits down in the chair next to me, cool as a cucumber.

"Well, for one he was covered in claret! And we've had to pull dental records because Mr. Lavelle was unrecognisable!" he snaps in a prominent London accent, as the door swings open and another detective steps into the room with a cup of coffee in a white mug in his hand. I notice he is the other detective, who questioned me after my accident. This detective is tall, lean with dishevelled, mousy brown hair, blue eyes with dark circles underneath them. His brown suit looks cheap, his shirt untucked and his tie is loose around his neck. Detective Maddox takes a seat next to Detective Fellows and taps the screen of a digital audio recorder.

"Interview with Brody Hart, at Bexleyheath Police Station, on Wednesday the ninth of December. The time is eighteen thirty four p.m. Present in the interview room is Detective Patrick Maddox."

Detective Maddox turns to Detective Fellows.

"Detective David Fellows and for the purpose of the tape," he nods at Vance and me.

"Brody Lennon Hart," I state.

"Mr. Hart's Legal representative, Vance Stryker."

Detective Fellows clears his throat.

"Walk me through what happened prior to the double murder of Mrs. Lorna Lavelle and Mr. Stefan Lavelle."

I puff out a tired breath, as I begin to go over and over the fateful day in minute detail. Reliving every poisonous word, every punch and everything that ensued. I leave out Lenny's involvement and every hour that passes feels like a fucking lifetime.

"Were there any witnesses of the alleged incident?" Detective Maddox asks. I squeeze my eyes shut, wishing that the whole thing were all a fucking dream and any moment now, I'm going to wake up.

"No, no one else was involved or saw what happened."

I run my hand through my hair and lean back in my chair.

"This isn't the first time you've had a brush with the law in recent times, is it, Mr. Hart?"

Detective Fellows says with a smug look on his face, and it makes me want to reach across the table and punch him square in his jaw. *Prick.*

"Detective Fellows, how is that relevant to the case?" Vance states sternly.

"Well, Mr. Hart has shown himself to be reckless and impulsive. He crashed his motorbike while high on a Class A substance. Now he's beaten someone to death. Were you under the influence of drugs at the time of the incident?" Detective Fellows presses. He's goading me, he's trying to get a reaction out of me. I take a deep breath and try desperately to remain calm.

"No, I wasn't, I'm clean. I've had problems with drugs over the years. It's been well-documented over the past few months, but that was just a blip. I'm clean and sober now, I attend regular NA meetings. I have a sober sponsor and I see a counsellor once a week," I explain, as Vance clears his throat.

"Detectives," Vance claps his hands. "As far as I'm concerned, there is no evidence to suggest that my client was more than a victim. You only have to look at the laceration on his arm, the obvious rope burns on both of his wrists, which suggest that Mr. Hart was restrained and there was a clear struggle. He has a single stab wound, which also point to Mr. Hart's back being turned at the time. All evidence points to self-defence. Now, are you going to charge my client? Because you can't hold him without charge," Vance states confidently, as Detective Fellows sinks his teeth into his bottom lip, his round face contorting with clear disdain. My head is pounding and all I want to do is sleep, I'm fucking exhausted, physically, and mentally.

"I want you to explain to me, again, what happened?"

I place my hands behind my head and look up to the ceiling.

"I told you before, Stefan found out about my affair with Lorna. She was a victim of domestic abuse... he beat her for years! She showed up at my house, bloody and beaten, I couldn't just do nothing, she was frightened of him. I took her back to her house to get some of her things, and the next thing I remember, I was restrained... we both were. Stefan sliced my arm, and he slit Lorna's throat in front of me."

My voice quivers and I try desperately to swallow back the lump in my throat.

"I managed to break free, he stabbed me, and I beat him in self-defence. He fucking attacked me like some sort of mad man! I was terrified for my life! He already murdered his wife in front of me and I didn't know what else he was capable of. I was trying to protect myself against a cold-blooded murderer!"

A stray tears slips down my cheek, and I drop my head into my hands, utter despair and devastation washing over every inch of me.

"Interview terminated at twenty one thirteen p.m." Detective Maddox flashes me a look of sympathy and Detective Fellows folds his arms across his chest.

"Mr. Hart, we're releasing you on bail, pending further enquiry and on the condition that we release you into the custody of a family member who will take full responsibility of you."

I nod, letting out the breath I didn't know I was holding. *Fuck me, I've never been so relieved in all my life.*

***

After hours of questioning, I couldn't wait to get home and hold my girl. As I step outside the police station, the flashbulbs go off simultaneously and the frantic shouts of the journalists echo through my exhausted brain. My heart beat starts to quicken, as I attempt to push my way through them. I can feel my chest start to tighten, as the fear grips me. I'm about to pull my phone out, when I hear someone call my name and I look up to see Sam flanked by Kai and Trey. I have never been so relieved to see them, as Trey shoves his way through the crowd. He nods curtly to me and grabs me, pulling me forward, shielding me from the glare of the paparazzi's lens. When I'm in the quiet confines of Sam's truck and it's then, I allow the true extent of today's' events to sink in.

"Well, you look like shit," Sam rasps, interrupting my misery and I close my eyes, sagging back in my seat.

"Thanks, prick."

I fold my arms, and I feel so exhausted I could sleep for England. Sam starts the engine and looks over his shoulder, keeping a watchful eye on the road.

"Raleigh was rushed into hospital."

I sit bolt upright in my seat, the fatigue turning into pure concern for the woman I love.

"What?"

Sam pulls away from the curb and glances in the interior mirror at intervals, as we make the journey home.

"Is she ok?" I ask, worry marring my features.

"She suffered a placental abruption. The doctors thought she was going into premature labour, but they stabilised her and she's been sent home and put on bed rest for the remainder of her pregnancy."

He explains.

"W...what the fuck? Why didn't anyone tell me?" I snap, a mixture of frustration and fatigue.

"Because you'd been arrested for fucking murder!" Sam rasps matter-of-factly and I narrow my eyes on him.

"Low blow, Sam. You've got no fucking idea what I've been through! I watched the woman I was sleeping with four years get her throat slit right in front of me! Her husband killed her! HE FUCKING KILLED HER, SAM!"

The dam that has been holding my tears at bay for the past few hours, breaks and I burst into floods of tears.

"She's dead, Lorna's dead," I sob, as Sam pulls over at the side of the road, offering me words of comfort and right now, I'm not sure I can come back from it.

22

Raleigh

In the hours that passed, the pain started to subside somewhat, but Brody was still nowhere to be found and I was becoming increasingly more worried as the time ticked by. The news was on the TV in the corner of the room and my head snaps up, as I hear Brody's name mentioned.

"...*Brody Hart from popular rock band Rancid Vengeance has been taken in for questioning in connection with an incident that left two as yet unidentified people dead. Hart, thirty-four is being held at Bexleyheath Police Station for further questioning. Forensics are gathering evidence at the scene to piece together what occurred in the hours leading up to the incident. We will keep you updated on any developments, as this story continues to unfold.*"

My eyes widen, as I turn to look at Liv in total disbelief and I couldn't comprehend what I'd just heard. *Taken in for questioning? What for? What the fuck is going on?*

"Rae?" Liv says, concern lacing her melodic voice, as my phone starts shouting an unfamiliar Rancid Vengeance song on the table beside the bed. I glance to see who's calling and Lenny's name flashes up. Liv hands me my phone and I answer apprehensively, suddenly terrified of what he's going to reveal to me.

"Hello?" I greet him wearily.

"Raleigh, love, it's Lenny. Brody's been involved in an...incident, he's been taken in to the police station in Bexleyheath for questioning. He needs you, sweetheart."

I shift uncomfortably, as a pain rolls through my already exhausted body.

"Len, I'm in hospital," I say, my voice laced with emotion, as I hear Lenny curse softly. A strangled sob escapes from my lips, Liv reaches for my hand and I let her take it.

"What happened?" I ask curiously.

"Lorna's dead, her husband murdered her, he stabbed Brody and Brody killed him in self defence," Lenny says, as if he's practiced it. I gasp at his words and I can't believe what I'm hearing. *The man I love is a murderer? What the fuck? Brody isn't a killer.*

"What?" I say incredulously, as I listen intently to Lenny's words.

"The bands' solicitor is on his way to the police station as we speak. It's going to be alright, sweetheart, Vance will take care of it."

As he says those words, I'm not sure if I believe him.

***

I was released from hospital a few hours after my placental abruption stabilised with strict instructions to rest for the remainder of my pregnancy. I was beside myself with worry and I was desperate to see Brody. But to take my mind off the whole thing, Liv drove me back to Brody's place and settled us both down on the sofa with duvets, blankets, pillows, large mugs of hot chocolate and marshmallows and a movie fest. It was a welcome distraction. We are half way through watching Forrest Gump, when I hear the door slam. Liv pauses the movie and we look at each other, she smiles in understanding. I move the duvet to the side, getting awkwardly to my feet and I go in search of the man I love.

Brody

I unlock the door and walk through the entrance hall, that's when I catch sight of her. *My girl, my Raleigh.* I stand there taking her in for a few precious moments, even though she looks pale, she still looks stunning. Her amethyst eyes look tired, she is wearing one of my bright red, oversized Rancid Vengeance hoodies with the sleeves pulled over her hands, a pair of loose jogging bottoms and a pair of black Ugg slippers. She moves to the doorway, and she's never looked as beautiful as she does now; her face free of make-up and her stomach swollen with our babies. I walk towards her, until I am inches from her. I take a lock of her hair between my fingers and twirl it.

"Kitten," I say softly and I don't know what I expected, but she throws her arms around me. I reciprocate and put my arms around her, holding her to me, breathing her in.

"God, you smell good, I've missed you, so fucking much."

I breathe and she lifts her head up, burying her face in my neck.

"I'm sorry, I'm so fucking sorry, for everything."

She shakes her head.

"Shhh, not now. Please just hold me," she whispers and it's as if she can't get close enough. I engulf her in my arms and she clings to me. We silently stand in the middle of the entrance hall way for long moments. As I hold her in my arms, I find the peace I have been so desperately searching for.

***

There's blood, so much fucking blood. It's on my hands, it's smeared across my face, I can taste the acrid, metallic in my mouth and it makes me gag. I stare down at the dead, pale, lifeless body of Stefan Lavelle. Unexpectedly, he sits bolt upright, pointing his index finger accusingly in my direction, laughing maniacally. His eyeball out of its socket and resting casually on his cheekbone. I take a few steps back, slipping on the viscous, crimson on the wooden floor, as I hear Lorna softly sobbing, blood pouring from the slit across her throat.

"Why didn't you save me, Brody?"

Tears roll freely down my cheeks, as I repeat the words 'I'm sorry' over and over and over again.

"This is all your fault!" She screams, as I shake my head vehemently.

"No! No! No! No!" I yell, as Stefan grabs her by her hair, dragging her away, calling her a filthy, cheating whore. I try to stop him, failing miserably as he keeps her from my grasp. I follow them both outside and he swings the car door open, shoving her face first into the back of the car. He gets into the car, as I straddle my bike. He revs the engine and I mirror his action revving my bike, as he takes off, kicking up gravel at me. The pleading look Lorna gives me from the back window spurs me on. She bangs desperately on the window, screaming.

"HELP ME! BRODY HELP ME!"

I speed up, but I can't seem to keep up with Stefan. I swerve to go around him, but he swerves with me, almost knocking me off the road.

"HELP! HELP! SOMEONE HELP ME!"

My heart beat kicks up a notch at the haunted look in her aquamarine eyes. No matter how fast I speed up, she's just out of my reach, I can't get to her, I can't save her from Stefan. I roar, as I make one last attempt to get to her. I speed up and suddenly she disappears from the back of the car. I frantically call her name, searching for her, while trying to keep my eyes on the road.

"LORNA! LORNA!"

I feel a set of arms wrap around my waist and the blood red of Lorna's nails morphs into a set of toned forearms.

"Boo!"

Stefan whispers in my ear, as he reaches up and grabs me around my throat in a vice-like grip.

"You took my wife from me! You ruined everything I loved, now you'll watch as I set your fucking world on fire!" he roars, the grip on my throat tightens. I'm gasping for air, willing him to just fucking finish the job...

I wake up screaming to Raleigh softly calling my name and shaking my arm gently.

"Brody, baby, you were having a nightmare."

My breath comes in sharp, erratic bursts, as I gulp in lungfuls of precious air. My heart is pounding and a sheen of sweat has formed on my forehead. I look down at my hands, as if to reassure myself that no blood is on them. Raleigh shifts closer to me and she goes to pull me into her embrace, and I flinch away from her, putting some distance between us. *I can't fucking do this.* I leap ungracefully out of bed and run into the bathroom, slamming the door and locking it behind me. I slide down the door and onto the floor with the remnants of my nightmare still clinging to me like a cloak of pure grief and despair. My stomach twists and I scramble across the bathroom floor, lift the toilet seat up and feel the contents of my stomach vacate spectacularly into the bowl. *Fucking hell.*

I rest my cold, clammy head on my forearm, as the door slowly creaks open. I lift my head up and catch sight of Raleigh stood in the doorway. She looks like a fucking angel sent to redeem me of all my sins, she wearing an oversized red Chicago Bulls baseball shirt, which looks like a dress on her, her long, slender legs bare. She looks at me with a look of pure anguish on her face and it causes my heart to slam against my rib cage.

"Brody?"

She moves slowly into the bathroom, regarding me with quiet concern. She looks beautiful, her huge baby bump protruding in front of her, the bagginess of the t-shirt doing nothing to conceal it. I take every inch of her in and commit her to memory, every curve, every inch, every blemish, every scar, every fucking inch of her perfect body. The powerful and formidable urge to get high rushing through my veins, gripping me tight and all I want to do is forget. My whole body begins to tremble violently with impulsive need and I want to get so high that it doesn't hurt anymore. Watching Stefan slit Lorna's throat playing frame by frame, in slow fucking motion is driving me further and further into the familiar darkness I spent fourteen years trying to repel. We stay silent for long moments, until I get unsteadily to my feet, as she watches me carefully.

"Come back to bed, babe," she encourages, as I rake my hand through my hair.

"I'm going for a walk to clear my head, I can't be here, not right now."

My voice void of emotion.

"Is that it then, you're just going to walk out without even talking to me?" she retorts, her voice filled with obvious resentment and clear anger.

"What's there to talk about? The fact that I watched the woman I thought I was once in love with get her throat slit right in front of me, or the fact that I fucking murdered someone in cold blood! Because that's the truth, Raleigh! I've got blood on my hands!"

I hold my hands out in front of me.

"Look! You're sleeping next to a fucking murderer! The father of your children took someone's life! Even though he fucking deserved it, it doesn't make it right! It doesn't justify the fact that he doesn't get to wake up and go on with his life, he's going to be cold and dead in the ground because of me! No matter how much you dress it up, I'm still a killer!" I bark, as I jab my thumbs into my chest harshly.

"You did what you had to! You did what you thought was right because you cared deeply about her! No matter how much it fucking hurts me to admit it, I know you loved her!"

Her voice uneven and thick with unshed tears.

"I'll always be second best!" her voice cracks and I let out a laboured breath.

"For fucks sake! This isn't about you! Why do you have to make it all about you?" I snap and she hangs her head.

"Because ever since the accident you haven't been here! You might have been here physically, but mentally, you've been somewhere else entirely," she admits honestly and I drop my head to my hands, feeling my control slipping with every second that passes. I start to get anxious and the thirst for a fix is so strong, my hands start to tremble and my mouth starts to water. The usual dull pound in my head becoming significantly less bearable.

"So, that's it, you're just going to bury your fucking head in the sand? I thought we were making progress!" she continues to talk at me, but I don't hear a fucking word she says. All I can focus on is the familiar safety of my sanctuary called oblivion.

23

Raleigh

After a restless and uncomfortable nights' sleep, I wake with a start to an empty bed. After his nightmare and our disagreement last night, Brody walked out on me and he didn't return home. I take a shower, get dressed and prepare for the day ahead. I'm browsing the internet on my iPad when I come across a series of Tweets about Brody. I never usually read gossip on the internet, I tend to stay away from it, but seeing his name trending, curiosity gets the better of me.

@Magicalmelxx FYI I ripped all his posters off my wall! #heartbroken

@VengeanceGirl R.V. are better off without him; Flash out plays him at every single gig!

@ForeverVengeance Why do those poor boys put up with his antics? Sack him! And there are better guitarists out there!

@WildBabexox So what he made a mistake? Big deal! Get over it! Rise up Snake! I still love ya! <3

@VampGirl619 Wanna hook up and be bad together Snake!! ☺ DM me!

I snap the iPad case shut, angry on his behalf. I know firsthand what it's like to have to live in the shadow of the paparazzi's lens and your life is no longer your own. It's fodder for the press to feed on and once the rumour mill has built up momentum, shit sticks, no matter how many times you set the record straight. I spend long minutes trying to occupy my mind by busying myself with mindless chores. But it does nothing to suppress the nagging feeling deep in my gut that this unwanted press attention and the fact that he could be thrown in prison for murder could potentially drive Brody back to his old ways. I pick up my phone and dial the only person I know who could offer me a new perspective on the whole situation.

"Hey babe!" Peyton greets cheerfully.

"Hey girl, are you free to chat?" I ask, desperately trying to quell the tears I feel stinging the back of my eyes.

"I'm at the shop today, I have back-to-back appointments. Seb is still in New York overseeing the works on the new shop, is everything ok?" she replies cautiously.

"It's fine, everything's fine," I say a little too enthusiastically, swallowing down the lump in my throat.

"Are you sure? I can do lunch, how does twelve thirty sound? Parker and Harley are here and Rocky Lee is in town guest spotting. I'm in charge until Seb gets back but there's been a huge delay on the opening of the new shop," she explains and I let out a huge sigh of relief.

"Twelve thirty sounds perfect."

A tear rolls down my cheek, as I respond.

"Great, I'll meet you at Swingin' Eli's. I don't know what's wrong, but I want you to know I'm here for you, Raleigh. You're part of our crazy family now."

She laughs and I find myself laughing along with her.

"Thank you, I'll see you soon."

With those words we say goodbye and I hang up the phone feeling a little more optimistic that everything will be ok.

***

I spend longer than my usual fifteen minutes under the shower, welcoming the feel of the warm water cascading over my exhausted and very pregnant body. When I emerge from the shower, I feel refreshed and ready to face what the day has to throw at me. My outfit for the day consists of a knee length red and white polka dot tea dress, white Converse, natural make-up and my hair styled into tousled waves. Trey drives me into Islington to meet Peyton, keeping a careful and vigilant eye on me and his surroundings.

We pull up at the curb to a quaint little bistro called Swingin' Eli's Bistro. Trey escorts me to the door with a curt nod and I silently smile my thanks. I step inside and I'm instantly transported back to the nineteen fifties, the decor is old school swing, with paintings of old swing artists scattered on the walls. Peyton is sat at a table by the window and I spend a few moments taking her in. Her dark hair with electric pink and purple flashes is styled perfectly straight on one side and shaved on the other side, she is wearing a pair of dark blue denim dungarees, a three quarter sleeved navy and white striped top underneath and a pair of matching blue Converse. She grins brightly as I approach her and she stands to greet me with a warm hug, standing on her tip toes to accommodate our height difference.

"Hey babe! It's so good to see you!"

I find her enthusiasm infectious and beam right along with her, as a tall, southern American man in his mid to late sixties, with coffee-coloured skin, greying hair, and a wide, infectious smile approaches us.

"Ladies! What can I get y'all?"

I take a seat opposite her and she orders a caramel hot chocolate for herself calling him by his first name.

"And you Miss?" he asks and I smile, as he hands us both menus.

"Just water, sparkling, twist of lemon, no ice, please."

He nods brusquely and leaves us to peruse the menu. She places the menu face down on the table regarding me intently and eyeing me carefully.

"Come on then, spill."

She places her finger thoughtfully to her chin and I feel my lip start to tremble. She reaches across the table for my hand and I let her take it in a gesture of sympathy and reassurance.

"How do you cope being the wife of a world famous rock star?" I ask her and she chuckles softly at my question.

"Believe me, honey, it doesn't come without its setbacks. Sam and me have had some times in our relationship when the press attention has tested us to the limits. It's difficult sometimes, but we deal with it together. There were times in the beginning of our relationship when I couldn't see us continuing, but we got through it because I couldn't imagine my life without him in it. We've been through something no couple should ever have to go through."

She shifts her gaze away from mine and I remember a conversation Brody and me had a while ago about Sam and Peyton's first wedding in Vegas. He didn't go into detail, but I remember hearing about it on the news at the time, it was bad. I give her hand a reassuring squeeze and she looks up at me through tear filled lashes.

"You probably saw it on the news at the time, but we fucking lived it and we've lived with the consequences every day since."

She puffs out her cheeks, and she looks so full of grief. My heart hurts for her.

"We lost nine people that day and it never gets any easier. Jax lost his fiancée, I lost my best friend and Sam lost his mum. We lost so many people close to us all, because of Sam's psycho sister. She burst into the chapel in Vegas..."

Her eyes glaze over and she pulls her hand away from mine, placing it in her lap.

"You don't have to explain," I say softly, as she smiles her thanks.

"I thought I'd lost Sam, no one knew the full extent of the massacre, not even the newspapers, they speculated, but they didn't know the real story. I'd been taken from Sam by J.D., but I'd never felt fear like that, I felt so...useless. All the press seemed to be worried about was a story. They camped outside the hospital for days looking for their golden egg. They don't care about us, not really; our feelings, our privacy doesn't matter. All we are to them is their next sensation, their meal ticket. This thing with Brody, he...might be a lot of things but he isn't a murderer. He had to have a good fucking reason to do what he did. I get that you're angry, we all are, but Brody is an all-or-nothing kind of guy. He's fiercely loyal, he'll do now and deal with the consequences later. He's not a bad person, quite the opposite. I know he loves you and those babies even though he might not show it or even voice it in the way you want. What I'm trying to say is, you need to put on a united front or the press will swallow you up and spit you out."

Our conversation is temporarily halted by the southern American man placing our drinks down on the table.

"Have you decided what y'all would like to eat? Or would you like some more time?"

He directs his question to Peyton.

"Can we get five more minutes, please, Eli?" He nods , his eyes crinkling at the corners with a kind smile, leaving us to it once more.

"It's going to be hard, probably one of the hardest fights of your life, but if you don't face it together, your relationship might not survive. I'm not saying that to be a bitch, I'm being honest. The accident changed him and it was hard on us all, not knowing if he was going to pull through, I can't imagine what type of strain that must have been on you."

I squeeze my eyes briefly shut.

"I love him so, so much. We rowed before and he walked out on me, I always get so fucking terrified that he's going to go back to the drugs again. Ever since the accident, it's like he's been somewhere else, it's like he's drifting away from me. Day by day, bit by bit, there's a distance between us that wasn't there before."

My voice is thick with unshed tears.

"I get that it's difficult. We've been through hell and back, not just me and Sam, but the rest of the guys too. But we've come out of it stronger. Please, don't give up on him and whatever happens, do not show weakness. The most important thing right now is you have to show them how strong you are, together."

As I listen to her explain, I understand a little more.

"The key to handling the press is you play them at their own game. You need to play them rather than being played by them. You of all people should understand that, you're from the same industry and you've spent a good portion of your life under the media spotlight. I'd had glimpses of it through my mum, my dad and the tattoo TV show, but my experience was limited. It wasn't until Sam and me first started dating that I realised how they twist things. It almost broke us in the beginning, but by then I'd already fallen in love with him and I knew wasn't going to give him up, not for anyone," she says with conviction. As she says those words, I vow to follow her advice.

24

Brody

The biggest lie addicts tell themselves is that they can stop whenever they want and I allowed the drugs to swallow me up and spit me out over the years. However, I no longer wanted to be a statistic and after my disagreement with Raleigh. Instead of meeting Kev to score, I ended up at the place I always seem to gravitate towards when I feel particularly out of control. Lenny's, the person who always knows the right words to say in any situation. The person who is always there no matter the time of day or night. He's the father I wish I had growing up. I don't think I'll ever stop needing him and I'm grateful to have such a solid role model in my life. I walk up the path and tap softly on the door. I see a familiar shadow in the frosted glass door and the door opens and I'm greeted by Lenny. The sleeves of his pale blue shirt rolled up to his elbows and his salt and pepper hair slicked back.

"I didn't know who else to turn to, Len," I say tentatively and let out an audible sigh. He flashes me a small reassuring smile and steps out of the doorway to let me into the warmth of his cosy house.

"To what do I owe the pleasure of this, son?" His voice is laced with wry amusement. I follow him down the hallway and into the kitchen. Nancy stands at the cooker, stirring something on the hob and my stomach rumbles at the smell of her cooking. She turns to face me, her silver hair cut into a short, pixie crop. The wrinkles on her face a roadmap of her journey so far, but she looks younger than her sixty-two years. Her light green eyes gleaming with energy and warmth.

"Brody, come here, my darling boy."

She moves towards me and envelopes me in her arms, standing on her tip toes to compensate for her lack of height. I put my arms around her and mirror her greeting, smiling to myself.

"You need fattening up, he's looking too thin, Len. You need a good meal!" she chastises softly and Lenny chuckles throatily.

"Leave the poor boy alone, woman! He hasn't come here for a bloody lecture!"

Nancy pulls away from me and rolls her eyes dramatically, as I laugh at their easy cameraderie. Lenny cocks his head to the side in a silent gesture for me to follow him. I kiss Nancy on the cheek, as we head into Lenny's office. The room a world away from the rest of the house. The other rooms in the house are bright, inviting and cosy but this is a complete contrast. The dark walnut wood of the bookcases full of books and the large desk matching the dark, dated décor. Lenny sits down in his deep forest green office chair, the leather of the chair creaking as he takes his seat. I sit down on the Chesterfield sofa in the same green tone.

"To what do I owe this surprise visit then, boy?"

I sigh and lean back heavily on the sofa, tipping my head back so I am looking up at the ceiling.

"I don't know what to do, Len. Me and Raleigh had another row. She doesn't get it. I love her so fucking much, but she doesn't understand any of it. I contemplated getting high, but I don't want to be that person anymore, that's why I came here. I know better than to leave those innocent children with my legacy, but I keep letting them down. I keep proving everyone right that I'm a fuck up."

I lean forward, bracing my elbows on my knees.

"I keep letting Raleigh down. It took me almost killing myself in that accident for me to realise that she's it for me, Len, she's my chance at redemption. I've been given a second chance at righting those wrongs, but I murdered someone... I took someone's life. I came here to get some perspective. You out of everyone seem to understand me the most because you've seen me at rock bottom. I clawed my way back up because of you, because you taught me that I'm worthy. I'm not like my mum and it took me so long to finally believe that, but now I'm questioning fucking everything."

I spill out all of my doubts and fears and Lenny just sits there silently, allowing me to purge my thoughts and feelings.

"I don't know what to do, Len."

I cover my face with my hands, willing the tears stinging my eyes not to fall.

"I never thought I'd see the day, son. You've turned a corner and I'm so bloody proud of you. You've come so far compared to that lost young man I met all those years ago. I couldn't save Daryl, but I helped you realise you were worth more than the drugs. I didn't want to watch you self destruct, I didn't want to see another boy I loved, buried in a coffin," Lenny says with a melancholy tone to his gruff voice. With those words I'm transported back to the day I met Daryl Dean Nicholas.

Brody
Past

I had very few memories of my mum Imogen Rose Hart. The memories I did have were ones of an addict who didn't give a shit about anyone or anything, except for where her next fix was coming from. I was ten years old when she died and even now, eight years down the line, it still has a profound effect on me. After she died, I remember feeling separate from other people from a very young age, I struggled to make any meaningful connections with anyone outside of Sam, Jack and Luke.

I had been in the tight grip of drugs for two years now, purely for the escape it bought me from the demons that roamed loose in my head. It seemed to be the only way I could sleep soundly just lately, without waking up in a cold sweat from the nightmares that haunted me on a nightly basis. I couldn't tell the boys, or Jamie-Leigh or anyone, they just wouldn't understand. At eighteen years old, I was using drugs on an almost daily basis, I begged, borrowed and stole to get my next fix. Cocaine was my drug of choice, it helped me talk more openly to strangers, it helped me be the best version of myself. I've never known what it's like to be truly happy, but when I was snorting coke, I was the happiest I could ever be in that moment and nothing else beyond that mattered. I was always chasing the next high, fuck it, you only live once.

I had recently met Kevin Adams, who was a known high-end drug dealer in the city, he dealt drugs to TV, music and movie stars. He was the man you go to if you wanted a little something to get the party started. We had just finished performing a gig in a dive bar in Brixton called The Pear and Partridge. We played in front of a crowd of barely fifty people on a Friday night. We had built up a reputation of being a local band who sang our songs and wrote our own music. We were yet to be signed, but we played gigs every weekend at various pubs, clubs, bars and small concert venues. Sam was just settling our fee with the owner, and I stood at the bar, having a well-earned drink with the boys after the gig. We were shooting the shit and laughing raucously among ourselves when I turn to see Kev. I had called him earlier, but I didn't expect him to show up here. He lifts his hand to wave and Jack eyes me suspiciously.

"Is he a friend of yours?" he asks and I smirk, slapping him on the back.

"More of an acquaintance, I'll be right back, mate."

I saunter casually over to Kev.

"Surprised to see me, Hart?" he says with an amused tone to his voice.

"Didn't think this was your scene?" I say, taking a sip of my bottle of Budweiser and he laughs.

"And what would you say my scene is?" he asks and I cock my eyebrow.

"Not this."

I gesture around the room, as we are joined by a tall, wiry guy, who looks like he's barely out of nappies. His long dark shoulder length hair is secured in a black paisley headband, he is wearing black skinny jeans ripped at the knees and a v-neck black-and-white striped t-shirt. He rubs his finger under his nose and observes the exchange between me and Kev with curious eyes. Kev turns to Daryl, and he clears his throat.

"Brody, this is Daryl. Daryl, Brody."

I lift my chin in greeting and Daryl nods warily, his interest in me growing. I was more of an introvert when it came to people I didn't know. My friendship circle was small, and I didn't trust easily. I was somewhat awkward around strangers except when I was high. When I was high, I'd talk the hind legs off a donkey about shit no one cared about.

"Did you want to buy some sweets, Brody?"

Kev looks at me and I was familiar with the code that Kev went by. He never talked about selling coke on the phone he was paranoid that the police had bugged his phone somehow. I was surprised he didn't walk around wearing a tin foil hat. He never used the obvious words, he always used obscure analogies. I nod at his question, as he turns and strides off with Daryl and me following him.

We end up going back to Kev's place to chill out and as soon as the coke works its way into my system, I feel all of my inhibitions leave me, all of my hang ups, all of my apparent shyness vanishes. The buzz making me feel like I could talk for England, Daryl and me talk as if we've known each other for years. We're lying on two bean bags in the corner of Kev's flat, staring up at the ceiling. All emotional barriers collapse around me and I find myself telling Daryl about anything and everything.

"My mum was an addict. I found her dead when I was ten years old with a needle hanging from her arm. I never knew my dad, she gave birth to me when she was twenty years old. According to her, my grandparents never approved of her relationship with my dad, so she left home right after she found out she was pregnant with me. She was on the street for a while and that's when she got hooked on the drugs. She was an immature, pregnant junkie, who sold her body for her next fix and I'll never fucking forgive her for that. I missed out on my childhood because the drugs meant more to her than I did. I was born with neonatal abstinence syndrome. I was born with drugs in my system and experienced painful withdrawal, up until I was three months old. There were a few rare occasions that she wasn't wasted or high and I looked forward to those moments so fucking much, but they were very few and far between. I'd come home from school and there would be a different bloke there and the fridge was empty. I spent so long hungry and neglected that I thought it was normal. She died on her thirtieth birthday and the moment I found her, still fucking haunts me. It keeps me up at night. The drugs help me deal with the emotional trauma, it blocks out for a little while, quiets those demons, ya know?"

Daryl nods in understanding.

"My mum and dad are my role models. They've never quit on me. I'm lucky in that respect, they've given up so much for me, my dad, Len, he's amazing. A little rough around the edges, but he's my hero, man. My mum is the sweetest woman I've ever known, it must have been so hard for you, I feel for you, dude," he says sympathetically and I let out an audible sigh.

"I don't want your pity, man, it is what it is. I made do with what I had. I was raised by the most amazing women, Lori, Jamie-Leigh and Ava. They all taught me what a mum should have been like. They took me under their wings and put me on the straight and narrow, I was moved from foster home to foster home, from one children's home to another. I never really settled, but I had a

family who raised me as one of their own. My friends and me, we're in a band. We've spent the last year and a half gigging... we're going to be big one day! We're gonna release number one fucking albums, tour the world, our fans are going to sing our songs back to us and it's going to be wild! Sex, drugs, women and rock n' roll, man!"

We both laugh and as we lay there staring up at the ceiling, the paint peeling at the corners, we had made a connection, a bond that could not be bought or sold. Fate bought us together, and it was rare for me to make that connection with a stranger. I was glad we met tonight, and I hoped it was the beginning of something new.

Brody
Present

I'm jolted back to the present by Lenny clearing his throat, as I move my hands away from my face and lean back.

"I had a nightmare, Len," I admit unashamedly, rubbing at my eyes. *I'm fucking exhausted.*

"Do you want to talk about it?" Lenny asks curiously and I shake my head ardently. We are silent for long moments and I puff out a tired breath.

"I think I owe you that Jaguar X-Type now."

I try to lighten the mood and subtely change the subject, as he laughs throatily.

"And three weeks in the Maldives," he says wryly.

"You drive a hard bargain, old man. Let's call it four," I quip and he laughs.

"Well, only if you insist! And less of the old, you little shit!"

He winks, as he pulls the drawer of his desk open. He takes out two glasses and a bottle of Macallan whiskey. He unscrews the lid and pours us both large measures. He pushes the glass across the table with his index finger, as he picks up his glass and tips it to his lips, regarding me carefully. I reach out and pick up the glass, while running my forefinger around the rim.

"I've not seen you this cut up in a long time, son," he observes and I shake my head tentatively.

"It's all such a fucking mess, Len, I watched him slit her throat in front of me. The fear in her eyes, the way she looked at me, it's burned into my fucking retinas. I've never felt that...out of control or that thirsty for blood before. It wasn't about revenge, not at all, but I wanted to watch the light fade from his eyes and I wanted it to be me that ended him. He killed her like a fucking animal!"

I clench my jaw and my hands start to tremble with rage, the liquid in the glass sloshing around with the force of it.

"The nightmare was about Lorna. No matter how fast I rode after her, I couldn't get to her, I couldn't save her, Len."

I let out a strangled sob and cover my eyes with my hand, not wanting him to see me so weak and vulnerable.

"I can't fucking pretend I didn't feel anything for her. It wasn't love, not really. Lust maybe, infatuation...possibly, but not love. She reminded me of my mum and I was so hell bent on saving her from herself because in my mind I thought she needed saving. But maybe it was me she needed saving from," I confess. I've never admitted that out loud to anyone before, surprising myself at how easy it was to divulge.

"Have you ever considered the fact that you see your mum in every woman you've ever been with? Raleigh was an abuse victim. She was an addict, and you met in rehab, for fucks sake," Lenny states matter-of-factly and I smile at his candour. I had never really thought about it before, but maybe he's right.

Rick touched on it before, he called it white-knight syndrome. He explained it as rescuing others, but losing yourself in the process. I was attracted to needy, damaged women, who all reminded me of my mum in some way or another. It was more common in people who grew up in a household with neglectful parents and there was a fine line between white-knight syndrome and co-dependency. I had a need to rescue people from themselves, Raleigh and Lorna being two prime examples of that. I based my self-worth on my ability to fix people and I pride myself on saving others when my life is a complete fucking car crash. I had severe emotional issues stemming back to my childhood and I had a history of still unhealed abandonment wounds. I was a classic case of an addict who avoided confronting their own struggles by focussing on solving the problems of their significant other. I was a psychiatrists wet dream in every sense of the word. I spend a few moments letting that thought sink in, as I look up to meet Lenny's expectant eyes. I cock my head to the side and clear my throat before I speak.

"You've probably got better things to do than listen to me fucking whining, Len," I joke and Lenny narrows his eyes on me.

"Don't ever fucking say that, B. Don't ever apologise for needing someone to talk to. My door is always open and I'm never far away."

I let out a breath and lean forward, as my phone starts buzzing in my pocket. I take it out and look down at the screen seeing Raleigh's name. I silence it and put it back in my pocket, Lenny laughs throatily.

"You've barely been together a year and you're avoiding her calls... that doesn't bode well!"

I knock my drink back in one gulp, relishing the burn as it slides down my throat and spreads warmth through my entire body.

"She's so different from all the others, Len. She's carrying my babies. I acted recklessly when I found out. She told me the night I had the accident, and I just left her like it meant nothing. In reality, it meant everything and I'll never be able to take that back."

I shake my head in disbelief, mentally running through the past few months in my mind.

"Go home, son, tell her how you feel."

He regards me intently, as I place my glass down on his desk. I get to my feet with renewed purpose and follow his advice.

25

Raleigh

"I love you."

I hear a husky whisper and warm breath tickling my cheek. My eyes flutter open and lock with familiar, twinkling silver eyes. He rests his head on my chest and I take a moment to breathe him in.

"You came back?"

My voice is thick with sleep. I must have fallen asleep on the sofa after I got back from my lunch with Peyton.

"I'm so fucking sorry, kitten."

He buries his head in my neck and the emotion in his voice causes my heart to slam against my ribcage.

"Hey, hey, it's ok," I reassure him softly, as he lifts his head up. The look in his eyes is somewhere between pure anguish and something else entirely. We gaze at each other for long moments, as he leans in and presses his lips urgently to mine.

"I need you," his voice low and desperate. I reciprocate his urgency, as he moves onto the sofa and settles himself between my thighs. He pulls my top and my bra down to expose my full, tender breast to him. He leans down to suck my now erect nipple, as I writhe beneath him and moan softly at the feel of his expert mouth on me. I close my eyes, biting down savagely on my lip, as he releases my nipple from his mouth with a loud pop. He leans back on his haunches and looks at me with such reverence, it makes me want to cry.

"God, you're so fucking beautiful," he whispers seductively and the sound of his voice makes me quiver with want.

"I want you naked," I practically pant out, and as he flashes me a grin, I almost spontaneously combust. His boyish grin really is a sight to beholden. This is the side I love, the side that no one but me gets to see.

"Your wish is my command, beautiful girl."

He pulls his t-shirt off lithely and I bite my lip at his ripped physique: his waist lean, his shoulders broad, his tattooed, defined abs and his visible six-pack. I watch him carefully and he winces as he straightens. My concerned eyes move to the angry stab wound, which starts on his right side and stretches around to his back. I reach out to run my fingers over it, but he shakes his head, moving slightly out of my grasp. He takes my hand and kisses my fingers one by one.

"Eyes up here, kitten," his voice a rough command, as I follow his gaze and my eyes land on his. He lowers the zip on his jeans, taking out his steel erection. My pussy is aching for him to be inside me after all this time, my pulse is racing and I'm burning for him.

"Clothes off."

I'm naked in record time, even if my movements and my actions are slower than usual. Every inch of my body is exposed to him, my large bump swollen between us. He lowers himself, until he's settled between my legs and my back arches, as he plunges two fingers deep inside me. I cry out in pure pleasure at the feel of him deftly twisting his calloused fingers in and out of my soaking wet heat. He increases his pace with each measured movement, finger fucking me thoroughly and driving me towards my release. I roll my nipples between my thumb and forefingers, moaning softly.

"Look at me, I need your eyes on me. I want to watch you fall apart as I lick you to orgasm."

He pulls his fingers free and I'm instantly bereft at the loss of contact. He immediately replaces his fingers with his split tongue, as his tongue swipes up my slit. I'm lost. His tongue gloriously assaulting my pussy in the most delicious way.

"Oh God, that feels so good. Don't stop, please, don't stop."

My breath is coming in short, sharp bursts, as he quickens his momentum, moaning softly at my orgasm building deep within me. His tongue flicks over my sensitive swollen nub and I feel the familiar flutters. My pussy floods as he continues punishing thrusts of his tongue inside me.

"OH FUCK! BRODY! I'M GOING TO COME! OH GOD! OH GOD!"

With one swift brush of his tongue, my orgasm tears through me like an explosion of pent up sexual energy. I scream out in pure ecstasy wave after wave of pleasure surging through me like a tidal wave. As I come down from my orgasmic high, I catch sight of him as he lifts his head up, his hair perfectly mussed and a lust-filled glint in his sparkling silver eyes.

"I missed you so much," I blurt out softly and then mentally scold myself, as I see the forlorn look on his face. He drops his head and shifts his gaze from mine.

"I'm right here, kitten, I've always been right here," he whispers so tenderly, he's barely audible.

"Let me show you. Let me worship you. Let me love you, Raleigh."

He offers me his hand and I take it willingly. He leads us over to the fur rug on the floor in front of the blazing electric fire, lowering us both down to the ground. He kneels down gloriously naked, settling me over him so I am straddling his lap. He wraps his arms around my back and my body erupts with goosebumps at the feel of his hands roaming up and down. I cup his face with both of my hands, pressing my lips softly to his, as the glow of the fire illuminates his face. He deepens the kiss, pulling me as close as I can get without my bump getting in the way.

"*Fuck me*, how did I get so lucky?" he says with a hint of disbelief in his voice.

"Make love to me, Brody, please," I practically plead with him. He flashes me a grin, as he leans back slightly. He lifts my bum up and his cock finds my entrance, impaling me on his waiting erection. We both moan aloud as he enters me. Our eyes lock and I see every emotion clear in his silver orbs. *This is how Brody Hart makes love.*

"Ride me, kitten," his voice urgent, as I lift myself up and lower myself down on his cock, building up a slow, steady rhythm. I feel his piercing rub my inner walls in the most delicious way.

"God, you feel so fucking good," he pants, as I increase my pace and he lets me take complete control.

"Oh God, Brody!" I scream and my eyes lock with his, silver to amethyst. He wraps his muscular arms around me and I see a thin sheen of sweat forming across his forehead, his jaw clenching tightly. Unexpectedly, he rolls us so I am spread beneath him, never breaking our connection, his cock still buried deep inside me.

"I'm not capable of slow and gentle, kitten. I need to fuck you."

He increases his thrusts and with every strike of his cock, I feel his piercing bump my cervix.

"Oh fuck, Brody! Brody! Oh yes! Fuck me, I need you to fuck me!" I pant desperately, as he builds up a punishing pace. He swivels his hips, and with each measured drive of his cock, I feel him push deeper inside me, hitting my g-spot in just the right place. I feel an intense orgasm cresting to the surface and I'm about to explode.

"OH GOD! YOU'RE GOING TO MAKE ME COME SO HARD! FUCKKKK!" I yell, as he continues his punishing grinds.

"TOGETHER, KITTEN, OH FUCK! I'M CLOSE, SO FUCKING CLOSE!" he barks and with another deep plunge of his cock, a powerful orgasm surges through me like a tornado.

"Brody! Oh Jesus! Fuck! Oh! Oh God! Brody!" I scream and Brody's release is right behind mine, as he growls out, filling me with his hot seed. We both come down from our orgasms, he pulls out of me and I shiver. He moves to lie down next to me, pulling me close into him and we lay there in quiet contemplation for a few moments. He traces idle shapes on my arm, before he breaks the silence.

"It's always been you, Rae. You know that don't you? From the very beginning. It's you I always come back to, it's you I want to spend the rest of my life with."

I gasp at his revelation. *Is this his way of proposing to me? While we lie here naked after we just had sex?*

"It's not a proposal. It's a promise that one day, Raleigh Storm, you will become Raleigh Hart and I'll spend the rest of my life worshipping you and making up for all of my fuck ups. Just know that from now on, it's only you."

He leans over to plant a chaste kiss on my lips, as a stray tear rolls down my cheek. "It's going to take time for me to forgive you. You cheated on me, and you've fucked me around our entire relationship. I got so used to being second best in my family and with Carter. I thought you were different, so please give me time, Brody. I love you, but I'm not sure I'll ever be enough for you. One day you'll get bored of being a one woman man and you'll screw around and I can't wait around for the shoe to drop. I'm carrying your babies, for fucks sake. I have to be the responsible one for once."

He shakes his head, as he lifts himself up, leaning on his elbow.

"You are enough, don't you see? What can I do to make you believe that I'm not that man anymore. The accident changed something in me, it flipped a switch. I'm not that selfish prick anymore, I was in a coma for three months! I almost fucking died!" he raises his voice a few decibels and I flinch at the sound. He rears back and his eyes widen.

"*Fuck*," he curses. "I'm sorry, I didn't mean to raise my voice. I need you to believe I'm nothing like Carter. I'd never lay my hands on you, except to worship every inch of your beautiful body."

He skates his hand down the length of my body and I shiver at the feel of his hand on me, giving him a contented hum of appreciation.

"It makes me feel physically sick that he did that to you. I couldn't live with myself if I ever hurt you like that."

The emotion in his voice is evident and I shake my head.

"I know you're nothing like him, I didn't mean to flinch. It was how I lived my life for so long... waiting for the next slap, waiting for the next cruel comment. I knew if I stayed, he'd never change," I say, almost disbelieving that I let Carter put me through that on a daily basis. His vindictive, spiteful, demeaning side far outweighed his loving side, and I can't believe it took me so long to realise.

"This life, here and now, feels like a totally different life compared to one I lived before. I no longer have to live in fear. I can finally breathe. I can sleep soundly at night," I admit and he twists the fibres of the fur rug idly between his fingers, as I find the strength to tell him the rest of my story.

26

Brody

I look at her, lying next to me naked, her body still slender except for the large bump that looks oddly out of place on her usually lean frame. I place my hand on her stomach and stroke gentle circles, as she shifts her gaze to me.

"I didn't always have short hair, my hair used to be long and platinum blonde. I grew up in Australia, and because of the sun, my hair was light and naturally wavy. Carter used to wind it around his wrist and pull it so hard, he'd pull clumps out, when we were having sex, or when we argued. I got so tired of it, I cut it all off myself in an act of pure defiance. I booked myself into the hair salon and dyed it lilac. I went to an awards ceremony that night and debuted my new look, it was all the newspapers wanted to talk about. Afterwards, he stormed round to where I was living at the time, which happened to be with Liv, but she was out at the time. He was so drunk he flew into a rage and we had yet another blazing row. He was yelling at me for daring to disobey him by cutting my hair and humiliating him on purpose. He punched me, kicked me, raped me, and left me on the floor of our apartment naked and covered in blood. Liv came back the next morning and I made up some bull shit that I got drunk and fell out of a taxi. I'm an actress, I made it look so believeable, it was Oscar worthy."

As I listen to her recount the rest of her story, I visibly shudder and tremble with pent up rage. *I should have ended him when I had the fucking chance.*

"I have so many stories of violence, I can't even remember a time when it was good, or we were actually genuinely in love. Looking back, I can't believe I was so weak that I allowed him to do those things to me without consequence."

She shakes her head as if ridding herself of a particularly horrible thought and I pull her tighter into me.

"I'll never do anything less than treat you like a fucking Queen. I'm so sorry for all of the shitty things I've done. I'll spend eternity making it up to you and our babies."

I stroke her stomach again, as I hear my phone start to ring, the familiar sound of *Linkin Park's In the End* singing from the other side of the room. She rolls her eyes and chuckles softly.

"No rest for the wicked, huh, babe?" she says with a chuckle, as I kiss her forehead and get to my feet to answer my phone. I see our managers name flash up and I swipe the screen to answer.

"M.J., hey," I greet him, warily wondering why he's calling me at this hour.

"Brody, how ya holdin' up, buddy?" he says in his familiar, over-the-top, Brooklyn drawl, as I pad across the floor and into the kitchen for a brief moment of privacy.

"I'm up on a potential murder charge, other than that I'm fucking peachy," I say wryly, as I hear him chuckle down the phone.

"That was what I wanted to talk to you about, Rancid Vengeance have gone viral, it's stratospheric! Record sales are up, all of the gigs sold out! Are you ready to go back on the road? I know it might be a little soon, but the fans are desperate for a show, dude!" He babbles enthusiastically and I groan at his persistence. *It's been barely forty-eight hours since I was released and he's already seeing pound signs? What the fuck is wrong with this prick?*

"I'm still recovering from the accident. I'm not strong enough yet and my memories are still jumbled on a good day. To top it off, I'm up on a potential murder charge because I beat someone to fucking death! And you want me to get back up on stage in front of thousands of fans like nothing happened? I've heard what they're saying online, M.J., I'm not a fucking idiot."

I try to keep my voice level, as I start to pace the floor and I'm about to speak again when he cuts me off.

"First homecoming gig in London at the end of next month. No excuses, don't let me down, Brody."

He hangs up before I get to protest. *Fuck my life.*

27

Raleigh

The weeks that followed, we fell into a picture of domestic bliss. We made
love on a nightly basis and we were closer than we had ever been. Christmas
had come and gone. We spent it with the rest of the Rancid Vengeance family
and Brody lavished me with gifts. It couldn't have been more perfect. We
saw in the New Year and vowed that this year would be so much better and
so different from the last. We were a few weeks into January and I had now
given up my apartment and moved in with Brody permanently. The doctors
were monitoring me closely, and they were pleased with how the twins were
growing. Although, there was a high chance I wouldn't go full term and
would have to undergo a caesarian section in order for me to give birth safely.
In the past few weeks, Brody has been rehearsing with the band for tonights'
up coming gig. But the past couple of days, he's been withdrawn and nervous
at the prospect of performing again after all this time.

He received a call last night to tell him that all murder charges were
being dropped against him under extenuating circumstances. Clear evidence
pointed to Stefan murdering his wife Lorna, after her four year affair with
Brody. Stefan restrained Brody, stabbed him and Brody retaliated in
self-defence. He was relieved to say the least, and it was as if a weight had
been lifted from his shoulders. It was as though the load he had been bearing
the past few months had disappeared and for a while, he was the Brody I
knew and loved from before the accident.

But over night, it was like a switch had been flipped and he's been off for
days, distant. My Brody is almost never distant, not since before the accident
anyway. He always has a cheeky grin, a cocky wink, or a wiggle of his split
tongue for me, no matter what mood he's in. It's like he's been replaced with
someone completely different and I didn't like it, not one bit. I am almost
eight months pregnant, I am aware I look like a fucking hippo. I am terrified
he is going to find solace in the arms of another woman. I have developed

trust issues and even though I have forgiven his past transgressions, I couldn't forget what he put me through.

He was having nightmares again and leaving in the middle of the night. I was waking up to an empty bed, and he was refusing to open up. I knew the nightmares were about her, I had no doubt in my mind, but no matter how many times I pushed for an answer, it would always result in an argument. This morning was a particularly bad one, he had just come back from his early morning run with Sam. He was in the kitchen drinking a tall hi-ball glass of water as I was preparing a breakfast of blueberry pancakes with bacon and maple syrup. He refused to look at me, instead choosing to stare blankly out of the window, which looked out across the acres of lush green land behind the house.

"When are you going to actually talk to me and open up like an adult? I thought over these past few weeks, we had turned a corner."

I couldn't keep the snark out of my voice. He ignored me and I couldn't help but let my eyes roam over his body, licking my lips at the sight of him standing there looking glorious, damp with sweat. His shorts hung low on his hips revealing the perfectly deliciously cut V on his lower abdomen.

"What are you so fucking afraid of, Brody? Are you afraid that I'm going to figure you out? That once I know your inner most secrets, you won't be such a mystery to me anymore, is that it? Or is it something else? Please, fucking enlighten me!" I raise my voice and I'm somewhere between flying into a blind rage, or breaking down at his feet in floods of tears. I set the bowl down with the pancake batter in on the kitchen island and brace my arms on the marble, pressing my lips together willing the tears burning behind my eyes not to fall. I move closer to him, until I'm within touching distance.

"Are you scared that I might find out you're a fucking fraud? That your little boy lost façade is all a fucking act?"

I know I'm goading him, but I can't seem to help myself. I walk forward, and with every step forward he takes a step back wards towards the wall.

"Or is it the fact that you see your mother in every woman you've slept with? Am I getting warmer?" I spit, my voice full of vitriol and I see the moment his eyes flash with fury.

"Don't ever try to get inside my head," he snarls, grinding out the words, as he spins me and shoves me back against the wall. My mouth falls open, forming a perfect 'O shape, in complete shock of his forcefulness. My heart beat quickens at the sudden switch of his temper, but I try to remain calm. *Deep breaths, Brody isn't anything like Carter, he won't hurt you.*

For several beats we stay there, almost panting labouriously, his grip crushing my wrists and the fear I felt from seconds ago disappears, suddenly replaced with lust. The feeling is short-lived when his stormy silver eyes soften.

"It's too dark for you, kitten."

He loosens his grip on my wrist and tucks my hair behind my ear. He strokes my face tenderly and as he loosens his grip on my other wrist, my hand flies out and lands across his cheek.

"DONT EVER FUCKING GRAB ME AND PUSH ME AROUND LIKE THAT EVER AGAIN, BRODY!" I yell, feeling an overwhelming burst of anger towards this stranger in the body of the man I love. Shame washes over his features and he looks horrified at the fleeting look of terror on my face, taking me back to a time I'd rather forget.

"FUCKKKKK!" he curses, as he launches the glass across the room. The glistening shards shattering and sound echoing around the room, as he turns and strides out.

Brody

As I stride out of the room, I grab the keys to my mustard yellow Lamborghini Urus, catching my reflection in the glass. I feel so full of hate, so full of pure disgust and complete self-loathing at my appalling behaviour. *Why the fuck did I grab her like that?* She doesn't deserve that, and it makes me feel sick that I put my hands on her like that. She's had so much of that in her life already. I'm nothing like that low-life, scum of the earth prick Carter. I want to go back and reassure her that I'm not that man. I don't ever want to see that fear in her eyes. I want to fall to my knees and beg her forgiveness, but an overwhelming feeling of guilt crashes through my body. No matter how hard I try to suppress it, all I want to do is get high to punish myself until the feeling subsides. *I can't be here. I need to be as far away from here as I can get. I have to leave.* It takes a few minutes for my brain to send a message to my legs and I leave the house, slamming the door with force behind me. I sprint with urgency to the bottom of the stone steps, unlock the car and climb inside.

Since the accident, I haven't been able to get back on my motorbike. Every time I think of it, the fear paralyses me, it causes my heart to pound and my skin to prickle. My motorbike was unsalvageable after the accident and it was a miracle I'd survived at all. I had managed to get away with points on my licence and a hefty fine of a cool twenty-five thousand pound for driving under the influence of a Class A substance. I have several top tier super-bikes lined up in my garage and none of them have been ridden. But every time I go in there, my breathing accelerates and I break out in a cold sweat. I know my fear is irrational. I'd been riding since I was seventeen and not once had I been in an accident. It was the only aspect of my life I was truly in control of, but the terror that stabbed at my chest tormented me.

I long to feel the exhilarating thrill of the speed and the blur of the horizon zipping past me. But even thinking about it unmans me, dread twists in my gut and panic surges through me. I had already faced my own mortality and each time my mind darts from one nightmare scenario to another. It reminds me that next time I might not be so lucky. Sam kept reminding me all too often that I was like a cat with nine lives, but I am now paranoid of when those lives will eventually run out. I'm not scared of dying, I just don't want to. I have a second chance at righting the wrongs of my past. I have another shot at making up for every wrong and questionable decision I had ever made. I want to seize every opportunity, I want to overcome my fears and I want to fall in love with riding again. But every time I merely think of it, my blood turns to ice and crippling terror holds me in a vice-like grip. I didn't want to rely on our security team to drive me around, so I bought a car. I feel safer on four wheels and it has to do for now.

As soon as I am within the quiet confines of my car, the guilt slowly starts tearing at my insides and ravaging my chaotic thoughts. I pull my phone out of my pocket and shakily dial the number I need.

"Ah, Brody. Well, well, well, wondered how long it would be," Kev greets cheerfully. He's the last person I want to call, but I need a fix so badly I can taste it.

"Kev, mate, it's been a while. I haven't got time for small talk but can you meet me in the usual place in thirty minutes?" I state impatiently, my heart rate accelerating in my chest at the thought of it. I hear Kev sniff on the other end of the phone and lean my head back on the head rest.

"Sure, works for me, Hart. The usual?"

I pause for a few seconds.

"A baller and a little something extra," I reply and he hums his answer.

"See you in thirty minutes," he says coolly and hangs up without saying goodbye. I push the start/stop button to start the car, the gravel kicking up, as I rev the engine and speed off down the driveway with renewed purpose.

***

I make it to our meeting place in Lewisham in record time; spending the entire journey stuck inside my own head and going over the events from the past hour in minute detail. I have no idea what I'm so afraid of, I've never been one to talk about feelings, but she makes me want to be better. She brings out a side to me that I'm terrified to explore further, her earlier words hitting me full force.

"Or is it the fact that you see your mother in every woman you've slept with?"

Have I really become that transparent? Or is it so glaringly obvious to everyone but me? My brain is working overtime and I can't allow myself to continue that trail of thought, not right now. All I crave is oblivion, and that's all my brain can focus on.

The bell chimes, signalling my entrance to the *Rise and Shine Café* and as soon as I step through the door, it feels like I am finally home again after all this time. The familiar smell of comfort food, freshly brewed coffee; it looks as if it has had a fresh coat of paint, but the old school décor of worn shabby chic and London themed designs throughout is still ever present. As I catch sight of Emmy wiping down a vacant table and I feel a sudden pang of guilt, I haven't seen her since the night of the accident. I approach her cautiously and as she glances up, she drops the cloth to the table, slapping her hand over her mouth. Her wide, expressive eyes glaze over and fill with tears, as I flash her a smile and hold my hands out to the side.

"Don't I get a hug from my best girl?" I ask, breaking the silence and she runs at me, closing the space between us. She throws her arms and legs around me. I catch her easily and hold her tightly to me, as she sobs softly into my neck.

"Hey, hey, I've got you, it's alright. I'm here."

I placate her. Every sob and every tear she sheds is like a knife to my heart, I can't fucking stand knowing I'm the reason she's crying.

"I thought you were gone, I thought I'd lost you," she mumbles against me, as I set her down on her feet, her arms still wrapped around me.

"It will take a lot more than that to get rid of me, babe," I chuckle, trying to joke, as she pulls away from me and begins to hit me.

"Don't ever fucking do that to me again, Brody!" she sobs, swiping the tears away from her eyes with the back of her hand. I move closer to her and gently take her wrist to stop her assault on me. I hold her hand in mine, pressing it to my chest.

"Hey, I'm here. Do you feel that? I'm not going anywhere, ever. You hear me, Ems?" I soothe softly and as she gathers herself, I take her in. Emmy is around five feet eight inches, quite tall for a girl her age. Her usual long blonde hair has been cut into a long sharp bob, which frames her face and the ends have been dip-dyed electric blue. Her eyes are an unusual shade of sea green, which emphasise the smattering of freckles across her newly pierced nose. Her straight up, straight down, gaunt figure replaced with a set of curves Marilyn Monroe would be jealous of.

"You're looking gorgeous as always, babe, Where did those rockin' curves come from?" I compliment and she blushes her usual adorable shade of pink, which I have missed.

"I've met someone," she admits shyly and I grin widely, happy that the little sister I never had has finally met someone.

"I'm so happy for you, Ems! That's fantastic!" I beam enthusiastically and she flashes me her familiar smile.

"I want all the gossip!"

I cock my eyebrow dramatically and she nods.

"Take a seat, I'll grab you a coffee and come sit with you."

I go to sit in my usual spot, at the back of the café in the corner. I sit down at the table with a black and white checked tablecloth, as Emmy approaches with a steaming cup in her hand. She places it down on the table and sits down opposite me, silently observing.

"So, I want details! Don't leave me hanging!" I say brightly and she fidgets with her hands.

"His name is Nate, and he owns a restaurant. We met online. He's older, and he has a daughter from a previous relationship. She's adorable, we've been out on a few dates. It's still early days, but I really like him. Like really, really like him," she admits with a dreamy sigh, as I reach across the table to hold her hand and she lets me.

"Age is just a number. Does he treat you well, or do I have to go and kick his arse?" I ask seriously and she laughs, shaking her head.

"He treats me like a princess... he gives me those butterflies I told you about," she confesses, almost nervously, as a wistful look crosses her face.

"Is Emmy Woods in love? I'm so happy you finally found someone, babe," I say genuinely, as I take a sip of my coffee. *God, I have missed this, Emmy makes the best cup of coffee in London.*

"I'm sorry I didn't come to visit you while you were in hospital."

Her voice is full of remorse.

"Don't be silly, you don't have to apologise."

She shakes her head, her bottom lip trembling. "I couldn't bear it if I lost you, I didn't want my last memory of you to be lying in a hospital bed."

My heart slams against my ribcage at her declaration and she is about to speak again, when a man calls her name, interrupting our moment. He waves his empty coffee cup impatiently at her and she nods, getting up from her seat, the chair scraping noisily across the floor.

"I have to get back to work."

She swipes tears from her eyes, walks over the man who called her name, takes his cup from him and scurries off back to the counter without another word. I hear the bell chime, signaling the arrival of another customer. As I look up, I see Kev Adams. He looks a little more dishevelled than usual as he scans the room for me, with his vacant, sludgy green eyes. I catch his gaze and put my hand up to alert him of my presence. He walks over to me and I silently gesture with a cock of my head for him to take a seat. He sits down opposite me, his eyes darting all over the place.

"Hart, long time no see."

He reaches across the table to shake my hand and I try to ignore the clammy feel of his hand in mine.

"It's been a while, mate, good to see you." I try desperately to keep the insincerity out of my voice, it's really not good to see him at all.

"Do I not get a cup of coffee this time?" he asks, as he smiles his rodent-like smile. I can't hide the repulsion I feel for this slimy fucker.

"We both know that's not gonna happen. We're both here to conduct a simple business transaction, so why bother with pleasantries," I say matter-of-factly with a nonchalant shrug of my shoulders. He cocks his eyebrow, shifting his gaze to Emmy. *Keep your eyes and your thoughts to yourself, motherfucker.*

"She's got a cracking arse, nice pair of tits too, wonder if she's single?"

He leers while licking his lips and I straighten in my chair.

"Lay one fucking finger on her and I'll bury you."

My voice level and steady, as Kev leans towards me in an attempt to appear menacing.

"I'd fucking ruin her pretty pussy," he goads. It takes everything inside me not to reach over the table and smash his fucking face in. *Deep breaths, Hart.*

"Relax, man, I'm just fucking with you."

He laughs anxiously, it grates on every nerve and every cell in my body. He holds his hands up defensively as he reaches across the table in a swift movement, handing me what I came here to collect. I slide a roll of notes in exchange, tucking it inside the pocket of my jeans, as he gets up from his seat.

"Until the next time, Hart."

He turns to leave and the craving for a fix grips me tight, refusing to let go. My chest constricts and I swallow hard to stop the roil in my stomach. *For fucks, sake, come on, Hart, get your shit together.*

"Brody?"

I look up into Emmy's concerned sea-green eyes.

"Is everything ok? You look like you've seen a ghost?"

I shake my head and plaster on a fake smile.

"Everything's fine, babe! Honestly!" I say a little too over enthusiastically and she narrows her inquisitive eyes on me.

"Don't bullshit me, Brody. Did you really come here to see me, or did you come here to score drugs from that guy?" she accuses, through gritted teeth. This isn't the Emmy I know and love.

"Of course I came here to see you, you're my best girl!" I say with a suggestive waggle of my split tongue, trying to lighten the mood.

"Stop lying! Don't treat me like a fucking child, Brody! I'm not seven years old anymore!" she raises her voice, attracting the attention of the other diners.

"Ems, babe, please. Just come and sit down with me, yeah?"

I gesture for her to sit at the seat opposite me and she shakes her head.

"What so you can lie to me some more? I'm not an idiot, so I'd appreciate it if you didn't treat me like one!"

I sit back in my seat, dumbstruck at her sudden change of mood.

"*Jesus Ems*, is someone on their period?" I try to joke, and she raises her hands in despair.

"Oh my God! You're unbelievable!" she yells, attracting the attention of the neighbouring table, their judgemental eyes observing the scene unfolding mere feet from them.

"You know what? Just go! I can't be around you right now!"

I can't hide the hurt as she says those words, they cut deep. She's never yelled at me or even spoken to me like that before. It's so out of character for her. She spins around and storms back behind the counter, as I get to my feet I hang my head in defeat. I take two crisp fifties out of my pocket, placing them underneath my now empty coffee cup, as Mandie flashes me a look of pure sympathy. I walk casually over to her; she brushes my arm in a gesture of sympathy.

"Don't take it personally, darlin', she was inconsolable when she found out you were in hospital," she says softly and my heart breaks for her. I hate that I was the cause of such anguish for my sweet Emmy.

"She idolizes you. She doesn't trust easily, but she trusts you implicitly with her life. I'd never seen her like that, seeing my daughter in pain like that, it broke something inside of me."

I pause briefly, suddenly feeling ashamed of my behaviour.

"What can I do to make it right, Mandie?"

She shakes her head, flicking her blonde hair over her shoulder.

"Just give her some time, sweetheart, she'll come around," she says with a smile, as she pauses wiping down the counter. She puts her arms around me and kisses me on the cheek. As she pulls away from our embrace, she strokes my face and looks at me longingly.

"I'm sorry," I whisper and she nods.

"I know, darling."

There is so much emotion in that one sentence, I can't help the tear that slips down my cheek and she silently wipes it away with the pad of her thumb. I take her hand in mine and place a chaste kiss on the back of her hand, as I turn and go in search of Emmy.

I find her sitting on the steps at the back of the café. I hear her quiet sniffles, as I approach.

"Ems?"

I sit down next to her.

"Fuck off."

She sobs softly, as I wrap my arm around her. She struggles against me for a few minutes, but as the fight drains from her, she goes lax against me and buries her face in my chest.

"Shhh, shhh, I'm here now, Ems. I'm not going anywhere," I soothe, feeling shitty that I'm the cause of her tears. She lifts her head up and the look in her eyes makes my heart slam against my ribcage. Unexpectedly, she moves closer to me until I can feel her warm breath on my cheek and she presses her lips softly to mine. She grips my t-shirt in her fist, it takes me a few seconds to realise what's going on, before I pull away and I wipe my mouth with the back of my hand. She touches her fingers to her lips and her sea-green eyes widen, as she realises what just happened. *I had no idea she felt that way about me.*

"Shit! That shouldn't have happened! I-I don't know what came over me, I'm so sorry," she says in a rush and she can't seem to get away from me fast enough.

"Emmy! Come back! Emmy!" I call after her, but she ignores me. *Fuck my life.*

28

Brody

I spend the rest of the day rehearsing and sound checking with the rest of the boys in preparation for the show tonight, unable to stop myself from thinking of the row with Emmy, the kiss, and my argument with Raleigh. I throw myself into work, but my head is somewhere else, the day seems to go by in an instant. Before I know it, it's time for us to perform our sold out gig in front of a crowd of twenty thousand dedicated and die-hard Rancid Vengeance fans at the o2 arena in London. It's our first gig since before my accident, and as I step out onto the stage with my guitar, the mass of Rancid Vengeance fans are screaming their familiar chant that I have missed.

"Vengeance, Vengeance, Vengeance."

I feel the tumultuous hum around the venue and the atmosphere is palpable.

"Do you want to raise a little hell with us, London?" Sam growls huskily into the microphone and I smile to myself at his ability to command an audience. He's become accustomed to it over the years and it's like a second nature to him.

"*Wow!* It's so fucking good to be back after all this time! Give me a riff, Flash."

Sam turns to Jax and flashes him a wink.

"We owe these guys a show, right?" Sam laughs into the microphone and the crowd scream.

"Let me fucking hear you, London! YEEAAHHHH!"

The cheering is so loud, but the screams of adoration no longer drove me to play harder, it no longer offers me the buzz I so desperately crave. I felt numb, empty, void of feeling. As I look vacantly out into the sea of bodies who are there to support us, I feel...detached. Jax starts to play the opening riff to *'Rock Me'* and the music just sounds like a dull cacophony ringing in my ears, my hands shake violently causing me to miss a note. Jax catches my eye and mouths "*what the fuck, man!*" I shake my head, muttering my apologies and take a breath, as Sam turns to me with a furrowed brow. *What the hell is wrong with me?* This feeling is alien to me, I've never felt like this before, so disconnected and so...out of control. The screams usually spur me on to play the best I've ever played, but right now, I can't do it. I just can't pretend anymore.

So I do what I've never done before in all my fourteen years in Rancid Vengeance. I stop playing, set my guitar down in front of Lucas' drum kit and rush off stage in a blind panic. I hear someone calling my name in a concerned tone, as my breathing becomes shallow and arduous. The sweat begins to trickle its way down the back of my neck and the bile rises in my throat threatening to choke me. My pace quickens and in my quest to get the fuck away from everyone and everything, I shoulder bump into M.J.

"Brody, what the fuck man!" he calls and I focus on making my way to my destination. I swing the door of our dressing room open and run to the toilet, the door smashing into the wall with the force. I drop down to my knees and vomit violently into the bowl. I hear the door creak open and heavy footsteps enter the room. I rest my head on my forearm, suddenly drained of all energy.

"Do you want to tell me what that was about, Hart?" M.J. asks calmly, seriously this guy is so laid back he could be horizontal.

"Not now, M.J." I say feebly, all of the fight just depleted from my exhausted body.

"I can't do this anymore, M.J., I can't."

I feel my chest tighten, my stomach roiling, as I dry heave into the toilet bowl and vacate my guts once more. A few more moments pass and once I feel my stomach settle, I reach for some toilet paper to wipe my mouth and flush the toilet. I manage to get unsteadily to my feet, wash my hands and look at my reflection in the mirror. *Fuck, I look like shit.*

"Brody?" M.J. says with more than a hint of concern in his voice. I turn to face our manager expecting him to unleash his wrath, but it doesn't come. We stay silent for long minutes, as I take him in with my hand tucked casually into the pocket of my jeans. He is wearing a plain black t-shirt, a leopard print blazer with the sleeves rolled up to reveal his tanned forearms, black ripped skinny jeans, his signature rhinestone encrusted cowboy boots and his familiar grey streak running through his perfectly styled and spiked sandy brown hair.

"I'm sorry," I mutter, unable to keep the shame out of my hoarse voice, my throat burning due to the gross expulsion of my stomach lining.

"No, I'm the one who should be apologising. It was too soon, I should never have pushed for you to perform. It was an error in judgement on my behalf and I can't apologise enough, man. Your welfare and your mental health is more important than making a buck."

His voice full of apologetic sincerity. I shake my head and let out an audible sigh

"You don't understand what it's like to live inside my head, M.J. It's dark, and it's fucked up. I was selfish for just running off stage like a coward. Those boys don't deserve it. They would be better off without me. Jax outplays me at every gig and all I ever do is bring them down, I don't know how they put up with my shit for so long. I've held them back for years, I've been nothing but a burden to them," I admit truthfully, my voice full of emotion and remorse for my actions.

"It's been a wild ride, but I think it's time I hung up my guitar. My fifteen minutes are up, I'm done."

I surprise myself at my admission and M.J.'s mouth falls open at my revelation. He's about to speak again, when the dressing room door swings open. One of our roadies, Donovan almost falling through it, his long black hair hanging down his shoulders and his face drained of all colour.

"Erm...Brody, your Mrs. has gone into labour."

Fuck it all to hell.

29

Raleigh

I'm in my familiar spot next to Peyton, front row, centre where Sam and Brody can see us both. He ran off stage in a blind panic, I was set to go after him when it happened. A strong, tightening cramp in my stomach and a rush of warm fluid leaking down my leg. I turn to Peyton, my mind sprinting at a million miles an hour and I'm terrified I'm going to give birth in front of thousands of people. I'm rendered speechless and I can't move, the pain freezing me to the spot.

"Raleigh?"

Her concerned voice filters through my foggy brain and I whimper wordlessly, just loud enough for her to hear. Her eyes shift to the puddle at my feet, as her blue eyes widen and she curses softly.

"*Fuck*, ok, give me a second," she pauses for a few minutes, desperately trying to keep the panic out of her voice, as another pain rips through me. I can't help the scream that erupts from deep within me and it seems to shake her into action.

"I need to get some help. I'll be right back, I promise."

She goes to leave and I grab her hand to stop her, shaking my head vehemently.

"Please, please, Peyton, please, don't leave me," I plead and she nods, my eyes landing on hers.

"Look at me, Raleigh. It's going to be alright, babe," she reassures, pulling her phone out of her pocket. I don't hear who or what she says, as I try to breathe through another constricting cramp. A deafening scream explodes from me, as a pain I've never felt before rushes through my body like a tidal wave and my legs buckle underneath me, causing a collective gasp from the people surrounding us. I drop to the floor and blink back the tears that are pricking the back of my eyes. The fear overwhelms me, as I'm resigned to the fact I could potentially give birth at a Rancid Vengeance gig.

***

I'm not sure how much time passes, but the gig has been temporarily halted. An ambulance was called and in the hours that passed, the contractions were coming more frequent and were significantly close together. No matter how early it is, our twins arrival is imminent. I am being prepped for surgery for a cesarean section because of the placental abruption and pre-eclampsia. I have never been more terrified. Brody hasn't left my side, whispering soft words of reassurance in my ear. I am grateful I no longer have to face this alone. I shift uncomfortably, as a pain rolls through my already exhausted body and I can't help the tears that fall. Brody holds my hand in his and presses his forehead to mine.

"It's going to be alright, kitten. You're doing so well, I'm so fucking proud of you."

His voice thick with unshed tears, as he kisses me softly on the lips. I know with Brody by my side I can get through anything.

Brody

My life so far had been defined by fame, rock 'n roll, drugs, sex and women. I wasn't truly fulfilled, until I saw our twins enter the world for the first time. As soon as I saw them, everything else ceased to exist. My legs felt like they were about to buckle beneath me and my heart felt almost too big for my chest. My daughter has Raleigh's nose and my son has my dimpled chin. I look at both of them and they fill me with a sunshine I never knew existed in the world. I want to drink this moment in; both sets of hands delicate, both sets of toes perfect and I have no doubt in my mind that from now on, I am their protector and my love for them will last for as long as there is breath in me. I watch them closely in the incubator for long moments, in awe of the two tiny humans in front of us that we created.

Raleigh was awake throughout and I refused to leave her side. I had never been more proud of her. She had been taken to a private recovery room after the birth and both twins needed immediate care. Neither of us was able to hold them after they were born, as they were both a low birth weight. They were transferred straight to an incubator, but were otherwise strong and healthy.

It has been a few hours since our twins had been born, who were both yet to be named. As I sit next to her bed, I hold her hand in mine, watching as her chest rises and falls. I listen to the dull beep of hospital machines surrounding her and wonder how today took such a turn. Her eyes flicker open and land on mine, the smile she gives me causes my heart to stutter in my chest and in this moment, I couldn't love her more.

"Hey."

Her voice thick with a mixture of sleep and pure exhaustion.

"Hey beautiful," I say with a smile, my jaw aching. I haven't been able to stop smiling since they came into the world.

"Where are they?" she says with a panicked edge to her voice and I place a chaste kiss on the back of her hand.

"It's ok, they're fine. They're both in the neonatal unit being taken care of," I explain and I see her shoulders visibly sag with relief.

"Can I see them?" she asks hopefully, she looks truly exhausted.

"You need some rest, kitten," I say softly, stroking the back of her hand. She shakes her head and moves her hand away from mine.

"No, I want to see our babies," she says a little more forcefully and I nod.

I take her to the neonatal unit in a wheelchair and as soon as she sets eyes on both of them, she bursts into tears.

"You're a daddy," she sobs, flashing me a watery smile and I swear my heart skips a beat, as I grin back at her.

"And you're a mummy."

She reaches for my hand and I allow her to take comfort in the warmth of my hand in hers.

"Hey, jellybeans, this is your mummy and daddy," Raleigh says and a lump lodges itself in my throat. *I can't fucking speak, I'm too overwhelmed.*

I move closer to the incubator and stare in awe of them for a few moments, suddenly aware that during the months of Raleigh's pregnancy we hadn't discussed names. As we stand there for long moments, I start to think that it's not until you actually see your babies for the first time, you can't be entirely sure what names will suit them. Our son and daughter will have their names for all of their lives, I didn't want it to be a last minute decision. In the beginning I was terrified at the prospect of becoming a father, that I refused to even acknowledge it. After the accident, it gave me time to come to terms with it, but even then it didn't seem real. I continue to watch them, swallowing hard, before I speak.

"Bowie Hendrix Hart," I whisper so softly, I'm not sure if she heard me. Raleigh squeezes my hand and I wrap my arm around her.

"I like it. Hello Bowie Hendrix Hart," she says softly, her voice full of awe.

"Azalea Iris Hart," she speaks again and I beam. *Welcome to the world Bowie Hendrix Hart and Azalea Iris Hart.*

30

Brody

After Raleigh practically forced me to leave the hospital in the early hours of the morning, I wake with a start, do my morning workout and take a shower. I'm sitting at the kitchen island with my morning coffee, eating cereal and scrolling through the news on my iPad, when something catches my eye.

Lorna Lavelle

"I hope to arrive at my death, late, in love and a little drunk – Atticus"

A funeral service will be held at 10am on Thursday 15th January at St Nicholas' Church, Chiswick.

In lieu of flowers, donations to Help For Heroes will be greatly received.

I look at the clock on the wall, I still have time before the funeral begins. I have to say goodbye to Lorna. My heart slams against my rib cage at the thought and it's like my heart breaks all over again, the pain threatening to suffocate me where I sit. It still doesn't seem real. I still can't wrap my head around the fact that she's gone and I'm never going to see her again.

***

As I arrive at the church, I come to the stark realisation that none of these people knew I was seeing Lorna. I didn't know her family, I didn't know her friends, or work colleagues. I knew nothing about her beyond the sex and the snippets of information she would feed me when she was feeling particularly chatty. My heart starts its familiar pound in my chest, as I stand awkwardly off to the side with my hand tucked in the pocket of my suit trousers. I approach the entrance and hear the dull cacophony of chatter, suddenly feeling more than a little self conscious and out of place. *I should never have come here, why the fuck did I come here?* I'm about to turn and walk away, when a middle aged woman approaches me calmly and cautiously. She has the skin the colour of café au lait, she reminds me so much of Lorna. She is wearing a black sheath dress, black heels and her black hair in tight curls, peppered with silver, is piled on top of her head. She comes to a stop in front of me, regarding me intently and I feel like my expensive tie is fucking strangling me. I don't wear suits, I'm more of jeans and t-shirt type of man, I feel so far out of my comfort zone wearing my uber expensive Ralph Lauren suit, expertly tailored to my body type.

"Tessa Reed, her mum," she offers me her hand and I take it. I'm about to introduce myself and she smiles, giving me a nonchalant wave of her hand.

"I know who you are, child. You were there weren't you?"

Her soft voice filled with such emotion and I nod, unable to find the right words. *What do you say to someone whose kid was murdered?*

"Come and find me afterwards, we'll talk," she states matter-of-factly and turns to walk away. *Fuck me, this is going to be a long morning.*

I make my way into the church and slip in at the back, not wanting to be the centre of attention. The sound of *Alter Bridge Watch Over You* fills the church. I watch as three men and young woman escort a white casket down the centre aisle, I don't register what they look like. I try desperately to quell the tears that are burning behind my eyes. The priest gives a brief opening sermon and as I listen intently to the people who knew Lorna the best, I realise I never really knew her at all. The kind-hearted, free-spirited woman they speak about, she's a stranger to me. With that thought, the fortress that has been holding my tears at bay abruptly gives way under the weight. The tears falling freely down my cheeks and I swipe them away, feeling more and more like a fraud with each moment that passes. *I have no right to be here.*

I manage to make it to the end, and by the time everyone is filing out of the church, turning their eyes to me, I feel emotionally exhausted. All I want to do is fall face first into a bag of cocaine and drown in the bottom of a vodka bottle. As we move from the church to the graveside, we gather around Lorna's final resting place.

After the burial, people are gathered in groups mindlessly chattering and others are dispersing. I stand over her grave for long moments, the grief coming in large tsunami like waves. I wanted to remember the happy times, but all I can remember is her silently pleading with me to save her. The tears flow hot and endless down my cheeks, as I cast my eyes down to the freshly dug soil, I want to sink to my knees and howl at the sky at how unfair life is.

"I'm so fucking sorry, L."

Emotional pain flows from my every pore, my face wet with tears, my grief threatening my composure and my sobriety. I feel a warm arm slide around my waist and pull me into a hug.

"It's ok, dear boy," Tessa says softly and I swipe the tears away with the sleeve of my suit jacket.

"Did you kill my beautiful girl?" she asks unexpectedly and matter-of-factly. I shake my head.

"No," I reply simply and resolutely, as she nods in approval.

"Did you love her?"

I squeeze my eyes shut briefly and turn to look into her dark, grief stricken eyes.

"Yes, I did," I whisper softly and honestly. In my own way, no matter how much I might have tried to deny it, I loved her.

"Did you kill that man for murdering her?" she spits, as if it's poison and I nod; a brief flash of the knife slashing across her throat barrels its way through my mind.

"Did he suffer?" she asks, her voice full of hatred.

"Yes," I answer, as a satisfied smile washes over her kind features and in that moment, I find absolution standing over the grave of Lorna Lavelle.

31

***

Raleigh

The weeks that followed were a blur of hospital visits and a whirlwind of emotions. Brody never left my side. He was a source of comfort and I had come to rely on his support. I was released from hospital after five days, but recovery was going to be a slow process. The twins were now out of the neonatal unit and we bought them home into their newly decorated nursery. Brody had resumed Rancid Vengeance's UK tour, I had begun reading through some new movie scripts and I had a start date to start shooting the second film in Damien Valentine's trilogy, titled *'Rock Me Harder.'* I was reprising my role as Stevie Lynn and I couldn't wait to begin. Brody and I couldn't have been happier, we were closer than ever and I don't know how I would have gotten through the past few weeks without him.

Today was a rare day off for him and I woke to the flick of his tongue on my sensitive clit. We hadn't had sex since before the twins were born and I was still recovering from the c-section.

"Mmmm."

I hum sleepily. It was still dark outside and as I uncover his head, his eyes sparkled wickedly. His hair is perfectly sleep mussed and I run my fingers through the softness, tugging it gently.

"Good morning, kitten."

He licks his lips, as he resumes his assault on my engorged nub. My pulse is racing at the feel of tongue grazing against my wet flesh.

"Oh fuck, Brody, that feels so good," I moan, throwing my head back against the pillow, every nerve in my body tuned to Brody Hart.

"I've got you. I'll take care of you, kitten."

He breathes against my clitoris and as he swipes his split tongue up my slick folds, I cry out in pure unadulterated pleasure and tug his hair a little harder than before.

"Fucking savage!" he murmurs against me, continuing his experts laps, as he thrusts his tongue up inside me.

"BRODY! OH GOD!" I yell, writhing beneath him and bunching the sheets in my fists.

"BRODY! OH BRODY! OH FUCK! BRODY!"

He looks up at me from beneath the covers and I desperately mewl his name.

"What do you want, kitten? Tell me, what you want me to do." he says with an assertive edge to his voice.

"I want you to make me come! Please, I need you to make me come," I pant out feverishly, teetering on the precipice of my pending release. I grind my pussy against the stubble on his chin and he chuckles softly against me, as I cry out at the delicious torture. The throbbing between my thighs makes my body light up from the inside out, as my pussy floods with pure want. With a few more expert swipes of his tongue, the first hard tremor of my orgasm hits me like a lightning bolt. My breath coming out in sharp, urgent gasps, as I cry out his name, clenching his head between my thighs.

"Brody! Oh Brody! Brody! I'm coming! Oh God!"

He milks every ounce of my release from me, leaving me spent on the pillow.

"My work here is done," he smiles, peeling the covers away to reveal his perfectly sculpted body. He reminds me of David by Michaelangelo; all effortlessly cut, clean lines, he oozes sex appeal from head to toe. I lick my lips at the sight of him and he rolls his eyes.

"Sometimes I only think you want me for my body!" he jokes and we both laugh. I turn over onto my side and snuggle back down.

"What time is it?" I ask, suddenly feeling exhausted. He kisses me softly on the lips, as he gets out of bed.

"It's still early, go back to sleep. I'm going for a run, then I'm going to do my morning workout."

I grab his hand. Since he's been back on the road, like clockwork he gets up at five a.m., he sees to the twins, goes for his morning run, he does three hours in the gym then sets about his daily routine.

"But wouldn't you rather I be your morning workout?" I attempt to sound seductive and flutter my eyelashes at him.

"I'd love nothing more, kitten, but you're still recovering."

Bless him, he's so sweet and considerate, but it doesn't stop me wanting him to ravish me like I want him to.

"Soon," he mouths with a wink.

"The baby monitor is on, but I'll sort the twins before I go and you can get some more sleep."

He tucks me back under the duvet and kisses my forehead.

"Love you," he whispers and before the door has even closed, I'm a slave to sleep once more.

Brody

It's still dark, as I gently open the door to the twins' nursery, careful not to wake them. Both sets of tiny toes peeking from the blanket they share. Bowie's arms are raised above his head and I slide my finger into his open hand, watching as they curl around it, as he continues to sleep. Azalea's tiny fists are clenched and her legs are bent at the knees. Both of them growing every day and as I watch them both in slumber, it robs me of breath. I want to drink in these precious moments. I never realised that being a parent would change me, until I held both of them in my arms for the first time. I never had a solid family unit when I was growing up. I never had a strong patriarchal father figure in my childhood, until I met Lenny in adulthood. My mother robbed me of a relationship with my father from a young age. I never even knew his name and the resentment I had towards her ran deep. I was surrounded by broken relationships and shattered bonds throughout my life. When Raleigh told me she was pregnant, I wanted to hide away from the responsibility. I was terrified I would infect any children that had my blood running through their veins with the very same poison I was subjected to. I pull my finger from Bowie's grip and kiss them both gently on top of their heads.

"I promise both of you, that I will never leave you. I'll teach you both that you're worthy of respect and I'll help you navigate the big, wide world. I promise to get messy with you; we'll build sandcastles, blanket forts, I'll jump in the leaves with you and dance in the rain with you. I'll always listen to your joys, your fears and your secrets. I promise to believe in you and love you wholeheartedly, whatever or whoever you decide to become. I promise you that I'll become a better man and a better role model for both of you. I'll make you proud to call me your daddy," I say softly, my voice cracking with emotion, as I turn and silently leave the room.

***

The frosty chill of the wintry air hits me as soon as I step outside and it seems to awaken my senses almost instantly. The dark inky sky is misty and overcast with thick clouds. The branches of the trees are laced with ice crystals and the chilly wind biting at my cheeks. The snow crunches beneath my feet, as I begin my morning stretches on the gravel driveway. It is part of my morning routine that keeps my body functioning and my demons caged. I finish my stretches and put my Apple AirPods in and set my running playlist on my phone to shuffle, starting the day off with *Train by 3 Doors Down*. I begin with a gentle jog around the perimeter of all five looming mansions that make up Vengeance Estates. All were modern concrete buildings with tall glass windows that gave panoramic views across the acres of lush greenery and woodland, which seemed to stretch for miles.

I enjoy the peace that running brings. It clears my mind, making me appreciate the simple things in life and bringing a fresh outlook. I breathe in the cool, crisp morning air into my lungs, making me grateful to be alive. The pounding beat of my music pushes me on and as soon as I hit my stride, I am pounding the snow covered dirt trail which leads into the dense woodland, at a punishing pace. I run for what seems like ages, my calf muscles deliciously sore. I stop briefly to catch my breath and bounce from one foot to the other. I look up to see Sam jogging towards me and I pull my earbud out, pausing my music.

"Morning," he rasps and I nod my greeting.

"Didn't fancy my riveting company this morning?" he says wryly and I chuckle softly.

"It's not like that, man, I've got a lot on my mind," I explain, as Sam cocks his pierced eyebrow and I roll my eyes.

"Is this where you start trying to analyse me? Newsflash, you're in the wrong job, Newbolt!" I joke and we both laugh, Sam adjusting his black beanie hat.

"Wanna talk about it?" he asks and I realise how grateful I am to have him in my life. Sam is my best friend and for years our friendship was toxic. He was my partner in crime, but we led each other down a dark path and we weren't good for each other. J.D. encouraged it, but everyone else saw it for what it was; two fucked up guys, barely adults, who had been thrust into the spotlight. We bought the absolute worst out in each other and if we had carried on down that path, we both would have been dead before we were thirty-five. I was the reason Sam ended up in rehab all those years ago. I almost destroyed him and I'll never be able to apologise enough. After he met Peyton, it was different. He gave up that lifestyle for her and I felt like I'd lost my wingman. It took a lot of talking, raised voices and a few tears, but we totally rebuilt our friendship and the bond between us couldn't be stronger.

I put my hands on my head and puff out a tired breath, my breath visible in front of me, as I look up to the sky.

"The night I walked off stage and Raleigh gave birth, I told M.J. I wanted to hang up my guitar," I confess and Sam nods regarding me carefully, his face impassive and void of shock. I feel the need to elaborate.

"I'm not like you. I've never shown the same dedication. I've never lived and breathed Rancid Vengeance and I always knew there was an expiry date. It wasn't until I held my babies in my arms for the first time, that I realised there's more to life than the fame. It's been fourteen fucking years, Sam, don't you ever get tired of it?"

Sam cocks his head thoughtfully, before he answers.

"All the fucking time! But I go out on that stage and it makes all those sacrifices worth it. We've sacrificed so much over the years. We've been to hell and back, don't you think I get that? Do you think you're the first person to feel that way? After I lost Peyton, I could quite happily have given it all up, my career and everything that came with it. I didn't give a shit about the fame, the money, the band, the music... none of it mattered, because I'd lost the one thing that meant more than any of it. She was the reason I got up there and performed. If it wasn't for her, I'd have given it all up a long time ago. When I got her back, she restored my love of performing again and I owe it to you guys and the fans to give them a good fucking show. I want them to come away from a gig and feel like they've had their money's worth. What I'm saying is, you're an amazing guitarist, man. Don't make any decisions yet. You need to find your passion for the music again. Take as long as you need, but I don't want you to make any irrational decisions that you're going to regret. I'm here if you ever need to talk."

I am grateful for Sam's perspective and over the years, we have come to a mutual understanding. He's there for me and I'm there for him to listen, to offer advice, or just a shoulder to cry on.

"Thanks, mate, I needed to hear that. I've spent so long in my head, going over and over it, and constantly coming up with the same conclusion. I just needed another perspective."

He slaps me on the shoulder, halting our conversation and swiftly changing the subject.

"Now, are we going to finish our run, because it's fucking freezing!"

We both laugh, continuing with our morning run and feeling a little more optimistic about the future.

32

Raleigh

As I lay back in bed, I stare up at the ceiling. I have been restless since Brody went for his morning run and I feel oddly horny. My thoughts drift to Brody licking me to orgasm just over an hour ago. I bite my lip at the thought of his hands caressing my skin and roaming gently over my body; the way he takes charge and dominates, the way he seductively whispers dirty things in my ear in that smooth voice of his, the way his hard, tattooed chest presses into mine. I bite my lip, cupping my still tender, swollen breasts in my hands and knead them, imagining they are Brody's hands. I pinch my nipples between my thumbs and forefingers and tweak them, causing me to gasp aloud at the pleasure pain. I slowly move my one hand down my abdomen and down to my pussy. I press one finger into my slit and surprise myself at how slick I am. I gently rub and tease my wet folds, as I continue to play with my sensitive, now erect nipple with my other hand, moaning softly. Unexpectedly, an idea forms in my brain and I stop what I am doing, in order to set my plan into action.

***

After breastfeeding the twins, changing their nappies and settling them back down for a few more hours, my plan was in motion. I quickly showered, shaved, moisturised, styled my hair, put on make-up and changed into the sexiest underwear I own. A black velvet and lace balconette bra with Swarovski crystals joining the middle and matching low rise thongs, which sit on my hips. I have a horizontal scar around twenty centimetres across above my pubic bone from the cesarean section. It has healed nicely and the doctors are pleased with my progress over the past seven weeks. I have been self conscious about being naked in front of Brody since the birth of the twins, but I feel ready to resume our sexual activities. I put on a pair of sky high heels and head down the stairs. I put the finishing touches to my make-up in the mirror and I am pleased with my smoky, sultry look. I put on some red lipstick and fluff my hair, as I hear the door close.

He is damp with sweat from his run and as he looks up and his mouth drops open when he catches sight of me. I walk wordlessly towards him, my heels clicking across the marbled floor of the entrance hallway. His eyes travel from my face to my full breasts and his teeth sink into his bottom lip. With every step forward I take, he takes a step back, until he collides with the door. I press my breasts to his solid chest and start to work my way down his body, until I am on my knees, face to face with his crotch. I yank his shorts down in one swift movement, freeing his already solid erection.

"Mmmm," I hum my appreciation.

"*Ah, fuck,* kitten, what are you doing to me?" he grinds out huskily. His eyes are hooded with lust, as they lock with mine and I shake my head.

"Please, let me take care of you, Brody. Let me do this for you."

I fist his cock in an up and down motion and take his length deep into my throat. His head hits the door with a thud, as he growls low in his throat. I swipe my tongue up and down his tattooed cock, taking him as deep as I can. I run my tongue over the bell-shaped head, flicking and taking his piercing between my teeth.

"FUUUUCCCKKKK!" he yells, as he presses the back of my head into his pelvis, careful not to make me gag. I take him further into my mouth, bobbing my head up and down, lapping and sucking as I go. I can feel his cock twitch with his pending release, as I cup his heavy sacs in my hand. I look up at him, his thrown back in pure unadulterated ecstasy.

"*Oh Fuck!* Raleigh, that feels so fucking good!"

I keep sucking and open my throat, taking him as far into my mouth as I can manage.

"*Shit! Fuck! Bollocks!* I'm going to come, kitten. *Jesus fucking Christ!*"

I continue sucking as he spurts his seed into my mouth, yelling and jerking, as he finds his release. He squeezes his eyes shut, shuddering from his orgasm.

I swallow every last drop and lick my lips, a satisfied grin spreads across my face. He opens his eyes and the look of awe on his face almost knocks me on my arse.

"You never fail to amaze me, kitten. *Fuck,* you look gorgeous," he offers me his hand and helps me to my feet, as I stand in front of him, exposed and feeling self-conscious at his close scrutiny. I shift my gaze to the floor and wrap my arms around myself protectively, second guessing my sexual prowess. He shakes his head, his brow furrowing and his eyes narrowing, tipping my chin up to face him.

"Don't ever fucking hide your body from me, Raleigh. You've given me the most precious gift of all, our children. Don't ever think I don't want you and never think that I don't find you attractive."

That's all the encouragement I need, as I tackle him again, my lips landing on his. Our kiss has a raw intensity, our tongues duelling, as I fight to peel his damp t-shirt away from his body so he is completely naked. He pulls briefly away from our kiss, as he discards his t-shirt and kicks his trainers off. The sight of him completely exposed and nude renders me a puddle at his feet.

"Let's take this to the bedroom, kitten," he commands, as he leads me up the stairs. We enter the bedroom and Brody stands close enough for me the feel his warm breath on my cheek. He stops in front of the full-length, gothic style mirror and stands behind me, his arms snaking around my midriff, careful to avoid my scar. In one gentle tug, our skin touches and it's like electricity pulsing between us. I feel him trace slow gentle lines across my neck and shoulder blades, placing tender kisses from one side to the other. He spends long moments caressing every inch of my body and as I look up, his eyes meet mine in the mirror.

"Look how beautiful you are. See what I see," he whispers softly, as he moves his hand slowly into my thong, pushing his long finger inside me. My head falls back onto his shoulder, as I let out a long satisfied moan of pleasure, his other hand moving up to rest on my throat. His musky scent mixed with sweat intoxicating me, as I breathe him in.

"I need your eyes, kitten. Look. Watch how you respond to me and watch me pleasure you."

I open my eyes and watch his hand move skillfully beneath the material of my thong, as he thoroughly finger fucks me. There is something erotic about watching myself being pleasured, my slow, measured breathing changing to sharp pants, my face contorted with pleasure. The visual sight of us in the mirror awakens something inside me, seeing myself from the same perspective as Brody. It's a turn on, pressing all of my hot buttons, as his fingers continue their assault, moving deep within my slick channel.

"Don't take those eyes off me, kitten, don't you fucking dare," he warns, as he introduces another finger.

"OH GOD! BRODY! BRODY! FUCKKKK!"

His eyes find mine and I feel like I am watching my very own porn movie.

"*Fuck*, you're soaked. Is this turning you on? Does this make you wet for me?" he asks. I nod and I can't tear my eyes away from him fingering me. I've never been this turned on.

"Watch yourself fall apart. Come for me, Raleigh, come now," he commands. His grip on my throat tightens a little and with one swift movement of his fingers, my orgasm detonates. My mind feels like it is short-circuiting, as I scream out. Brody is drawing every ounce of pleasure from my body. As I come back down to earth after finding my release, my eyes find his and he flashes me a boyish grin. It makes me want him again. I turn around and rest my hands on his hard, damp chest, leading him gently in the direction of the bed. The back of his thighs collide with the softness of the mattress, as I push him down and move to straddle him.

"Mmm, someone's feeling frisky! Not that I'm complaining!" he laughs, and I put my finger to his lips.

"Shhh, this time I'm in control. So you be a good boy and I'll take care of you. I'm going to drive you crazy, take you right to the edge, stop, then do it all over again until you beg me to finish it. Even then, I won't, I'm going to do every wicked thing to you, until your mind and your body explode," I purr seductively, as I move my thong to the side and direct his cock into already soaking wet pussy. I'm drunk on lust and I'm so turned on, I can't think straight. There's something about him that lights me up from the inside and as I drop down onto his steel erection, he roars out loud. I look down at him, his eyes searching mine, as his large hands grip my waist.

"God, how did I get so fucking lucky? You're so beautiful."

His voice is strained, as I lift myself up and drop back down on his cock, his piercing rubbing my inner walls in just the right way.

"Do you like that, baby?" I moan softly.

"OH FUCK! YES! YES!" he yells, as I increase the pace, desperate to make this moment last. He grits his teeth, as I build up a punishing momentum, my breasts bouncing with each measured drive.

"That's it, oh God!" I cry out, as I move the cup of my bra down and take my nipple between my thumb and forefinger. In one quick movement, he rolls us so he's on top and I'm spread beneath him. He flashes me a cheeky wink and in a split second every nerve in my body is tuned to Brody Hart's frequency. My brain electrified as he leans down and presses his hard, toned body into mine. I wrap my leg around his lean waist and dig the heel of my shoe in the soft flesh of his arse. He curses softly as he presses his lips to my neck, igniting a fire inside me that had lay dormant. I am writhing underneath him as he strokes every part of me, flesh on flesh. He establishes a rhythm and I meet him thrust for thrust, feeling his piercing rub my g-spot, as he pounds me into the mattress.

"Wrap those fucking legs around me, kitten," he grunts, driving me higher and higher towards my orgasm. I wrap both of my legs around his waist and dig both of my heels into his arse. He snarls like a man possessed.

"BRODY!"

He impales me so deeply, I feel his cock crash against my cervix.

"OH FUCK! I'M CLOSE! I'M SO CLOSE!"

He quickens his pace.

"Come for me. I want you to come all over my hard cock!" he demands, his face covered in a thin sheen of sweat.

"OH GOD! PLEASE DON'T STOP! DON'T YOU DARE FUCKING STOP!" I plead desperately, his strokes becoming more frantic with each expert swivel of his hips. That's all it takes to tip us both over the edge, sinking my nails into his thick, tattooed biceps.

"OH FUCK! BRODY! I'M COMING! FUUUUCCKKKK! I'M COMING!"

I let out a primal, animalistic scream, as my sex ripples and erupts around his pulsating shaft. His orgasm is right behind mine, as he growls out his climax.

"JESUS FUCKING CHRIST! I'M COMING!"

I feel him pump his hot seed inside me, as I milk every last drop of his release from him. He stills and I go lax beneath him, waiting for my breathing to return to normal before I speak.

"Wow!"

I feel his shoulders shake with laughter and I wince as he pulls out of me, the warmth of his semen inside me reminds me that he didn't use a condom. I shake that thought away, as he collapses on the bed next to me, pulling me into his side and wrapping me in his arms. I rest my head on his pec, relishing the heat of his body against me.

"Well, that was definitely a great way to start the day, kitten," he chuckles softly, as he presses a kiss to my forehead, stroking my hair.

"We should start our days like that more often."

I look up at him and in that moment, I couldn't be more in love with him.

33

Brody

I'm lying in bed naked, with my hands behind my head, staring up at the ceiling after our marathon early morning love making session. The sound of both of the twins screaming their lungs out on the baby monitor startles me into action, as I swing my legs out of bed and go to pull on a pair of boxer shorts.

"I've got them, babe," I hear Raleigh call. I head in search of her and stand in the doorway of the nursery observing her for a few moments. She is unaware of my presence and she is sitting in the grey cuddle chair in the corner with both twins in her arms, breastfeeding. I am in complete awe of the way her mothering instinct pushed her to persevere after the first time and the way she handles the two of them as if they are made of glass.

"Mummy's here," she whispers tenderly, as I continue to watch her.

"Shhh, shhh, mummy's got you, I'm here," she coos softly, as she rocks them back and forth. I couldn't be more in love with her if I tried. She challenges me every day and I need her more than the bag of cocaine I have hidden underneath the floorboard in my studio. I love her like I'd never loved anyone before. It makes my stomach fill with the butterflies Emmy was so obsessed with and I understand now why it's so important to her. I lean against the door frame and as she looks up, her eyes lock with mine.

"Hey handsome."

The smile she gives me makes my knees weak and my heart rate quicken.

"Hey gorgeous," I smile warmly, as I move further into the nursery.

"You've never looked more beautiful," I tell her honestly, and she chuckles softly.

"I feel like a fucking cow!"

I laugh at her, her eyes darkening wickedly.

"Would you think I was greedy if I said I wanted you again?" she admits, sinking her teeth into her bottom lip and I shake my head.

"Not at all," I state, as I pull my boxer shorts down and step out of them. I turn my back to walk out of the room, flashing her a roguish wink over my shoulder.

"You've already made me miss my morning workout, so meet me in the shower in ten minutes, kitten."

My voice is playful and full of promise. I pad across the floor and into the bathroom, flipping on the shower awaiting all of the tempting things to come.

***

Taking a shower after my morning workout is one of the pleasures of my day. I love the sting of the hot water, as I stand under the spray. It awakens me in a way that nothing else can. The water cascades down my rippling abs and a slight breeze causes the hairs on the back of my neck stand on end and I instantly know she's there. I can feel her eyes on me. I run my hands through my wet hair and open my eyes just in time to see her step out of the sexy black lingerie she teased me with earlier and joins me in the walk-in shower. I move to the side to accommodate her, as the rivulets of water hit her rocking body. Since she has given birth, her breasts are larger and fuller than they were before, her waist is a little thicker, but I couldn't possibly want her more. The water glistens and trickles over her naked breasts and over her curves, it takes everything I have not to slam her against the wall and take her like I need to. Wordlessly, she moves closer to me and grazes her soft, plump lips against mine and what starts out as an innocent kiss, turns into instant hunger. My arms snake around her, as I press her back against the cool tiled wall, our lips melting into one and her tongue seeking out mine. She sucks on my bottom lip and a moan escapes from deep within my throat.

My cock thickens between us and I'm so fucking hard, it's painful. I lean down and seal my mouth over her left breast, lavishing it with the attention it deserves. She moans instantly and all of a sudden, it's a mess of limbs and lips... we can't seem to get enough of each other. I part her legs with one of my hands and slide it between her thighs, placing my thumb on her sweet spot, and using my index fingers to lightly trace the outside of her pussy lips. She starts panting and moaning desperately, the sound echoing around the shower cubicle, as my fingers continue their journey across her slick folds. She crashes her lips to mine once again, the kiss wet, hot and urgent, water running down both of our faces. I push two fingers deep inside her and she cries out.

"OH GOD! BRODY!"

I pull my fingers free from her and she whimpers at the loss of contact.

"I'll take care of you, kitten. Hands on the wall."

She places her hands on the tiled wall, bracing herself so she is bent over in front of me, her delectable arse presented to me on a silver platter.

"Bend your knees," I command and she does as she is bid. I don't give her time to adjust to the position, as I impale her on my waiting arousal. She screams as I penetrate her deep, moving my hand around and playing with her clitoris, the hot water trickling and cascading between us.

"OH GOD! YOU FEEL LIKE FUCKING HEAVEN AROUND MY COCK!"

Her breath hitches, as I continue to possess and entice every inch of her beautiful body. She pushes back to meet my urgent thrusts with her hands braced on the shower wall, moaning softly. I feel the familiar ripples of pleasure sparking between us, as I quicken my pace with one hand on her hip and the other one reaching down to tease her aching cleft.

"Brody, I need to come again. I need you to make me come!" she pleads almost desperately, as she pushes back against me. I move my hand from her hip and bring my hand down on her right bum cheek. She moans aloud, feel her pussy flood around my throbbing member and my senses are in total overdrive, my mind blanking as the pleasure washes over me. I move my hand back around and skate my finger through her wetness, teasing her for a few seconds, as she writhes and bucks loudly against me.

"Shhh, I've got you, kitten."

My thrusts were coming hard and fast, she squeezes her inner muscles around my cock.

"Fuck! You're close, I can feel you gripping my cock, that feels so good!" I grunt.

"Brody! I need you to fuck me, HARD! I need you to make me come!" she demands, as I increase my feverish, deep drives into her, fucking her hard, almost aggressively. I feel the slap of my balls against her, as I feel her body convulse, screaming out her orgasm.

"BRODY! BRODY! I'M COMING! I'M COMING! OH GOD!"

My body tenses as my orgasm is right behind hers. I grip her hips harshly, finding my release.

"RALEIGH! FUUUCCCKKK! I'M GONNA COME!"

My hot seed spurts inside her, causing a second orgasm to detonate from deep within her. She cries out, as she shudders with tiny aftershocks. We come down from our orgasms, the shower cubicle silent except for our breathless pants and the sound of the water raining down on both of us. I pull out of her and she straightens, tackling me to the wall and angling my face to hers until our lips lock. The caress of her lips softer, as I move her wet hair from her face, leaning over her to grab the natural sponge. I pour Pineapple and Papaya shower gel onto it and I turn her, so I can wash her down, starting at her neck, across her collarbone and down between the valley of her breasts. She arches her back towards me and I scrub down her abdomen, placing a kiss on her c-section scar and she shivers, letting out a small moan of contentment. I move down soaping both of her legs, down to her feet and across her back, down to the fleshy globes of her pert bum. She takes the sponge from me when I'm done, as she starts to wash me, across my chest, shoulders and my tattooed torso. She places a kiss on my scar from the stab wound and I smile softly at her reverence. She turns me around washing my back, over my bum and down each leg in turn. I was exercising restraint, but the way her hands deliberately brush every part of my body, it makes me want her again. I have a photoshoot with the band I need to get to and I know I'm already going to be late, but I can't seem to help myself.

She seems to read my mind, as she sinks down to her knees, grabbing the base of my dick and guiding it into her mouth. A moan escapes my lips, as I brace myself against the wall, leaning my head back and closing my eyes, allowing myself to focus on the sensation of her wet mouth on me. She moves her hand down between her thighs and pushes a finger inside herself, as she takes her tongue and traces from the base to the tip of my cock, then uses her tongue to draw circles around the head, flicking my piercing as she goes. I curse low in my throat, as her lips form a tight seal around the head. She slowly sucks, moving her head back and forth, taking me deeper with each bob of her head. My cock swells and I feel the tip hit the back of her throat, causing her eyes to water. She continues to work her mouth up and down my shaft, as she fucks herself with her fingers, moaning against me, causing the vibrations to drive me closer to blowing my load.

"OH FUCK, DON'T STOP, DON'T STOP, I'M GONNA COME. SHIT! I'M GONNA' COME!"

I feel my legs start to shake and my dick start to tense and swell within the confines of her mouth. She leans her head back, her mouth open and her tongue out, before my seed spills all over her chin and drips down her neck onto her chest, as she pleasures herself to climax.

"FUCCCKKKKK!"

I look down at her.

"I didn't hurt you, did I?" I ask, and she smiles up at me, shaking her head.

"I love being able to do that and watching you lose control like that."

I help her to her feet, pulling her into my wet chest, our lips colliding and in perfect sync with each other. In that moment, with her body pressed against mine, I was finally home.

34

Brody

A strategically placed hand and a guitar are all that is going to be between my cock and a closed set full of onlookers. Rancid Vengeance and some of rock's finest bands, have all come together to do a naked charity calendar shoot to raise awareness of Men's Mental Health. Sam is an ambassador and patron of the charity which is a cause close to his and all of our hearts. Sam's battled mental health ever since we formed Rancid Vengeance all of those years ago and has since been diagnosed with bi-polar disorder. When we were approached about posing nude, reluctant as we were, we all agreed wholeheartedly.

Currently, my body is in the best shape it's been in for a long time and my shoulders have gotten broad from working out like a beast. I've been doing five a.m morning runs with Sam and then gruelling four hour workouts, all before breakfast. Working out has become part of my daily routine and it helps to calm the demons that roam freely in my mind.

"Mr. Hart, Max is ready for you on set now."

A nervous young woman enters the dressing room, she is wearing a red and black striped t-shirt, black combat trousers, New Rock boots and black-rimmed glasses, her hair in pigtails. I flash her a wink and reassuring grin. I brush her arm and she literally swoons on the spot. *Bless her heart.*

"Thanks, sweetheart. No need for formalities, please, call me Brody."

She returns my smile and nods, as I get up from my chair and follow her down the hallway to the open plan studio, wearing a navy-blue robe. The rest of the boys are already there, I was late because of my marathon sex session with my insatiable temptress and by the time I finally arrived, I was last in hair and make-up. They all give me a rowdy round of applause, as they catch sight of me and I bow elaborately.

Max Harper, Peyton's dad, is the photographer on this shoot. And to be honest, I'm somewhat relieved it's someone that we know and respect. Max is at the top of his game, he's been in the industry for over forty years and he's been part of some of the most famous ad campaigns and some of the most prestigious photo shoots of the last four decades. He's a legend and his work is renowned all over the world.

"Brody! Good to see you, mate! You're looking well!" he shakes my hand with a firm grip, and I greet him equally as enthusiastically.

"Max, good to see you too. It's been a while!"

He smiles warmly, as he looks down at his camera on the tripod.

"That is has. How are the twins doing?"

He looks up and I nod, smiling fondly, as I think of my son and daughter. I still can't believe I'm a dad.

"They're great, really great thanks. Growing every day, keeping us up all night, but that's kids for you."

Max looks at me sympathetically, and by the look on his face, he just gets it. He's a father to Peyton, Dexter, and Eden, so he knows what being a parent entails.

"Don't ever be afraid to ask for help, son. Marnie looks after our Freddie and Zachary and she's recently started looking after Thea, you should consider her, she's brilliant. I'm not just saying that because she's Dexter's girlfriend! Dex calls her the child whisperer!"

We both laugh. Marnie Breckenridge is Peyton's brother Dexter's girlfriend. He lost his fiancee Grace in the wedding massacre in Vegas three years ago. He took some time off his job as a police officer to grieve the loss of the woman he loved and went travelling for a year. He met Marnie on a beach in Bali where she was travelling too and they have been together for a year. She is a part-time Instagram influencer with over a quarter of a million followers and a part-time nanny. She looks after Freddie and Zachary while Peyton is at work and when she comes on tour with us.

"I'll consider it. Thanks Max, appreciate the advice."

He slaps me on the back, as he points the light meter at me, the light flashes and he glances down at the reading. He presses a few buttons on his camera and fires off a few test shots, causing the model lamps to flash in unison, temporarily blinding me.

"Anytime, son, anytime. You're all welcome at mine and Sophia's. It's quiet now all of the kids have flown the nest so it would be nice to have some life back in the place," he says with a melancholy tone. I smile at his invitation, as he moves behind his camera and I take a breath, preparing for my close up.

"Can you lift your chin slightly for me, Brody?" Max instructs and I do as I'm bid, while trying to remain professional.

"Perfect!"

He lifts his hand up in an '*ok*' sign, as he resumes the 'click, click' of the shutter.

Photographs capture precious moments. They depict some of my best memories and they are snapshots of days gone by and document times in my life, which may otherwise be lost to the past. The power of a picture is to reveal the truth in one single image. They visually show pure joy, love and real happiness. The traditional flair of taking a photograph with a camera seems to be a dying art these days since almost everyone has become a photographer. It is the age of almost everyone taking selfies with their smartphones and posting them on Facebook and Instagram.

I have always been very self-conscious in front of the camera and photos of me have never looked natural. They looked forced and some look like I'm straining for a shit. I don't think I've ever taken a serious photograph without me pulling a stupid face, or sticking my tongue out. On the rare occasion when someone has managed to capture an image of me smiling and looking natural, I hang it on the wall in my house for all to see. There aren't many photos of me as a child because I hated having my picture taken. Hell, even now I'm not fond of it. Max has done a number of photoshoots with us over the years and after all this time, he has grown used to our camaraderie and our laid back way of working, both privately and professionally.

I continue to pose for the camera with my hands strategically placed. Max is calling instructions and words of encouragement from behind the lens, when I hear whispering and raucous laughter getting closer. I look up to see Jax running towards me, stark bollock naked, he hovers over me and simulates sex with me, thrusting his hips forward. I can't help the bark of laughter that escapes from deep within my throat.

"WOOOO! RIDE 'EM COWBOY! OH BRODY! OH GOD BRODY! YOU'RE SUCH A STUD! YOU'RE THE BEST I'VE EVER HAD!" he mocks sarcastically in a high pitched voice. Max moves from behind his camera and desperately tries to stifle a smirk.

"Boys! Come on, now, focus!"

He claps his hands once, as Jax resumes the thrusting of his hips, as he throws his head back and flicks his long blonde hair over his shoulder.

"OH GOD! I'M GONNA COME! OH! OH!" he moans long and loud, as I feel a cool wetness land on my cheek. I'm about to headbutt the prick, when I look up from my position on the black leather chaise lounge and see Lucas trickling water on me, laughing wildly. Max stands with his hands on his lips and sighs exasperated.

"Boys! *Jesus Christ!* You're like a bunch of bloody kids!"

Jax gets to his feet, bows dramatically and flashes me a cheeky wink. He turns his back to me and shows me his arse. I reach over and slap his bum cheek and he looks over his shoulder at me, pouting.

"You're the best!" he says in his high pitched voice and blows me a kiss. As he skips away, I can't hide my amusement, my shoulders shaking with laughter.

Max puffs out his cheeks, he pulls the curtain back into position and resumes his place behind the camera.

"Can you position the guitar on the lower part of your body and lay back with your arm above your head, please? Try to relax, nice and natural."

Max points to the custom Fender Stratocaster guitar emblazoned with the Rancid Vengeance logo of a skeleton playing a burning guitar on the back of a motorbike. The guitar is leaning up against the bottom of the chaise lounge and I move to position it, as he directs. I lay back to pose for the camera and Max nods his head.

"Good, hold it there."

He presses the shutter, firing off a series of photos, the lights flashing with each click.

"Perfect! Try to relax, you're doing brilliant!" Max encourages, as I hear shuffling and familiar laughter coming from behind the curtain. *For fucks sake!* I'm alternating between smiling and moody poses, as I feel a light tickle on my left ear. I ignore it, trying to focus and continuing to hold my position, as I feel another light tickle on my ear. I turn and see a dick poke me in the ear. *What the actual fuck!* I leap up from the chaise lounge and pull back the curtain, to see Sam holding his knob in his hand, his wedding ring glinting in the bright artificial studio lamps.

"What the fuck, man!" I yell, Jax and Lucas are rolling around on the floor in their boxer shorts in fits of hysterical laughter.

"For fucks sake!" I hear Max grumble.

"I'll get you back, you fucker!" I warn Sam and he laughs throatily.

"I'd expect nothing less, mate!"

We all laugh rowdily and I shake my head.

"The size of that thing still isn't normal, man!"

Sam looks smugly and cocks his pierced eyebrow. Max pulls back the curtain and shifts his gaze.

"I know I'm your dad, but for fucks sake, Sam, put it away!" Max chastises Sam. We all 'snicker' and 'tsk' at the father son-in-law interaction. Sam smirks, pleased with himself and Max rolls his eyes, mumbling about smart arses and fucking kids. In that moment, I embraced the madness of Rancid Vengeance and the close relationship we all had between us. It was rare, and I'd never been more content. I had people I felt comfortable around, the love of a good woman and a precious gift of two children who I'd kill for.

35

Raleigh

I walk through the door of Saint Sinner Ink, the door bell signalling my presence. The shop is a fairly large and open space, decorated in a simple black and white, with black-and-white floor tiles throughout. There is a large work area, split into three sections for each tattoo artist. Each station has a leather chair that folds down into a bed, a small desk, a sterilising machine, and each has a large shelf with various inks and a drawer section which holds various tattoo paraphernalia. At the front of the shop, there is a reception booth with a large desk, a comfortable, leather office chair, a large screen iPad Pro set up with a wireless keyboard, a printer, and telephone. There is a small waiting area with a small leather sofa and a coffee table in front of it with various tattoo magazines and design books neatly piled up. The walls are adorned with various tattoo designs and as I take in my surroundings, I hear a soft chuckle from behind me. I turn to see Peyton. She is wearing a Motley Crue t-shirt tied at her midriff, black ripped jeans and a pair of black and white Vans. Her hair is loose and styled perfectly. She moves towards me and throws her arms around me, as I return her embrace.

"It's so good to see you, babe! You look fab! Motherhood looks good on you!" she giggles enthusiastically, as she pulls away from our hug. I find myself mirroring her excitement and laugh along with her. In the time I have known her, she has become a close friend and someone who can relate to the ups and downs of dating a rock star. She is a genuinely kind and loving person. I feel privileged that she had taken me under her wing and welcomed me into the Rancid Vengeance family.

Tattoos may be skin deep but sometimes their significance goes deeper. It is a form of self-expression. It is visual proof, a snap shot of your journey in life so far. All of my tattoos are unique, individual and they have helped me heal. For many years self-harm bought a sense of relief from my emotional pain and after I had my first tattoo, it quelled the need to mark my skin in a negative way. Tattoos helped me celebrate my scars, they helped with my self-esteem and it offered me a healthy coping mechanism.

Getting tattooed also helped me come to terms with my past and move forward to a better relationship with my body, mind and my spiritual self. I wanted to add to my collection, so I was getting a huge back piece dedicated to Brody and the twins signifying closing the chapter on a part of my life I'd rather forget. It was important for me to depict it on my body to show I'd slayed those demons. I was getting a black and grey tattoo of an Archangel fighting a demon, with the hand prints and footprints of our babies on either side, with their names and dates of birth.

I had seen Peyton's work, and I had no doubt in my mind that she would do it justice. She was the best in the business and I have wanted to get tattooed by her for a long time. At just thirty-one years old, she has earned her reputation as one of the best female tattoo artists in a male dominated industry and she was dedicated to her profession. She had honed her skills over the thirteen years she had been tattooing, specialising in black and grey work and new school traditional. I admired her for continuing to be a working mum when she was married to a world famous rock star and juggling two kids. I often wondered how she did it and I was in awe of her devotion to her job, her husband and her children.

***

Peyton has been tattooing me for a few hours now and something about the buzz of the tattoo machine that soothes me. I am relaxed lying on my stomach on the full length black leather bed, resting my head on my folded arms.

"How are the twins?" she asks and I smile when I think of our babies Bowie and Azalea. There are so many experiences of love that can change you as a person and parenthood did that for me. There were no words to describe the unconditional, life-changing love I felt for both of them equally. I was still adjusting to being a new mother, but they made me want to be the best mother I could be and every day was a constant learning experience.

"They're great. Liv's looking after them today. They're growing every day and I still can't believe they're here," I admit with an awestruck tone to my voice and she giggles girlishly.

"I wish Freddie and Zachary were still babies sometimes. They're growing so fast."

I smile when I think of Peyton and Sam's sons Freddie and Zachary Newbolt. Both are mini versions of Sam and Peyton, two very different characters. Freddie is confident and a true entertainer exactly like Sam. He's going to be on stage one day following in his father's footsteps. Zachary is more laid back and reserved, a little like Peyton, but both are adorable.

"Do you want more kids?" I ask curiously and she smiles thoughtfully, as she pauses tattooing me.

"I'd never say never but obviously I'd love a baby girl! I loved the whole experience of being pregnant. It was definitely easier the second time around but I couldn't have gotten through it without Sam. He was my rock," she says wistfully and I smile at her sentiment.

"I sometimes can't help thinking that maybe life would have been...simpler if I'd never met Sam. But I wouldn't be wearing his ring and I wouldn't bear his name. I wouldn't have given birth to two of the most important people in the world, our boys. We deserved our happy ending. There were days when I thought we'd never get there, but I wouldn't change it for the world. You and Brody deserve your happy ending too, after everything you've been through, you deserve this, both of you. I've never seen him this happy and that's all because of you. He might have done some questionable things, but don't ever doubt his love for you. Brody's the man he is today because of you, you've changed him for the better, just like Sam in the beginning, he used the women and the sex as a crutch because his life was unfilled, but we made them both see that there's more..." I look up at her from beneath my lashes taking in her words, Brody was my chance at building a strong, stable family that both of us lacked growing up. It was a chance for us to finally be happy and I was going to hold on to it with both hands and never let it go.

As she continues to tattoo me. The look of concentration on her face and the delicious sting of the needle piercing my skin makes me feel alive somehow. It reminds me that this is a pain I can control, and I was making progress to beat my addiction with each day that passed. I spend long moments relishing the silence, except for the buzz of Peyton's tattoo machine.

"How are you and Brody now, babe?" she asks and I look up to meet her curious blue eyes.

"We're really good for the most part. He's the man I wished for him to be way before the accident. He's loving, he's attentive, and he's not afraid to admit his feelings. There are times when he gets this faraway look in his eyes and I know he's thinking about her."

I can't keep the bitterness from my voice, as I watch her listening to me intently.

"You're the woman he goes home to. You're the woman he sleeps next to at night. She's insignificant. Those women who wish they were the ones that were naked in his bed, none of them matter. It's a fantasy. The ones who scream their names and burst into tears when they look their way, they're...irrelevant...inconsequential." she explains.

"Did you know about...her?" I ask and suddenly, I'm afraid of the answer.

"It wasn't any of our business, it wasn't our story to tell. He never spoke about her, we didn't know her. We've never lied to you, Raleigh, you have to know that."

I nod and her answer has my curiosity piqued.

"Has Sam ever cheated on you?" she shakes her head.

"Never. I trust him implicitly. It's the other women I don't trust," she says simply and I understand completely. She doesn't work without Sam and he without her.

"When I chose to love someone who was damaged, I chose to take on the weight of his past and all the pain that goes with it. I've tried so hard to be strong and to move past it, but it's always there in the back of my mind."

I let out a sigh, as Peyton cocks her perfectly plucked eyebrow, suppressing a smirk.

"Which self-help book did you get that from? I must remember to never read it, because you and I both know that's a load of absolute bullshit."

She pauses tattooing me and I burst out laughing.

"I can always rely on you to be honest, babe!" she laughs along with me and in that moment, I knew I didn't have to hide behind a mask with Peyton.

I had found a true friend, she had accepted me for who I am, flaws and all. I could be myself around her and I have never been more grateful to have her in my life.

Brody

That first hit of caffeine in the morning, compared to the way I feel when I wake up next to Raleigh fucking Storm, nothing else can compare to that euphoric high. Not even the thrill of performing to a crowd of thousands. I had just discovered earth-shattering, mind-blowing, steal-your-fucking breath love, and that was all thanks to her.

After spending the morning at a charity calendar photoshoot, all I wanted to do was go home and lose myself in my girl. However, the rest of the day was reserved for sound checks, and rehearsals for tonights' gig in front of two thousand die-hard Rancid Vengeance fans at Shepherds Bush Empire. It is a fairly small and intimate gig compared to the rest of the tour. Shepherd Bush Empire was an award winning venue, and it is an iconic spot on London's cultural map.

***

As Donovan finishes fitting Sam's headset and hands me my new custom Fender Stratocaster guitar. Lucas is spinning his drumsticks, psyching himself up, and Jax is tuning his guitar with a look of pure concentration on his face. We're all getting in the zone; it's become our ritual before every show.

"Are we fucking ready for this, boys?" I shout and the other boys yell in unison.

"Let's do this shit!"

Sam and I go out first and take our places in the centre of the stage. As soon as I step out into the spotlight, all of the doubts of wanting to hang up my guitar fade away almost instantly, as I look out into the crowd of fans and I find myself grinning. The electrifying atmosphere is what I live for. It lights me up from the inside, it gets my adrenaline pumping. As I strum the opening guitar riff, I am immediately consumed by the music. Jax moves across the stage until we are standing back to back and we play in perfect sync, allowing ourselves to feed off the crowds raw energy.

As the opening song draws to a close, Sam steps to the front of the stage, looking out at the ocean of fans that have turned out here for us tonight. Every time Sam gets up on stage and has the crowd singing to his tune, it never fails to amaze me. Me and the other boys are happy just to stand back and let him do his thing. The atmosphere is thrilling, and I can feel the blatant enthusiasm reverberating through this small venue.

"*Wow!* How the fuck are you lovely people doing tonight? You're all looking so fucking beautiful out there!" Sam growls into the microphone, as he looks out at the sea of people with a look of awe on his face and I find myself grinning.

"Right! We're gonna change it up a bit this evening for all you lucky fucking people! We're going to do a bit of audience participation! Are you all up for that?"

The audience goes wild, and the screams are deafening.

"When I say Vengeance, you say rock! Can you do that?"

They all shout '*YEEEAHHH!*' and Sam laughs throatily. I'll never get bored of listening to him expertly command the crowd like he was born to do it.

"Vengeance!"

"*ROCK!*"

"Vengeance!"

"*ROCK!*"

"YEEEAAAHHH! You're so fucking good at this!" he chuckles.

"One more time for me, London!"

The crowd screams.

"When I say Vengeance, you say rock! Vengeance!"

"ROCK!"

"Vengeance!"

"ROCK!"

"Vengeance!"

"ROCK!"

"FUCK YEEEAAAHHH! LONDON!" he roars and jumps up and down.

"Give me a beat, Axeman! Let's rock this place to the motherfucking ground!"

Lucas pounds a drum beat, as I join with a riff and Jax breaks out an impressive solo. Sam moves to the centre of the stage and is bathed in a soft spotlight. He wraps his hands around his microphone and starts to sing, completely losing himself in the music.

"Through the sea of pain and skies of fire, your love lifts me higher..."

As Sam sings, the crowd are feeding off his potent energy and I feel goose bumps begin to form, the hairs on the back of my neck standing on end. There's no feeling like it, gone is the feeling of complete detachment, the buzz was back and it felt like the very first time I performed all over again. I felt a renewed sense of purpose and I bounced from one side of the stage to the other. I was so fucking high on adrenaline, I didn't need a chemical high. I didn't crave that artificial feeling of euphoria... I had it coursing through my veins and I hadn't felt like this in a long time. As the song draws to a close, the crowd goes wild and the whole venue seems to pulsate with their vehement high-spiritedness.

"Let me see those fucking hands in the air. Let me hear you, Shepherds Bush!" Sam rumbles into the microphone.

"Vengeance, Vengeance, Vengeance."

The crowd start their familiar chant and as I look out into the sea of people, I have never been happier, I don't ever want this to end.

36

Raleigh

As I looked into the eyes of my son and daughter, I had never felt love like that ever. Not even the love I feel for Brody compares to the way I feel as I rock them in my arms.

In the months that passed, I have learned a valuable lesson, that being a parent isn't easy. It didn't come with a manual. I ran on caffeine and cuddles most days and some days I wake up and I don't know how I'm going to make it through the day. I'm starting to think that exhaustion is a permanent state of mind. I had good days, I had bad days, but it was worth it to see their smiles and their wide inquisitive eyes as they look up at me.

Before I had kids, I had a million ideas of how I would raise them. Now that they're both here, I only have one... just love them. Love them through their tears, their smiles and their tantrums. I am their safe place, their whole world and their protector all rolled into one. Every day they do something new and every day is a challenge but I couldn't have gotten through the past few weeks without Brody. He is my rock.

He has completed the UK leg of Rancid Vengeance's tour and was about to leave for the US tomorrow. He will be gone for three whole months and as I crawl into bed, I watch him standing at the floor to ceiling window. He looks magnificent under the moonlight filtering in, casting him in shadow. His boxer shorts are hanging off his lean, narrow hips, his powerful thighs look thick and muscular. I watch his back bunch and flex, as he runs his hand through his hair, damp from his shower. He turns to face me and flashes me a wink. I melt all over the bed.

"You're beautiful you know. I've never told you that before," I admit softly, almost shyly. The smile he gives me in return renders me speechless, as he climbs into bed and pulls me close to him, my back to his hard, warm chest. His arms feel so right wrapped around me; he makes me feel safe. I am going to miss him so much while he's away. He nuzzles his nose into my hair and breathes in my scent.

"You smell good," he murmurs into me, wrapping his arms tighter around me.

"I'm going to miss you so fucking much, kitten," he whispers and my heart clenches in my chest, causing a physical ache. It takes everything I have not to burst into tears.

"I'm going to miss you too, Brody, so much."

He pulls me closer to him, and before I know what's going on, he flips me onto my back and straddles me.

"Let me love you, Raleigh."

I look up at him and he looks at me with such reverence it makes me want to weep.

"My love for you is infinite, Raleigh. It goes on until I say it does, which is when I'm cold, dead and fucking buried. There is no me without you, kitten."

He kisses a burning trail from my neck to my collarbone, skating his hands across every inch of my upper body.

"Every inch of you is fucking perfection," he whispers roughly, focusing on the feel of his hands all over my body.

"I don't want to just fuck tonight, kitten. I want to make love to you as if it's the first and the last time. I want you to feel me, every fucking inch; I want to explore every beautiful inch of your body. I want to make you come in a thousand different ways. I want to swallow your moans and I want you to scream my fucking name. You belong to me, Raleigh, from the very beginning, I don't want us to fuck about any more. We've wasted too much time already, I don't want to waste another second."

With those words, he cups my breast softly in his large hand, and leans his head down and takes my nipple between his teeth. Tonight has the power to change everything between us and the feel of his split tongue lapping at my erect buds lit me up from the inside, causing my body to erupt with goosebumps. His silver eyes flicked up to mine, and it felt as those he was looking straight into my soul, causing a shiver to spread over my skin. He releases my nipple with a pop, as his warm, soft lips continue to explore every inch of my body.

"I'll never stop wanting you, Brody," I pant out, as desire pooled deep in my core at the feel of his mouth on me. He moves his hand lower to cup my sex and I gasp at the contact.

"Make love to me, Brody. I need you, please, I need you inside me," I say, sounding breathy and almost desperate, as he rubs my sex through my sleep shorts. I writhe beneath him.

"Mmm," I hum, as he rips my shorts off in one deft movement, I pull my vest top over my head until I am naked before him.

"I'm wet for you, what are you going to do about it?" I challenge and he cocks his eyebrow, as he removes his boxer shorts. I lick my lips at the sight of his taut, tattooed biceps. He grasps his throbbing erection in his hand and slides gently into me, inch by glorious inch.

"That feels so good," I moan out loud.

"You feel like heaven around my cock. I could spend hours between your legs and it still wouldn't be enough."

His voice almost sounds pained, as he moves agonisingly slow, and I feel every warm throbbing inch of his magnificent cock. I moan softly, wrapping my legs around his waist to pull me deeper into me.

"*Brody,*" my breath hitching, as he thrusts his hips forward. The rhythm he sets is slow and sensual, while tirelessly filling my soaking wet pussy.

"Raleigh! God you drive me fucking crazy," he barks and with each unhurried, languid drive, I feel my climax unfurling deep within me.

"I can feel you around my cock, you're close."

He swivels his hips, and with each lazy plunge of his cock, I can feel him deep inside me. His piercing hitting my g-spot and rubbing my inner walls in just the right way.

"Oh God! I'm gonna come! Harder! I need it harder!" I plead and he sinks deeper into me, pulling my leg up to rest on his shoulder, as he builds up a punishing pace. An intense orgasm building up to its crescendo.

"Come with me, kitten, I'm close, fuck!" he growls, and with those words, I feel my orgasm tear through me so powerfully, I see stars.

"BRODY! OH GOD! I'M COMING! I'M COMING!"

A second later, Brody finds his release and fills me with his hot seed, shouting out my name repeatedly. In that moment, what we shared together could never be replicated with any other person. My love for Brody Lennon Hart anchors my soul and he wis the reason my heart was beating. He gave me a purpose, he was right, the love we have for each other was infinite, it is never ending. I fall asleep soundly with that thought at the forefront of my mind.

Brody

Instead of going for my early morning run, I chose to spend those precious few hours in bed with my girl. I spent long hours worshipping every part of her delicious body, which in the months that passed, had gone back to the way it was before she had the twins with the help of gentle exercise and healthy eating. I wanted to commit every inch of her to memory because after today, I would have to make do with FaceTime calls for the next three months. We are embarking on a tour across America starting in Los Angeles tomorrow evening. Our flight is scheduled for midday and I want to spend as long as possible with Raleigh and the twins.

The twins are growing every day. Every day they do something new and filled me with the hope that despite my traumatic and awful childhood, theirs will be worlds away from the abuse and suffering I went through. They will want for nothing and I am determined to be the best father I can be. I want to be there for them, I want to be present in their lives and I want to be a good role model. I am not perfect, but I am trying for Bowie, Azalea and Raleigh. As I'm lying in bed staring at the ceiling, a flash of inspiration hits me and I have to write it down, I have to put down on paper what I can't say out loud. I'm not good at putting my feelings into words, which is why people misunderstand me sometimes. I swing my legs out of bed, careful not to wake her and pad quietly across the floor, down the stairs and into my recording studio. I sit down in my leather recliner, pull out my notebook and a pen, and allow all of my thoughts and feelings to come flooding out.

I want her to know how I feel about her and when she doubts my feelings for her, she can read the words I can't say out loud. It is there in black and white for her to see. A letter is a reflection of my thoughts and feelings and I have so much to say to her that I feel I can write it better than to say it out loud. As the pen dances across the page, the words flow easily and I spill out my heart until I have no more words left to say. As I sit writing, I come to the realisation that I want nothing more than to spend the rest of my life with Raleigh. I want to make an honest woman of her and I want her to bear my name. I'll-spent the rest of our lives together righting all of the wrongs I had put her through. Now more than ever, I am determined to make her Mrs. Raleigh Hart.

Raleigh

"I love you, so fucking much."

He cups my face in both of his hands, as tears spill down my cheeks. I promised myself I wouldn't cry, but as soon as he held me in his arms, I broke down.

"I love you too, more than anything," I sob, as he presses his lips to mine, handing me an envelope. I take it from him, glancing down at my name in his elaborate penmanship.

"Don't read this until I've driven away," he says softly and I look up at him expectantly. He flashes me a grin, but it only makes me sob harder. I cling to him as he snakes his arms around my waist, pulling me into him. I breathe him in and commit every hard inch of him to memory.

"I don't want to let you go," I murmur into his neck and he nuzzles his face into my hair.

"Never," he whispers and pulls away from our embrace. He takes my face in both of his hands and presses his lips greedily to mine. His kiss is deep, his tongue probing mine, possessing me so completely by putting everything he has into one kiss. He pulls away and looks into my eyes, mouthing the words 'I love you' as he turns to get into the waiting car at the curb. As he climbs into the car, he takes my heart with him.

***

It's only been a few hours, but I miss Brody terribly. I have settled the twins down for a nap after feeding and changing their nappies. The envelope that Brody gave me before he left is taunting me from the low glass coffee table in the living room. I settle myself on the sofa, reach over to pick it up, turning it in my hands for a few moments, before I open it carefully and pull out the piece of paper which lies inside. I skim my fingers over the words on the page and start to read.

Kitten,

I am writing this letter in the hopes that you will read it on the day you think you have absolutely nowhere else to turn, or nobody left to talk to. I am here. I always think of you on my worst days and my very best days. Your face, that beautiful, crooked smile is always there when I close my eyes. On your darkest days, when the doubt and lack of esteem seem to be kicking your cute arse, remember the world is better with you in it, you are enough. In those moments, you forget those truths, but I am always here to remind you of those things you seem to forget.

Do not let your darkness in and put out the beautiful inner light you have, that calls out like a beacon to those that feel lost themselves. The light that drew me to you that day, which feels so long ago now. You told me once that you feel everything too damn much but you will not always feel this way. That's when you have to put that beautiful smile on and come out swinging. Just keep fighting.

I promise that you will make a difference. You are more than enough. Do not allow your own inner demons wrap you in chains. Trust your own feelings that life will get better, but you have to keep pushing forward. Life is better with you in it.

Please don't doubt my love for you, it's the only thing I've ever been sure of. It might have taken me a long time to admit it and say the words out loud, but I loved you from the first moment I laid my eyes on you. I never knew the true meaning of love until I met you. You're my best friend, my soul mate, my one and only. I want to spend the rest of our lives together proving I am worthy of you and the unrelenting love you give me. Your strength never fails to amaze me. You're the strongest, bravest woman I know and I need you to be strong while I'm gone. When I come home, know that I'm coming home to you. Keep fighting. Keep going for yourself, for me and for Bowie and Azalea.

No matter what time, or place, anywhere, know that this heart inside my chest, beats solely for you. Every breath I take and every battle I fight, it's all for you.

I love you.
Love Always

B x

A tear drips onto the page causing the ink to run as it hits the paper and I swipe it away from my face. Reading his words made my heart sing and I know our love has been a rocky road so far, but I wouldn't have wanted it to be any other way. When I fell in love with Brody, I fell in love with his soul. I was his from the moment I heard him call me *'kitten'* for the first time.

As the months have passed, we have healed each other in ways that I thought impossible in the beginning and I can't imagine my life without him in it. He is my happy ending and I am his. He is the other half of my heart that I had spending years seeking. Things are so perfect right now I can't help but think that something or someone was going to come along and ruin it for us.

Brody

Tonight is our first show on American soil. We are performing in front of six thousand people at The Greek Theatre in Los Angeles. It is an outdoor amphitheatre, carved into a hillside of Griffith Park and some of the best rock bands of our era have played here. For us as a band, it is the first time we have performed here and it will be a career-defining moment for Rancid Vengeance. We flew us and our entourage eleven and a half hours in our private jet from London to LAX and we are all exhausted. We came straight from the airport to the venue and we are sound checking in preparation for the gig tonight. I am looking forward to performing to our American fans, but even though it had only been almost twelve hours since I saw her, I miss Raleigh terribly. I can think of nothing else but her and the twins, the apprehension of her reading my letter was driving me to distraction. Sam has his hands wrapped around his microphone and he has his eyes firmly fixed on me.

"Oi! Earth to Brody! Pay attention silly bollocks!" he shouts into the microphone and the other boys laugh rowdily.

"For fucks sake, stop pining!" he grumbles, turning to Jax. "Give me a riff, Flash, 2-3-4."

Jax starts to play the opening riff to Corrupted and Sam nods his head. I move my hand up and down the fretboard, joining in and matching Jax note for note. Sam stops, pulling out his ear piece.

"Stop! Stop! I can't hear! Again!" he barks, his eyes darkening. I'm pretty certain that Sam is having another one of his episodes. Since he's been diagnosed with bi-polar he's been medicating, and they haven't occurred often. But over the years, we've begun to spot the signs, even when he thinks we don't know. He tries to hide it, and he hides it well, until he starts to behave erratically and his moods are up and down. He's off his medication, which he takes to balance his moods. He's self-medicating, taking drugs and he's drinking heavily. I started to notice it at the calendar photoshoot and I didn't want to be right. He's pushing everyone away, including the woman he loves. She hasn't said anything and I know it terrifies her as much as it does us. Jax looks from Sam to me and to Lucas and back again. We all shake our heads, concerned for our friend, our brother. As he wraps his hands around his microphone, I spot the visible tremor in his hands.

"Sam?" I shout across the stage, he turns to me and Jax stops playing.

"You good, man?" I ask, as he briefly closes his eyes. A screech of feedback echoes around the venue, as Sam crashes the microphone to the stage floor and storms off. *For fucks sake.*

I find him sitting on the steps to the terrace off the side of the stage.

"Is everything alright with you, mate?" I ask carefully and he laughs bitterly.

"Everything's hunky-fucking-dory, mate," he says with an unconvincing edge to his voice. I get up and move to stand in front of him, narrowing my eyes on him, regarding him intently.

"Peyton's pregnant," he drops his head into his hands.

"That's brilliant news, right? Congratulations!"

He shakes his head. "I should be ecstatic. I should be the happiest man to walk the earth, but I'm fucking terrified, Brody," he admits.

"Why didn't you say something?"

He looks up at me.

"We didn't want to jinx it by saying anything before it was safe. I wasn't there when Freddie was born, I missed out on the first six months of his life, Brody. I can never make up for that, J.D. stole that from us and I'll never be able to get that time back."

As I listen intently to Sam's words, I start to think of what fatherhood means to me.

"The story of fatherhood isn't about the last page, it's about every word, every sentence, every paragraph that make up the story. You cherish every single fucking moment. When Raleigh gave birth, I was shit scared I wouldn't have what it took to raise them, to look after them as well as I could. I didn't have a father growing up, so I didn't have anything to work from and since the twins were born it's becoming more apparent that I'm just fucking making it up as I go along! There isn't a book of rules, you can read all the baby books in the world and it still wouldn't prepare you for what it's like to hold that helpless bundle of joy in your arms for the first time. Nothing prepares you for that first night when it's just you and them without the safety net of the doctors and nurses. Peyton knows you would have been there if you could have. J.D. took everything from us back then. Freddie is a good kid, and he adores you. If Bowie looks at me the way he looks at you, my heart would literally burst because you're their hero. Any idiot with a pair of eyes can see that, he worships the ground you walk on and so does Zachary. That baby growing inside her has your blood running through its veins, so it's your fucking duty to look after all of them."

I surprise myself at my brutal honesty, as Sam leans forward bracing his forearms on his knees and twisting his wedding ring around his finger.

"Every time I hear Freddie and Zach call me daddy my heart feels like it's almost too big for my chest. I keep punishing myself because I wasn't there to see Freddie's first smile, his first breath. I feel like I missed out on so much, I feel robbed and cheated out of that. I saw Zachary's first everything and being a parent changed me. It's my job to protect them, to nurture them into good human beings. I would walk through hell for all of them without hesitation, but Peyton sacrificed so much to bring Freddie into the world. I'm in constant awe of her, she protected him with her life. Even when she thought she was going to die at the hands of J.D. she still protected him. His life was more important than her own and I'll never have the bond they have.

I'm jealous. How fucking pathetic does that sound? I'm jealous of the bond my wife has with our son!"

He runs his hands through his hair and puffing out a breath.

"Someone told me once that not all storms come to disrupt your life but some come to clear your path. That was your storm. Her coming back to you cleared your path."

He chuckles softly.

"I never thought I'd see the day, you giving me advice," he says wryly and I cock my eyebrow with a smirk.

"Just something new I'm trying out, don't get used to it!"

We both laugh, then go silent for long minutes.

"I'm thinking of asking Raleigh to marry me," I blurt out, as Sam's eyes widen and he nods coolly.

"I'm happy for you, man, about fucking time!" he rasps and I lean against the wall with my hands tucked in my pockets.

"She's my end game, Sam. It took me almost losing my life for me to realise. I don't work without her. I've done some stupid shit in my life and she's forgiven me for it all. I don't deserve her, but I want to prove to her that I've changed, that I'm worthy of her."

Sam lifts his head up and looks me in the eyes.

"She knows the real me, Sam. I've never had that with a woman before. She's different to all the other women and I've never loved anyone the way I love her. She's my soul mate, she's my fucking Queen, she completes me in ways I could never imagine."

Sam smiles a genuine smile, and he gets to his feet, pulling me in for a manly hug.

"Congrats, mate, now are we going to finish this fucking sound check?" he jokes and I laugh.

"Yeah, man, I'll be there in a sec."

He pulls away from our hug and strides off back up the stairs to the stage. I hear Jax and Lucas give him a round of applause, I smile to myself as I take a few moments to gather myself.

I'd never thought about marriage before as I'd never been with anyone longer than one night to even contemplate it. Lorna was the exception, but I push that thought to the back of my mind. When I met Raleigh, I was in a dark place and she dragged me back into the light. She healed me in ways I could never have imagined and I would be forever grateful to her for sticking by me through thick and thin, through good times and bad times. I wanted to spend the rest of my life with her, I wanted her to be mine for all eternity. She was my reason to get out of bed in the mornings, she was my safe place, my sanctuary, she was my home and nothing could separate us.

***

After we completed the sound check, we went back to our hotel. We are staying in The Waldorf Astoria Hotel in Beverly Hills. We are performing two sold out gigs at The Greek and we had booked out all the Penthouse suites for the next three nights until we move onto the next state. I am staying in the Presidential Penthouse suite; it is three thousand two hundred square feet of pure luxury. The large bedroom has a plush California King Bed and floor to ceiling windows looking out onto the private terrace. It also came with a dining room, home entertainment and media room, a fully stocked bar, a bluetooth enabled surround sound system, a separate shower room and master bathroom. It also has a mini-gym and private spa.

I just showered in preparation for tonight's gig and pad from the bathroom into the vast master bedroom. I have a towel wrapped around my waist, my body still damp. I am exhausted and jet lagged, but I have thought of nothing else other than Raleigh since we landed. I pull out my iPad and swipe the screen to FaceTime her. I finish drying myself off and settle down on the bed. She is eight hours ahead of us and it is nine a.m. in London. It rings three times before it connects and the screen fills with her beautiful face.

"Hey gorgeous!" she greets me brightly, rewarding me with the smile I love so much.

"Morning kitten," I say with more than a hint of amusement to my voice.

"How are you? You look exhausted."

I laugh.

"Is that a polite way of telling me I look like shit?" I state dryly and she laughs along with me.

"You know what I mean!" she says softly.

"I know, kitten, I'm just fucking with you! I'm good. Just getting ready for the gig. We've sound checked for a couple of hours and I'm back at the hotel. The car's coming for us in a little while to take us to the venue. How are you? You look gorgeous as always."

Her faces turns the most adorable shade of pink and she smiles softly, making her eyes sparkle.

"I'm ok, the twins kept me up half the night, but I'm good. I miss you."

Her voice full of sadness.

"I miss you too, I know it's going to be a long three months, but maybe when I come home, I can take you away. Just you, me and the twins. Grab a map, stick a pin in it and we'll go."

I smile and she nods.

"I'd like that! The movie starts shooting in a week. We had a cast meeting over Zoom yesterday and Marnie has agreed to look after the twins while I go back to work."

I nod, genuinely happy for her that she's returning to her job that she loves so much.

"That's great news, babe. I'm so proud of you."

She pauses for a few minutes, biting down on her plump bottom lip.

"Something on your mind, kitten?" I ask, my voice low.

"Only you, handsome," her voice seductive.

"Do you need me to take care of something?" she nods slowly, as I position myself so she can see me better. She whimpers as soon as she catches sight of my tattooed chest.

"God, you're so fucking hot," she states with awe and admiration in her voice, as I flash her a wink.

"All for you, kitten," I whisper softly.

"I'm so fucking horny right now, I wish you were inside me," she admits shamelessly.

"Take your top off," I command and she pulls off her t-shirt. I lick my lips at the sight of her as she isn't wearing a bra. Her breasts are pert and full, as her nipples pebble into hard, erect pink buds.

"Play with your nipples for me."

She does as I ask, and she tugs her nipples between her thumb and forefinger, rolling and rubbing them. She closes her eyes and the noises coming from her cause my dick to thicken.

"Mmmm," she moans.

"Good girl, are you wet for me, kitten?"

She moans softly and bites her lip again, nodding her head yes.

"I had this hot dream about you last night. I woke up soaking wet."

I wrap my hand around my cock and fist it up and down for a moment.

"Touch your clit for me, play with your pussy, show me how wet you are," I say firmly.

"Oh God!" she pants.

"Show me your fingers."

She lifts her fingers up and they are glistening with her juices.

"Fuck," I curse, as I start to move my hand up and down my cock.

"What was your dream about, kitten? Tell me," I breathe.

"I was handcuffed, and you were fucking me from behind, pulling my hair and spanking me."

She seems reluctant to admit it, but listening to her recount her dream causes my dick to swell to the point of pain.

"Does that turn you on?" I ask and she nods.

"Oh God, yes! Yes it does!" she pants.

"Tell me what you're doing," I grind out with a clenched jaw, I'm wound so tight.

"I just got a new sex toy, do you want to hear me use it?"

I swallow hard and nod, I can't speak. She holds up the mint green rubber monstrosity.

"Fuck yourself with it and pretend it's my cock," I order as I hear the buzzing, she grabs her breast with one hand, kneading it softly.

"This toy feels so good, but nothing compares to the way your cock feels inside me."

I move my hand up and down my cock, with twisting strokes from base to top.

"Oh God! Brody!" she screams, as I quicken my pace, growling low in my throat.

"Fuck! Don't stop!" I say through a clenched jaw.

"I wish you were inside me. I need your cock. I love the feel of you on top of me."

Her voice is desperate and breathy with pleasure.

"I need you to come for me, Raleigh, come NOW!" I command, her moans getting louder and the buzz constant.

"Brody, I'm coming! Fuck! I'm coming!" she screams, and my orgasm is right behind hers.

"JESUS! FUCK! RALEIGH! I'M COMING!"

I feel the warmth of my come spurt between my fingers, as we both ride out our orgasms together. I flop back on the bed, exhausted and sated. I look up at her and she looks perfectly fucked, her hair a dishevelled mess and her cheeks pink.

"I love you," she whispers softly.

"I love you too. That was...intense."

We both laugh as our breathing returns to normal.

"Those three months are going to fly by!" I reassure her, as I hear a loud pounding on the door.

"Shit! Someone's at the door, I have to go. Give the twins a kiss from daddy."

I blow her a kiss, as we say our goodbyes and the last thing I see is her beautiful face. In that moment, looking into her wide amethyst eyes, I couldn't be more sure that I wanted her to be my wife.

37

Raleigh

The three months that pass are a blur of sleepless nights and endless days, which seem to blend into one. I have been dividing my time between shooting 'Rock Me Harder', the sequel to 'Rocked' my first film working with Damien Valentine. The script is just as witty and edgy as the first film and I am reprising my role as Stevie Lynn, the feisty female guitarist in fictional band 'The Forsaken.' I am starring with Nick Slade and Gavin Kincaid and I looked forward to acting alongside them each day. We had done endless interviews to promote the film, and I was back doing something I loved.

The twins are now four months old. I have tried to occupy my mind and keep myself busy, but he has never been far from my thoughts. Despite the eight hour time difference, we have managed to keep in daily contact via FaceTime. Today is Saturday and the day he returns home. I'm counting down the hours until he can hold me in his arms. I have my morning shower, dry my newly short bubblegum pink hair, styling it into messy spikes and wearing a black skull print headband. I apply my usual natural make-up and put on some red lipstick, opting for black cut-off shorts and a denim shirt tied at my mid-riff. I jam my feet into my black and white skull Vans and put in a pair of simple diamond studs.

I spend the day with the twins and try to keep my eyes from flicking to the clock above the stone fireplace. I have settled Bowie and Azalea down for their afternoon nap, when I hear the front door slam shut. I sprint down the hallway and skid to a halt, as I stand there taking all six foot of him in. He flashes me a lazy dimpled smile... he looks delicious. His dark hair is perfectly styled and manipulated to the side, he looks leaner and more defined. His skin is extremely tanned, the black vest he is wearing showcasing his sculpted, tattooed biceps. My mouth forms a perfect *O* shape, as I take in the sight of him before me. It takes me a few minutes for my brain to catch up before

I'm running full pelt at him, throwing my arms and legs around his waist. He catches me easily and holds me tight to him. I breathe in the scent of him and it takes everything I have not to burst into tears.

"I've missed you so much," I murmur into his neck.

"I know, kitten, I know," he whispers tenderly and I cling to him. I move my head up to look at him and he crashes his lips urgently to mine. His lips are so soft, the contrast of his week old stubble scratching my cheek. His tongue delicately caresses mine, and I get lost in his kiss in the middle of the hallway, relishing our bittersweet reunion after long months apart.

***

The next morning, I wake to Brody blanketing me with his cock buried inside me. His face nuzzled into my neck.

"Mmm, good morning to you too," I greet him sleepily, as he lifts his head up, flashing me a lazy grin. His skin is warm pressed against mine, feeling his hardness slip in and out at a languid, unhurried pace. My grasp slips over his broad shoulders, my fingers running through his soft hair. I lift my legs up and wrap them around his waist, pulling him deeper into me, moaning in his ear, taking his lobe between my teeth and biting down. He thrusts his hips forward, building up a slow, sensual rhythm. He moves his head so he's looking down at me and lowers his mouth to mine. There is heat in his kiss and it seared through both of us. My blood pounds in my veins, as he devours my mouth. I am as hungry for him as he is for me. My tongue plunders his mouth and he skims his hands across my body, stroking my hair softly. I revel in the feel of his body, as he drives his cock deep into my aching channel. I had missed the feel of him inside me after three whole months of FaceTime sex and nights with my battery operated boyfriend. My breasts are pressed against his broad chest, he moves up my body and straddles me, I move my hands up to feel his solid muscles. It has been so long since I felt his skin, his touch, his body, his cock. My skin heats at his touch, as he quickens his pace then slows, alternating between deep drives and leisurely thrusts. He is driving me crazy with want.

"*Fuck*, I've missed being inside you, kitten. It's been a long, lonely three months," he says softly.

"Mmm, you feel like heaven."

It feels so right with him, as he moves in and out of my slick heat. I moan softly, trapping my bottom lip between my teeth. He tilts my chin, forcing me to look up at him.

"I need your eyes, kitten. I want to watch you come, I want you to feel what I feel."

My eyes lock with his, silver to amethyst, as his pace starts to quicken. I squeeze my inner walls around his cock and he curses long and low in his throat. He continues to piston in and out of me, as I explode around him.

"I'm coming, *fuck*, Brody, Brody! I'm coming! Oh God! I'm coming!" I cry out on a half sob of pleasure, his orgasm is right behind mine, as his hot seed coats my womb. The only sound in the room is our breathless post orgasmic pants, as we come down from our perfectly in sync climaxes. He pulls out of me, rolls over and lays down on the bed next to me. He shifts me so I am tucked under his arm, with my head resting on his pec. Our breathing returning to normal after a few silent moments. It had been so long, I craved his touch,

"We should start every day like that," I quip, as I idly trace shapes across his torso. I feel his body shake with laughter and he kisses me on top of my head.

"Noted."

I hear the twins crying on the baby monitor, as he takes my hand in his halting my journey across his smooth skin. He shifts me onto the pillow and plants a chaste kiss on my lips.

"I've got them."

I lick my lips at the sight of his bare arse.

"What did I tell you about eye-fucking me?"

His voice is amused and I pull the covers over my head, embarrassed at being caught ogling him. In that moment, I feel a wave of contentment wash over me and I couldn't be happier if I tried.

Brody

After waking up buried inside Raleigh and making slow, unhurried love, I hear our twins crying on the baby monitor. I head out of the room, feeling her eyes burning into my back. I smile to myself that I still have that effect on her after all this time. I pull on my black and white custom-made Rancid Vengeance robe, as I pad across the soft grey carpet into the nursery. They look so different to the last time I saw them, their features more prominent. Bowie is my double, he has my nose, my chin and a mop of dark hair. His wide silver eyes look up at me from the crib his shares with his sister. She looks exactly like Raleigh. She has her nose, her eyes and two deep dimples in her cheeks. I pick Bowie up and cradle him to me, He nuzzles his chubby face into the soft material of my robe and I hold him close. He lifts his head up and the tiny boy who is my mirror image is smiling up at me. The connection is instant and I feel guilty for being away from them both for three whole months. I check on Azalea and she has fallen back to sleep so I move across the room and sit down in the grey corduroy cuddle chair with Bowie in my arms.

I sing Ed Sheeran's Perfect softly to him, as he turns his head, nuzzling his face back into my chest. His tiny fingers find my thumb, gripping it tightly in his fist. His little body rising and falling with my breathing help put everything back into focus. When I found out Raleigh was pregnant for the first time I felt unprepared and unable to be the father they needed or deserved. As soon as I held them both in my arms for the first time, my parenting instincts took hold immediately and the bond was there from the very beginning. Since they were born I embraced fatherhood and the challenges that came with it. Standing over their incubator in the hospital, I vowed to be a better father than my non-existent dad ever would be. I read all the baby books, but nothing could have prepared me for that first night home from the hospital. I would never have the bond that Raleigh has with both of them. They grew inside her for almost nine months, she felt them kicking, moving and developing right before her eyes. I would never comprehend the unbreakable connection they had, but as I rock my boy to sleep I now have a better understanding of what unconditional love is supposed to feel like.

38

Brody

After travelling across America, we have a well-earned month off, before we start writing and recording our sixteenth studio album. We have flown to The Maldives, which is a secluded oasis that boasts it own stretch of beach. We are staying in a large eight bedroom villa, which belongs to Jax. It has four fifty five inch plasma TV's all with satellite channels, DVD players and mp3 cables. It has a large open plan dining area and living area leading out onto the beach, three outdoor showers, eight bathrooms, a twenty-four-hour gym at the resort down the beach. All eight bedrooms have four-poster beds, with glass floors, offering views of the marine life living in the tranquil turquoise waters of the Indian Ocean below us.

Raleigh, me, the twins, Jax, Zeppelin, Sam, Peyton, Freddie, Zachary, Cole, Amy, Addison, Dexter, Marnie and our security team are staying in Jax's luxury villa. We flew out on our private jet, Air Vengeance, and took a twenty-five minute speedboat ride from the airport. The villa, has its own housekeeper, cleaner, and chef to tend to our every need. This is exactly what we need to relax and recharge our batteries, after a crazy few months.

Raleigh's skin was glistening with the coconut sun cream she was wearing, her lips tasted like the salt from the ocean and she smelled like the sweet, strawberry daiquiri she'd just finished. Her eyes were back to their usual sparkle and her smile was genuine. I'd never been more in love with her than at that moment. Even though, deep down I feel unworthy of her love. I've put her through so much and I wake up every day feeling lucky that she's the one lying next to me and not some nameless skank I met when I was off my pickle on drugs. I look at her and wonder why she's with me, but I push those thoughts to the back of my mind. I take every inch of her in and commit this moment to memory. She's never looked as beautiful as she does now. Her lean, slender frame, encased in a Hawaiian print bikini, her Ralph Lauren sunglasses perched on top of her bubblegum pink hair, which had become lighter from the sun. The smile on her face genuine and the sound of her melodic laugh gives me hope that I've finally found the woman I want to spend the rest of my life with. Her golden tan compliments her array of full colour and black and grey tattoos, her toenails painted blue and a silver ankle bracelet around her left ankle with 'B' and 'A' dangling from it.

As I relax on the white sand, with my hands behind my head, my Ray Bans shielding my eyes from the fierce sun. I watch her interacting with Peyton, who is almost four months pregnant with a baby girl, her small bump bare and protruding in front of her. She is wearing a red bikini and pink Ray Ban aviators. Zeppelin is Jax's new girlfriend, they haven't been seeing each other for long but they met online. Her short blonde hair in damp tousled waves with her Michael Kors sunglasses perched on top of her head. She is wearing a pink polka dot bikini, and she is giggling along with Peyton and Raleigh. I lay back feeling relaxed and content, as I'm joined by Jax, Sam and Lucas.

"So, are you going to ask her?" Sam asks quietly, I swallow hard at the thought of asking Raleigh to marry me.

"What if she says no?"

Jax bursts out laughing.

"Then it will be one more thing we can take the piss out of you for!"

I narrow my eyes on him and Lucas jabs him playfully.

"Have you thought how you're going to ask her?" Lucas cocks his head to the side and I shake my head, continuing to observe my girl.

"She's not going to say no, you know that don't you? Have you seen the way she looks at you? It makes me want to hurl!" Lucas jokes, as Raleigh turns to me and blows me a kiss. I pretend to catch it and place my hand on my heart. The boys all laugh boisterously and make vomiting sounds.

"On a serious note, how are you going to ask her?"

The truth is, I have no idea. Proposals are an intensely personal and emotional experience. Choosing to spend the rest of your life with one person is a big fucking deal and I wanted it to be memorable. I wanted her to remember it for the rest of her life, I could perform in front of a crowd of thousands and be as steady as a rock, but even thinking about it my knees felt weak.

"How did you ask Peyton?"

Sam smiles the smile all the women go gaga over.

"Which time?"

We all laugh at his droll answer.

"First time, it was in Vegas. I had it planned for weeks. I got into the tank at the Mandalay Bay Aquarium and showed her signs, then when I got out I dropped down on one knee and asked her. Second time, wasn't so slick. It was on stage at The Roundhouse."

I listen intently to him recount him asking Peyton to marry him, I haven't the first clue about romance or asking a woman to marry to me.

"What about you? How did you ask Ruby to marry you?"

I ask Jax curiously and he gets this faraway look in his eyes, dropping his head down with a sigh.

"I pretended to be a busker outside Brent Cross tube station. I played a song I'd written for her, then got down on my knees and asked her to do the honour of being my wife," he swallows, as he explains and Lucas brushes his arm in a gesture of sympathy and reassurance.

I had spent countless hours thinking of the right way and the right words to ask Raleigh to be my wife. I loved her with every fibre of my being and I had never been as ready as I am now to take that leap of faith and marry the woman of my dreams. The woman who bought me back to life.

"It doesn't have to be an elaborate romantic gesture, it just has to come from here, man."

Sam puts his hand on his chest and I know he's right. I hate the fact that he's right and as I lie there, the sun beating down on my skin and watching my Raleigh, an idea flashes in my minds eye. I know what I have to do... I know the perfect way to propose.

Raleigh

As the sun sets over the Indian Ocean, the red and gold hues blossoming creating a rainbow-like flame, blazing across the evening sky. It is our first night in The Maldives and as I'm getting ready for dinner, applying my make-up in the mirror, I feel his eyes on me. I smile to myself.

"Hey handsome," he chuckles softly.

"How did you know I was here?"

I cock my perfectly plucked eyebrow, as I'm applying my mascara.

"I have a Brody-dar!"

We both laugh.

"Completely made up word, but I like it."

He moves closer to me and wraps his arms around my waist, resting his head on my shoulder, as our eyes meet in the mirror.

"I have a surprise for you."

I narrow my eyes on him, trying to gauge his mood.

"What surprise?"

He smirks.

"If I told you, it wouldn't be a surprise, kitten. That's the whole point!"

I finish applying my make-up and straighten my black sun dress, my bare shoulders on display. I push my feet into my black diamante flip-flops, my curiosity piqued. He takes my hand in his and leads me into the open plan living area, which is unusually deserted.

"Do you trust me, Rae?" he asks softly and I turn to him, suddenly full of apprehension. I nod, as I bite my lip. He takes out a scrap of black material from his pocket and ties it around my head to cover my eyes. My heart beat kicks up a notch at having one of my senses temporarily taken away.

"Relax, kitten, I've got you," he reassures softly, as he takes my hand leading me forward. I stumble a little and I shriek, as I'm lifted unexpectedly from my feet and carried in his arms.

"Where are you taking me, Brody!" I giggle, as he sets me down on the beach, the sand soft beneath my feet.

"Walk forward, kitten, keep walking."

I let him lead me across the sand and I hear the sound of the waves lapping. He brings us to a stop, and he takes off my blindfold. The sun temporarily dazzling me and robbing me of sight. I blink a few times and he stands in front of me, almost shyly. His hands tucked in the pockets of his denim shorts, his white v-neck t-shirt showcasing his chest tattoos. As I look down I see the words '*Will You Marry Me?*' etched into the sand. I cup my hands over my mouth in shock, my eyes glistening with tears.

"Not a day goes by that I don't think about our future together. I want to grow old with you. You complete me and I can't imagine my life without you in it, Raleigh Storm. I wrote you a letter not so long ago, telling you the things I felt at the time I couldn't say out loud. But now, I want to shout it from the fucking rooftops! When we first met, I was instantly taken aback by your beauty and I knew I wanted to spend the rest of my life with you."

He drops down on one knee and pulls a small black velvet ring box from the pocket of his shorts. He opens it up and presents it to me.

"Will you do me the honour of being my wife?"

My head bobs up and down in a nod and I sink down to the sand, throwing my arms around his neck. I am overwhelmed by his gesture and I let out a small sob. A mixture of emotions barrelling through my body.

"Yes! Yes! Of course, I'll marry you!"

He lets out a huge sigh of relief and I press my forehead to his. He pulls away for a moment, taking my hand in his and placing the ring on my finger.

"You don't know how happy you've made me, kitten... soon-to-be Mrs. Raleigh Hart."

I can't stop smiling, as we look at each other. His eyes are brimming with tears, as he places a kiss on the ring he just placed on my finger. I look down at the ring and see it is a simple, yet stunning platinum love-knot style ring with two interlocking rows of full-cut diamonds and beautiful amethysts surrounding it. He helps me to my feet and stands to his full height, wrapping his arms around me and pulling me into his hard chest. I wish I could freeze this moment and keep it for all eternity, because life couldn't be more perfect.

Our moment is interrupted by Sam, Peyton, Jax, Lucas, Zeppelin, Amy, Cole, Marnie, Dexter and our security team, all peering around the doorway of the villa.

"Is it safe to come out now? I don't like hide and seek!" Addison exclaims, with her hands on her hips. Everyone laughs and Brody nods.

"Of course it is, Princess!"

She sighs dramatically and rolls her eyes. "Did she say yes?"

She runs full pelt at Brody and he swings her up in his arms. He nods.

"I told you she would!" she says proudly, as she plants a wet kiss on his cheek. He laughs, setting her down on her feet. Everyone joins us on the sand, giving us a rapturous round of applause, swallowing us up in words of congratulations. Marnie brings the twins out and hands Bowie to Brody and Azalea to me.

"Did you hear that, buddy? Mummy agreed to marry daddy!" he coos and my heart feels too big for my chest, as I watch the interaction between father and son with glossy eyes. Bowie lets out a huge squeal of excitement.

"That's what I felt like doing too, mate!"

Brody kisses him on his chubby cheek, I join him and kiss him softly on the lips, the words *will you marry me* ringing in my ears. I had never contemplated what it would be like to belong to someone so completely. I never envisioned what it would be like to wear white and get married to a man I was hopelessly in love with. I wasn't like other girls who dreamed of the lavish wedding and the tall muscular groom. My mum and dad didn't exactly have the perfect marriage, but as I stand on the white sand on the beach in The Maldives, I allowed myself to get carried away in thoughts of white dresses and what it would be like to become Mrs. Raleigh Hart.

39

Raleigh

As I'm sat in front of the mirror, I'm fanning my face with both of my hands. I'm so nervous I feel like I'm going to throw up. Today is our wedding day. After a week of preparations and meticulous short-notice wedding planning, we gathered a small group of our close friends and family, flying them first class to The Maldives. Liv and Jensen, Maverick, my mum, dad, little brother Jagger, Lenny, Nancy, Emmy, her boyfriend Nate and his daughter Melody, Mandie, Malakai, Nick, Gavin, Damien and the rest of the band's entourage, had all been flown over to witness Brody and I get married.

The sun was beating down, there was a white canopy with pink hibiscus flowers hanging from it and at the end of each seated aisle hung pink fairy lights. Spread down the centre aisle were pink rose petals, on either side of the aisle sat white chairs set up on the sand.

"Here, drink this, you look like you need it!" Liv passes me a glass of champagne and I take it from her with a shaky hand, downing it in one go. My mum rolls her eyes at me and I ignore her. *She's not going to ruin today.*

"You're marrying the man of your dreams, Rae, you should be happy!"

I chuckle softly, placing the empty glass down on the dressing table.

"I am happy! Blissfully happy! I'm just nervous!"

I begin fanning my face with both of my hands again, my stomach roiling. Liv adjusts my veil and I catch my mum's gaze in the mirror. She smiles softly and moves closer, Liv looks from me to my mum.

"I'll leave you to it. Yell if you need me, babe!"

She does as she says, closing the door behind her with a click.

"I've never told you this before, but I'm so proud of you, Raleigh."

Her eyes glistening with unshed tears, I swallow the lump that has formed in my throat.

"Don't you dare set me off, mum!"

We both laugh as I get to my feet. I throw my arms around her and she holds me in her arms. For the first time in thirty years, my mum is acting like the mum I wanted her to be all those years ago.

"That rock star better take care of my baby girl." She pulls away and cups my face in her hands. "Do you hear me?"

I nod, desperately trying to hold back the tears.

"You look beautiful. I couldn't be more proud of you, I might not have been the best mother over the years, but I want you to know that I love you, I've never stopped loving you, even when I was wrapped up in work."

She kisses me softly on the cheek, pulling out a necklace from her pearl encrusted clutch bag. The necklace is a simple silver chain with a blue sapphire pendant hanging from it, encrusted with smaller sapphires surrounding it. My mum fastens it around my neck and I gasp as I catch sight of it in the mirror.

"It's beautiful," I whisper, my voice thick with tears.

"It was your belonged to your grandmother. She wanted you to have it on your wedding day. It's your something blue."

I hug her again and the tender look she gives me, causes the tears I was desperately trying to hold back, spill down my cheeks.

"That's enough tears, baby girl!"

She starts patting away my tears with her handkerchief and I laugh softly at her gesture.

"I love you, mum."

She smiles.

"Love you too, Raleigh."

With those words, my mother Avril Storm had redeemed herself and made up for thirty years of mistreatment and put downs.

After Danny re-did my hair and make-up, I was greeted by my father, Vince Storm. He looked better than the last time I saw him. His eyes had their familiar sparkle back, and he was wearing a pair of light grey trousers, a white shirt open at the collar and grey moccasins.

"You look...good Lord, Raleigh, you look beautiful."

I beam at him, as he offers me his arm to escort me to my husband to be.

Brody

Our wedding is a celebration of the love I felt for my Raleigh and all of those who came to share it with us. I am standing at the altar on the sand wearing a short sleeved white shirt, open at the collar and a pair of light grey trousers. My hair is manipulated to the side in side-swept undercut. Sam, who agreed to be my best man, nudges me, as he holds my son Bowie, wearing an outfit to match mine. He looks adorable.

"You good, mate?"

I nod, suddenly feeling nervous, as I cuddle my daughter into my chest. She is wearing a silver dress to match the bridesmaids. She looks equally as adorable as her twin brother. Sam glances to the side, then back to Jax who is standing to the left of Marlowe Newbolt, who wholeheartedly agreed to marry us, after he was ordained online to officiate Sam and Peyton's wedding. He is wearing a clerical collar, a short sleeved black shirt and sunglasses shielding his eyes. He looks ever the rock star, as Jax starts to play a rock version of the wedding march on his electric guitar. I turn and catch sight of her, my Raleigh. The sight of her renders me speechless and it takes everything I have not to burst into tears. I swallow the tennis ball sized lump that has formed in my throat, as I watch her gracefully walk down the rose petal lined aisle. I have no words, she looks breath-taking and...glowing. She utterly captivates me with each step closer she takes. I hand Azalea to Marnie, who plucks her from my arms.

Her bridesmaids, Liv, Peyton, Addison, Maverick and Thea, are following close behind her, all wearing matching silver dresses and matching Converse, personalised with their names drawn onto the side of each shoe. She is gripping her dad's arm so tightly, I can see her knuckles turning white. As she approaches ever close, I take in all five feet seven inches of her. She's enchanting and so fucking beautiful.

Her white dress is simple and strapless with a plunging neckline, a satin silver sash wrapped around her waist, the tulle skirt, flows down to her knees and she is wearing white Converse trainers with *'Mrs, Hart'* etched in elaborate script lettering. As her dad escorts her closer to me, my heart beat starts to quicken. Vince hands her over to me and I realise this is the first time I've met her family. He flashes me a reassuring wink and I smile, shaking his hand firmly but I don't miss the wordless warning in the tight squeeze of my hand. She takes her place next to me and smiles with glossy eyes, letting out a long laboured breath, as she turns to face me.

"*Jesus Christ*, you look stunning, kitten," I whisper, as Marlowe clears his throat and begins to speak.

"Friends, family, and everyone in between, we are gathered here today to celebrate the marriage of Brody and Raleigh. This is my second Rancid Vengeance wedding!"

He pulls a face and everyone starts to laugh at his joke. Raleigh takes my hands in hers and I feel her trembling. I give her clammy hands a squeeze in a gesture of reassurance.

"Eyes on me, kitten. It's just you and me, no one else," I whisper so only she can hear me, as her eyes lock with mine and she nods, offering me a watery smile.

"No tears, not today. Just pure happiness."

I flash her a wink and suggestive waggle of my tongue and she starts laughing. I clear my throat and begin to pledge the rest of my life to this beautiful woman who saved me from my addiction and bought me back from the brink.

Raleigh

Marlowe looks between the two of us and then out to the guests.

"Does anyone object to this marriage? Speak now or forever hold your peace," he asks, and he is met with silence for a few agonising moments. He breaks out into a wry grin.

"Thank God! That's always the awkward part!"

Everyone laughs at his humour, as Brody clears his throat, breathing in through his nose and out through his mouth, readying himself to say his vows.

"I take you Raleigh Alyssa Storm to be my lawful wedded wife., to have and hold from this day forward. Do you remember the very first day we met? I knew the very first moment I saw you. I knew we were meant to be together for all of our days. You have become my lover, my companion and my best friend. There's no one else I'd want to build my life with. I get to have you by my side, my love, my wife, my light, my soulmate, for all eternity. My today and all of my tomorrows, you're my redemption, my absolution."

He finishes on a grin, as Freddie steps forward in his white shirt, shorts and silver dickie bow. His raven black hair a mirror image of his fathers as he presents the rings on a silver velvet cushion. Brody takes the ring off the cushion and chucks Freddie's chin, flashing him a reassuring wink. Brody places the diamond encrusted platinum wedding band on my finger. I take a deep breath and take a few precious moments to gather myself, before I begin to speak.

"I take you, Brody Lennon Hart to be my lawful wedded husband, to have and to hold from this day forward. I love you with my whole heart, with a passion that can't be expressed in words. I'm madly in love with you, my husband. Not only do I promise that my love for you will grow with each day, but I promise to be your friend and partner every step of the way. I will be there for you, every day or night, in richer, in poorer, in sickness and in health. I trust, appreciate, cherish and respect you. I promise to share with you my hopes and dreams, as we build our future together. You are my everything, my ride or die, my end game."

I choke on a sob as I finish, all the while not taking my eyes off his. His eyes are glistening with tears, as Freddie steps forward again to present Brody's ring, I take it from the cushion and smile warmly at him. I shakily place his simple, plain wedding band on his finger.

"I love you," he says so softly and full of emotion it makes me want to break down in a sobbing heap at his feet. Marlowe smiles, clapping his hands together.

"I now pronounce you man and wife. Ladies and gentleman, Mr. and Mrs. Hart."

Everyone breaks out into a euphoric round of whooping and clapping, but my attention was firmly focussed on Brody.

"You may kiss your bride."

Brody sweeps me in his arms and elaborately dips me low and plants a pant-melting, searing, steal-your-breath kiss on my lips. His split tongue caressing mine, I feel my aching core flood with heat, as my boobs press against his chest and he growls into my mouth. He temporarily disarms me and I grip his shirt in my fist, suddenly forgetting there is a crowd of people awaiting our attention.

"Right, where's the bar!" Marlowe shouts, as Brody takes my hand in his, the sunlight making our rings sparkle.

"Wife," he says proudly and I chuckle softly.

"Husband," I mouth and we make our way down the aisle as man and wife. I finally have the knight in shining armour, the white picket fence and the happy ever after I always dreamt of when I was a little girl.

***

We are swept up in an unprecedented number of congratulations and I am reluctant to let go of his hand. It feels so right in mine and suddenly a wave of emotion hits me like a freight train. *We're actually fucking married.* I laugh, as we conclude our walk down the aisle, the boys grab him again and he's forced to let go of my hand, as they lead him away from me.

"Let's go commiserate boys! We've just lost another wingman to the fucking dark side!" Lucas quips, his voice laced with amusement and the boys all boo in unison. I find myself smiling along with them, there bond clear for all to see.

"That deserves a very large fucking drink, fellas!" Jax jokes and we all laugh animatedly. I encourage him to go with the boys, he silently asks me with his eyes if I'm ok and I nod, shooing him away. He flashes me his signature grin, and it tells me all I need to know. *Life couldn't be more fucking perfect.*

As the day progresses, we are swept up in the day and we don't leave each other's side, only to interact with our guests and to refill our drinks. The subtle hand brushes, the possessive touches, let people know that I belong to him and he belongs to me. I watch Brody make his way over to the bar, which has been set up on the beach. I can't take my eyes off Brody as I watch him tuck his hand casually into the pocket of his denim shorts, which he has changed into. I lick my lips at the sight of his pert arse, as he saunters over to the boys.

"If only he swung my way, I'd die an extremely happy man! Or any of those delicious boys were on my bus! I'm not fussy!" George whisper sighs in my ear and I chuckle softly. George is the band's tour bus driver, he is a six feet seven inch teddy bear and he never fails to make everyone smile with his dry sense of humour and razor-sharp wit. He became a great friend, ally and confidant while I was on tour with Rancid Vengeance. and

"You're terrible, you know that?" I say wryly and he pretends to look offended, placing his hand dramatically on his chest.

"How very dare you! That's why you love me, babe!" he says with a flamboyant flick of his hair and I roll my eyes.

"Someone's got to!" I retort and he links my arm through his, as I pick up my dress with the other hand.

"You look beautiful by the way!"

He looks especially handsome today wearing a white suit, with a black shirt and skinny black polka-dot tie. His long shoulder length, blonde hair, reminds me of a lion's mane and his usually full beard, has been neatly trimmed. His blue-grey eyes are misted with tears, as he looks down at me.

"No tears, you tart! You'll set me off and it took Danny all morning to make me look this beautiful!"

George rolls his eyes theatrically.

"*Oh please!* I'm sure you sleep with a make-up artist beside your bed, you wake up looking gorgeous! Bitch!"

I playfully punch him in the arm.

"It takes an immense amount of effort to look this good, babe, trust me. I've had twins! I definitely don't look like this at two in the morning, when I'm breast feeding Bowie and Azalea, with one kid hanging off each tit! I feel like a fucking cow!"

We both laugh, as he offers me his hand.

"Dance with me, love?" he asks in his strong Bristolian accent and I smile softly.

"Of course."

I take his hand and he leads me onto the dance floor. He puts his hand on my waist and spins me round on the make-shift dance floor to *Let's Stay Together* by *Al Green*.

"Don't look now, but the rock star is looking at you like you're dinner, and he wants to ravish you in front of all these people!"

His mouth forms a perfect O shape and I giggle girlishly. I catch Brody's silver gaze from across the sand. The smile and cheeky wink he gives me makes my heart stutter in my chest. I've never been more in love with him, as I sway in time to the music with George. I feel a presence and George clears his throat, I look up to see Brody standing cockily behind us with a smirk on his face.

"Would you mind if I cut in, mate?" he asks and George winks at me.

"Of course, she's all yours."

George spins me round, kisses the back of my hand and hands me over to Brody. George cheekily squeezes Brody's arse.

"What have I told you! Not in public!" Brody laughs mischievously and George blows him a kiss, as Brody wraps his hand possessively around my waist.

"Finally, I've got you all to myself again, *wife*."

I smile shyly.

"Don't go getting shy on me, I've seen you naked remember? Repeatedly." he whispers, and I feel his warm breath gust out close to my ear. I gasp and we both laugh out loud.

"And here's me thinking you were a gentleman, Brody Hart."

He cocks his eyebrow.

"It's been a while since I've been called one of those, kitten. Arsehole, prick, wanker, yeah. But gentleman? Not so much!"

He chuckles softly, as he leans closer and moves us across the dance floor. The song changes to *The Calling's Wherever You Will Go*. He pulls me close to him and I bury my nose in his chest, taking in his familiar scent, Dior Sauvage and pure Brody Hart.

"Kitten," he says throatily. I can't get close enough to him, this beautiful man who is now my husband. I never thought we would get to this day, after everything we had been through in such a short space of time. I thought I had lost him after the motorcycle accident and after I thought he would go to prison for a very long time after killing Stefan in self-defense.

"Hey."

He tips my chin up to face him, as we move in time to the dulcet tones of Alex Band.

"There's my girl."

My eyes glaze over and I'm overwhelmed by the sight of him. His dark hair neatly styled, the buttons of his white shirt, open at the collar revealing the smooth planes of his tattooed chest. He really is a sight to behold.

"You know I hate it when you cry, talk to me."

He moves my hand up to rest on his chest and I shake my head.

"No, they're happy tears, I promise. I'm just a little overwhelmed that's all. This day...I never thought I'd ever meet someone I wanted to spend the rest of my life with. Then I met you, in rehab of all places."

We both laugh and he wraps his arms tighter around me. He turns us and takes hold of my hand.

"Let's go somewhere quieter, kitten," he says, his voice low and sultry and without hesitation, I blindly follow him with his hand in mine. He grabs a magnum of Cristal champagne off one of the tables set up on the sand and stalks with purpose around the back of the villa, onto a short boardwalk overlooking the burnt orange sunset and the turquoise of the ocean. The water softly lapping around us and for the first time today, I can finally breathe. I hear Brody pop the champagne cork and he tips the bottle up, taking a long pull. He turns and offers it to me and I do the same. We both laugh and sit down on smooth wood.

"I've finally got you to myself, Mrs. Hart," he says seductively.

"It's taking all my fucking self control not to lay you down and fuck you into next week. I think you need a reminder of who you belong to."

I shiver at his dirty talk.

"Raleigh," he growls in warning and I can't help teasing him. I ghost my fingers over his crotch and he places his tattooed hand on top of mine, his wedding ring sparkling in the evening sunlight.

"Now, it's not nice to tease, is it, kitten?" he says with an amused tone to his voice.

"I have no idea what you're talking about, Mr. Hart."

I continue to stroke him, not caring that someone could potentially catch us in the act and he growls animalistically.

"*Fuck,* I need to be inside you. I haven't been inside you for at least twenty-four hours. I have a lot of making up to do."

He places the champagne down on the wooden boardwalk and before I know what is happening, he flips me and I find myself pinned beneath him. I grind myself against his cock and he tightens his grip on my wrists. I feel his cock growing harder and my heart beat starts to quicken. The look in his silver eyes is smoky and smouldering, he leans down blanketing me with his body and, kissing me passionately on the lips in a breath-stealing kiss. The feel of his soft lips on mine, he tastes of the champagne he just drank, as he coaxes my mouth open and his tongue strokes mine. His tongue piercing tickling the inside of my mouth. His kiss is so tender and so gentle it makes me want to weep. I deepen the kiss not wanting it to end and he swallows my moans as I reach down and rub his growing erection. I hear someone behind us clear their throat, as Brody pulls away from our kiss and presses his forehead to mine.

"Get a fucking room, you pair of filthy animals!" Sam laughs, and Brody rolls his eyes, cursing softly under his breath.

"I'm all for sex in public places, mate, but at your own wedding? *Fuck me,* you could at least wait until your guests have gone back to their rooms!" Sam quips, as Brody gives him the finger and he reluctantly climbs off me, pulling me up with him, shielding his visible hard on.

"You're a prick, you know that, Newbolt?" Brody grumbles and Sam grins, flashing his infamous dimples.

"So, I've been told, Hart! Tell me something I don't know!"

I hear someone call Brody's name, as he presses his lips to mine.

"Duty calls, kitten. Hold that thought."

He winks, and I practically melt on the spot. *When will he stop having this effect on me?* Sam takes a long pull from his drink.

"Congratulations, sweetheart. I couldn't be happier for you both," he rasps warmly, and he wraps his arm around me, as we dangle our bare feet off the edge of the boardwalk.

"Thank you," I whisper.

"Brody's the man he is today because of you. You've changed him for the better, sweetheart. He would have been dead before his thirty-fifth birthday if it wasn't for you."

I smile softly at his kind words, picking up the bottle of champagne and taking a long gulp. The bubbles exploding in my mouth.

"You deserve to be happy, sweets. After everything you've been through, you deserve this. I've never seen him this happy, and that's all because of you. He was heading down a dark path and you led him back into the light."

I swipe away a stray tear and hear the approach of footsteps. My skin prickles, the hair on the back of my neck stands on end and I know without looking up that it's Brody. *He's the only man who has ever had that effect on me.*

"Raleigh." My name sounds like a love song, as he looks from me to Sam and back again.

"I'll leave you two to it."

Sam leans in and kisses me softly on my forehead. "Congratulations again, sweetheart."

He gets to his feet, gripping my hand in his tattooed one and pulls me up with him until I'm standing and he leaves us alone. Brody moves closer to me until we are standing toe to toe. He cups my face in both of his large hands. I feel the cool metal of his wedding band against my cheek and I'm reminded that we're married. He smiles and not the first time today, his killer grin temporarily disarms me and renders me a wet, hot, horny mess. I instantly find myself swooning on the spot at the realisation that this beautiful human being, is my husband.

"What have I told you about looking at me like that, kitten? I'm not a piece of meat!" he says, with amusement in his voice, as he skates his hand down my back, pulling me closer to him.

"Fuck, my cock is so hard right now."

I feel his steel erection pressing against my abdomen and feel my pussy grow slick.

"I need to bury my fucking cock in that tight pussy of yours, Rae."

His voice is thick with arousal and I reach down to boldly stroke his erection through his trousers. He growls primally, and he slips his hand inside my dress, cupping my aching breast in his hand.

"Fucking hell, you're wearing too many clothes, kitten!"

I chuckle softly, and I lift my dress up, allowing him full access. He bends down, taking me in his arms and lowering me to the cool wood of the boardwalk. The distant sound of idle chatter and soft music surrounding us, reminding us that our wedding guests are mere feet away. That thought is soon pushed to the back of my mind, as I wrap my legs around him and he crashes his lips to mine. I'm mindless with want, as he kisses a burning trail from my bare neck to my collarbone and I involuntarily shiver at the feel of his lips on my skin. I close my eyes and enjoy the feel of my husband pleasuring me like only he knows how. He plays my body like he plays his guitar on stage; with expert precision, effortless grace and quiet control.

He reaches down to expose my bare breast and leans over to suckle my erect nipple in his mouth. I run my fingers through his hair and tug gently.

"Brody," I moan inaudibly, and he reaches underneath the layers of my dress to caress my pussy over my lace knickers.

"*Fuck*, your knickers are damp for me, that's so fucking hot."

He moves my knickers to the side and runs his finger through my wetness. He teases me for a few seconds, driving me to the brink of orgasm and pushes his long finger inside me, taking me by surprise. I gasp at the feeling of his finger moving in and out. He introduces a second finger, rubbing my inner walls with every stroke. My eyelids flutter closed, and he bites down on my nipple.

"Eyes on me, kitten. Don't take those gorgeous eyes off me."

I open my eyes and my amethyst eyes lock with his smouldering silver ones, as he increases his pace. He takes my nipple out of his mouth with a '*pop.*' The movement is rushed, as I manage to unzip his shorts and he twists his fingers inside me, causing me to cry out. He shushes me gently.

"*Oh, fuck Brody,* that feels so good."

I reach into his boxer shorts and stroke his erection, causing him to growl against my neck. He pulls his fingers free from my pussy, leaving me bereft at the loss of contact. He pushes his shorts and boxers down at the same time, fists his cock. He rips my knickers off with one sharp tug, until the sound of the delicate lace ripping echoes around us. The head of his cock finds my entrance, and he shoves forward, impaling me on his waiting firmness. His cock feels good inside me and I whimper softly. He bites his lip and throws his head back, as he cries out with pleasure.

"*Oh Jesus,* fuck, Raleigh. You feel like...heaven on earth."

He picks up his pace, moving in and out of my slick heat. I wrap my arms around his neck and stroke the shaved hair at the nape of his neck. It feels so good, I moan in his ear. As his pace quickens, I feel my orgasm cresting to the surface. He lets out a satisfied hum, as he pistons in and out of me and I explode around him.

"I'm coming, *fuck*, Brody, I'm coming," I yell, and he moves his hand over my mouth.

"That's it, Raleigh. Come for me."

His orgasm is right behind mine, as his hot seed spurts inside me, causing a second orgasm to detonate from deep within me. I cry out around his hand and as we come down from our orgasms. The only sound is the water lapping around us and our laboured breaths.

"Our first fuck as man and wife," Brody whispers, biting down on my earlobe and we both laugh out loud, as he pulls out of me. He tugs me up right and adjusts his still solid erection back into his shorts. He straightens my dress and kisses my neck, the rough tickle of his stubble against my skin makes me want to fuck him all over again.

"You look fucking beautiful and you smell of me. *Fuck,* I'm hard again just looking at you."

He smiles against my neck, as he pulls us both to our feet, holding me to him.

"Before I met you, I didn't know what love was. I thought love was something that happened to other people, that love was just being the best version of yourself that you could be. As soon as I saw you that day outside my therapy room, I knew none of what I'd seen or heard about love was true."

His words render me speechless and as his tall frame towers over me, I can't think of anywhere else I'd rather be, but with my husband.

40

Raleigh

We head back to our wedding reception hand in hand and Lucas wolf whistles.

"We know what you've been up to!"

He chants in his familiar American drawl, and Brody rolls his eyes.

"SHOTS!"

All the boys shout in unison and drag Brody off to the bar. He kisses me quickly on the lips and I find myself laughing at their camaraderie. As I watch their interaction, the love I feel for him in that moment, eclipses everything we've been through together and I can't help the dreamy sigh that escapes my lips, as I continue to observe my husband, Brody Hart. It still doesn't feel real, I don't think it ever will. I can't believe we're married... the ceremony, us exchanging vows, him placing the ring on my finger, Marlowe Newbolt pronouncing us husband and wife, it all seems like a distant blur now and it was over all too quickly. I kick off my shoes, suddenly wanting to be alone for a moment to gather my thoughts and reflect on the day. I feel my feet sink into the soft sand and the cool ocean breeze washes over my skin, the last hours of the sun's heat beating down on my face, I start to feel a little more relaxed than I've felt in a long time. I feel like I'm a million miles away from our crazy life back home. This place is idyllic and there's something about the sound of the sea that soothes me. The calming lap of the waves and the quiet that follows is so peaceful, as I continue my slow stroll across the white sand.

"Now, why would my wife be walking along the beach on her own on her wedding day? I wonder?" I hear Brody say from behind me.

"I just needed a breather that's all, I'm a little overwhelmed," I admit, as he catches up to me. He spins me around and takes my hand in his, stroking his calloused finger over my wedding ring.

"This ring symbolises my love for you, Raleigh. It symbolises our future together. It won't erase the past and the shitty things I've done, but I consider myself the luckiest fucker on the planet because you chose me. You chose me on a day when I thought I wasn't worthy of the breath that filled my lungs or the blood that ran through my veins. I've never told anyone this before, not even Lenny or the boys, but I read something the day Sam found me lying unconscious on my bathroom floor. He gave me CPR because I stopped breathing, I didn't fucking care if I lived or died, I never read the news or shit on the internet because it's so fucking negative, but there was something that stuck in my head that day that tipped me over the edge. *Somewhere out there is a tree working very hard to replace the oxygen Brody Hart consumes on a daily basis. He should go and apologise to it, and he does realise that people just tolerate him, but I don't think they have the time or the crayons to explain it to his dumb ass."*

My heart hurts for him, as I continue to listen.

"Seeing those hurtful words in black and white, it fucking stung, and it made me feel like a worthless piece of shit that didn't deserve love or kindness. But as soon as I laid eyes on you, I knew you were the woman that would eventually deem me worthy of love. I'll make a promise to you right here and now. I promise that I will prove to you that I'm worthy of your love that I deserve to wear this ring."

He lifts his hand up and points to his wedding ring. I cup his face in both of my hands and press my lips to his, halting his words. We get lost in each other, as the sunsets over Kuda Huraa beach and we begin our forever together as husband and wife.

Epilogue

Six Months Later
Brody

"My name is Brody Hart and I'm a recovering drug addict."

After a fifteen year love affair with cocaine, those are words I thought I would never say out loud. We are all born to crave and live with healthy addictions, some people are addicted to chocolate, some people are addicted to pizza. I considered my addiction unhealthy, and it caused me to spiral out of control. I looked in the mirror and I didn't recognise the pathetic, hollow eyed junkie that was staring back at me. I saw my mother staring back at me, I had become someone I didn't want to be and that thought terrified me. When the going got tough, my brain made a million excuses to cave in, but I only ever needed one and I hated myself that I was so fucking weak. Marrying Raleigh six months ago gave me a whole new outlook on life. I am no longer reliant on that artificial chemical high that addled my brain and ravaged my body like poison. The only high I need is her and the adrenaline that pumped through my veins when I perform in front of a crowd of our adoring fans.

It had been six months since we married on the idyllic beach in The Maldives. Being married taught me that marriage is a thousand little things. It's loving someone enough that you make sacrifices every day to make sure that the person you're with is happy. Every day I wake up glad to be alive and content to lie in bed next to my wife. I belong to her and she belongs to me. She has stuck by me even when I haven't deserved the unrelenting and unconditional love she so willingly gave me. She gives me the best of herself every day and she gave me the most precious gift when she gave birth to our twins Bowie and Azalea. She accepted me as a beautifully broken adult and she taught me that the hardest thing isn't to lose yourself. It's to find yourself again amongst all of the chaos. She dragged me from that chaos. Being in love with Raleigh was all I needed, but admitting it to myself was the hardest part. I will spend the rest of my life making up for all of my wrong doings. We deserved our happy ending and as I spent three months lying in a hospital bed in a coma, there were days when I thought we would never get to where we are now. Maybe life would have been simpler if we'd never met, but she wouldn't be wearing my ring and she wouldn't bear my name. I would rather tear my own heart out than put her through that heart ache ever again. I want to give her the life she deserves and I possess her as much as she possesses me. As I lie here watching her sleep, I come to the stark realisation that she was my redemption and my absolution all rolled into one and that was all I would ever need.

The End

www.ingramcontent.com/pod-product-compliance
Lightning Source LLC
Chambersburg PA
CBHW031225020726
47499CB00002B/649